The MIRACLE

Other Books by Gilbert Morris

Charade

Jacob's Way

Edge of Honor

Jordan's Star

God's Handmaiden

The Spider Catcher

The Singing River Series

The Homeplace

The Dream

The Miracle

GILBERT MORRIS

The MIRACLE

THE SINGING RIVER SERIES

BOOK III

ZONDERVAN®

ZONDERVAN.com/
AUTHORTRACKER
follow your favorite authors

 **ZONDERVAN®**

The Miracle
Copyright © 2007 by Gilbert Morris

Requests for information should be addressed to:
Zondervan, *Grand Rapids, Michigan* 49530

Library of Congress Cataloging-in-Publication Data

Morris, Gilbert.
    The miracle / Gilbert Morris.
        p. cm. — (Singing River series ; bk. 3)

        ISBN: 978-0-310-25234-4
        1. Depressions — 1929 — United States — Fiction. 2. Domestic fiction. I. Title.
    PS3563.O8742M57 2007
    813'.54 — dc22

2006033495

Published in association with the literary agency of Alive Communications, Inc., 7680 Goddard Street, Suite 200, Colorado Springs, CO 80920.

All Scripture quotations, unless otherwise indicated, are taken from the *King James Version.*

Some of the poems in this book first appeared in *Those Who Knew Him: Profiles of Christ in Verse*, published by Fleming H. Revell, copyright © by Gilbert Morris 1997. Used by permission.

Interior design by Michelle Espinoza

Printed in the United States of America

To June Jordan

The world is short of virtuous
women, but there are a few left.
You, June, are one of those
wonderful examples of what
a wife and mother should be!

The MIRACLE

PART ONE

A Romance for a Doctor

⁕ CHAPTER 1 ⁕

A grinding cold had settled down over Stone County and most of northern Arkansas. As Lanie Freeman hurried to slip into her dress, she noted the frost on the windowpanes and shivered. Her upstairs bedroom had a small wood-burning fireplace, but she only used it when she stayed up late reading or writing. Her dress was made of gray lightweight wool with long sleeves, a high neckline, and a fringe of black lace around the edges. Even so, it did not provide enough warmth against the early morning chill.

Moving over to the mirror above her dresser, she studied herself with a critical eye. A faint memory brushed the edges of her mind, pulling the corners of her lips into a smile. The memory brought back a day when she had cried because she was so skinny. One of the boys at school had called her "Rake handle," and she had flown at him in a rage. Only Davis had been able to pull her off of the boy.

"Well, I'm not skinny anymore." The young woman gazing back at her from the mirror certainly was no rake handle! As Lanie considered the lissome curves clearly outlined by the dress, she remembered an entry she had made in her journal when she was much younger.

Moving to the pine chest of drawers against the wall, she opened the bottom drawer and pulled out one of many notebooks concealed beneath her folded clothing. She opened the book and, ignoring her shivers, read the entry dated April the twelfth, 1928:

I had to kill Lucille today, and it broke my heart. I hated to do it, but I had to admit she was delicious. I fried her for supper, and we ate all of her. Mama only ate a little bit of the breast and some of the gravy. I'll be glad when the baby comes and Mama's strong again, and I'll be glad if I ever fatten up a little bit.

Lanie felt a keen sense of pain as she remembered her mother, who had, at the time, only a short time left on earth. She was carrying Corliss and would give her life to bring the baby girl into the world.

She leafed through the journal, sometimes smiling as her words brought touching memories, sometimes frowning as her words brought with them pangs of sorrow. When she came to an entry where a letter marked the place, she smoothed back the page and read her words again, just as she had many times before.

They're going to put us in a foster home if something don't happen. But I've heard about my daddy's aunt who's in a nursing home in Oklahoma. We're going to try to get her to come and live with us so the government won't break our family up.

Lanie next opened the letter, which was from her Aunt Kezia to her father.

Forrest, my husband has died and the fool spent all his money on a hussy from Muskogee. I'd have shot him if I had caught him and her too. He didn't leave a cent, and I'm living in a room in a rundown boarding house full of idiots! Got a little money, but when that plays out, they'll put me in some kind of old folks' home. Bah! I'll shoot myself before I put up with that.

A wave of affection for Aunt Kezia filled Lanie. In spite of her advanced age, the old woman had brought safety to the Freeman household. With Lanie's mother dead and her father in prison, the state had almost broken up the family, but Aunt Kezia had provided a safe haven for them all. Her sharp tongue was sometimes difficult to live with, but Lanie loved her.

She thumbed through the pages and stopped abruptly at the entry marked July the fourth, 1931. That had been the last Fourth of July, and the memory of it was etched clearly on her memory. As she read her words, her cheeks turned warm.

> *At the fair today I was standing at the Ferris wheel afraid to get in because it reminded me of the day Mama died. Suddenly Owen was there, and he teased me into getting on the Ferris wheel with him. We got in and I hung on, but I was scared. He put his arm around me, and when the car started rocking I just threw myself against him and hung on as if I was a little girl and he was my daddy.*
>
> *But it wasn't like that. As I was pressed against him, I knew he was aware I wasn't the little girl he always thinks of when he thinks of Lanie Freeman. And I knew he wasn't the father figure either. I could have let go but I didn't want to. I just held onto him and pretended I was frightened. I know it was wrong, but it'll never come to anything else. He's engaged to Louise now, and I've had to put that dream away.*

For a long moment Lanie stood in the center of the room staring down at the words. She had written things in this journal she would never share with anyone else. The thought drew her to her writing desk. Still shivering against the cold, she pulled on a sweater and rubbed her hands together to warm her fingers. Then she opened the notebook, picked up a pen, and began to write:

> *December 27, 1931*
>
> *Owen is not married to Louise Langley. That's the biggest thing in my life right now. She broke their engagement, and when I heard of it my heart nearly jumped out of my chest.*

Roger wants me to marry him, but I can't. I've got too many problems. I've got to handle all of these things:

1. *Davis can't read.*
2. *My sister Maeva has a wild streak that's liable to bust out at any time.*
3. *Daddy's in prison and may not be out for a long time.*
4. *I want to be a writer but there's no way I ever can be.*
5. *The Depression is getting worse, and I don't see how we can pay the bills.*
6. *I've got Cass to think of. Davis brought her home and she's going to have a baby, and I've got to help her somehow or other.*

She held her pen poised over the journal for a moment, and then she added one note:

In less than a week, it's going to be a brand new year. I'm going to trust God for every one of these problems.

Firmly she blotted the ink, closed the notebook, and put it back in the lower drawer of the chest. Then she rose and left the room, her head high.

As she started down the hall toward the stairs, she stopped by the room that Maeva shared with Cass. She opened the door and saw her sister propped up in bed, wearing a heavy mackinaw coat to keep off the cold. She was reading a copy of *True Romance* magazine. Looking up, she grinned. "You ought to read some of these stories, Lanie."

"Never mind those stories. Get out of bed. It's time to go to church."

"I'm not going to church this morning. It's too cold."

"You've got to go to church. You know that, so let's not argue about it."

"You can't make me go. I'm bigger than you are."

Indeed, it was true that Maeva, almost seventeen and one year younger than Lanie, was larger. She was also stronger and more athletic. Lanie stared at the girl and tried to think of a way to convince her. "You know," she finally said, "I can't make you go, but if Daddy were here, you'd go, wouldn't you?"

Maeva bit her lower lip, threw the magazine on the floor, and came out from under the covers. "All right. I'll go to church." She glared at Lanie. "I'm telling you, you need to read a few love stories. All you ever think about is money!"

The words hurt. Of course she had to think about money. Somebody had to pay the bills, and considering the desperate times of the Depression, it was a tight squeeze. Almost everybody in Fairhope, in Stone County—in the whole country, for that matter—was enduring hardship.

As she turned and went down the stairs, Lanie thought of Maeva's charge that she had no romance. *I've got as much romance in my heart as you have, Maeva. I just don't fly a flag about it.* The angry thought bounced around in her, but she put it aside firmly as she went into the kitchen.

The warmth from the wood-burning cookstove greeted her, and she saw at a glance they were all there: Aunt Kezia, Davis, Cody, Corliss, and Cass, the newest member of the household. Cass was wearing an old dress of hers and a coat that had belonged to her mother. The girl had been in pitiful shape when Davis had found her riding in a boxcar. He had brought her home, not knowing what else to do, and when it was discovered she was only sixteen years old and going to have a baby, by common consent they had agreed to keep her.

"Well, is everybody ready to go to church?"

"Not yet," said Cody, a wide-eyed young man of fourteen with red hair and green eyes. He was short and stocky with a head as packed with ideas as an egg is packed with yolk. The fact that most of these concepts never got off the ground never seemed to trouble Cody. His eyes gleamed.

Davis, his older brother, said, "We got a new invention, Lanie." Davis was tall, lanky, and had auburn hair and blue eyes. He looked like his father and was a good athlete like him too. "We don't know what it is yet. He won't tell us."

"We don't have time for that, Cody," Lanie said. "We've got to get to church."

Aunt Kezia grinned. She never wore old ladies' clothes but, instead, wore whatever suited her. The dress she had on today was a bright red and white, fit for summer, and over it she had on a coat with a fur neckpiece that was rather bare in spots. She was ninety-one now, but her mind was as sharp as ever. "What is it this time, Cody? Is it a perpetual-motion machine?"

"Nah. I'm working on that, but I ain't quite got it yet. Here it is."

Lanie moved closer to see the invention. It was a strange-looking device, but Cody was an expert at creating strange-looking things. It had a steel rod in the middle and blades of some sort that seemed to circle around it.

"What is it, Cody?"

"Why, can't you see? It's a potato peeler. Here, lemme show you how it works. Give me a potato, Lanie."

Maeva pulled a potato out of the bin and tossed it to him. "I bet ya a nickel it won't work."

"You ain't got a nickel." Cody grinned. "Besides, you already owe me a nickel." He plunked the potato down, impaling it on the upright pole, and then reached for a wheel that was on one side. "You watch this now. No more sitting around with a knife trying to get that skin off of there and picking out them little eyes. Cody Freeman's never-fail, surefire, always-on-the-spot potato peeler is going to make us rich!"

"Let's see the silly thing work," Aunt Kezia said. "I peeled enough infernal potatoes that it'd be a good thing if you could put a stop to that."

"Here we go." Cody turned the wheel, and the blade slashed and circled the potato. It was all over in a few seconds.

Davis began to laugh. "Look at that. You peeled that potato, all right."

Lanie couldn't help but smile. The blades had not just peeled the skin off; it had removed all the potato except a stubby round shape no more than an inch thick.

Maeva snorted. "I told you that dumb thing wouldn't work. Now you owe me a nickel."

"No, I don't. You wouldn't bet." They all waited to see how Cody would defend his failure, for he never admitted defeat. "It's gonna work. It just needs a few adjustments."

"We got to do something about this lack of confidence you got, Cody." Davis grinned.

"You just wait." Cody nodded firmly. "I got another invention. It's going to work too."

"What is it?" Lanie asked.

"It's a chicken-plucking invention."

"Oh, that'll never work." Maeva shook her head and scowled. "You probably want to pluck 'em while they're still alive."

"We can argue about that some other day," Lanie said, "but right now we've got to get to church. So let's go."

She picked up Corliss, who had been watching the doings of the grown-ups. At the age of three, she was the pet of all the Freemans. She was her mother all over again and all they had on earth left of her. She would have been spoiled rotten, but she was the sweetest-tempered, smartest child any of them had ever seen. "Going to church," she said with a bright smile.

"Yes. Going to church." Lanie kissed her on the cheek and said, "If everybody in the world were as sweet as you, it'd be a good world."

They piled into the ancient Ford pickup, the girls in the front, and Davis and Cody in the back. The engine turned over slowly and burst into a cacophonous roar. "I'm sure glad Pardue put a self-starter on this thing," Lanie said to Aunt Kezia.

Kezia was bundled up to the eyes. "I wish there wasn't nothing but horses. You didn't have to crank them. Just get on and go."

Since Aunt Kezia had grown up in the world where the horse was king, the girls could not argue. Lanie moved the Ford away from the curb. As she drove down the street, she waved at the neighbors, who waved back. In a town like Fairhope almost everyone went to church. The Catholics had already gone to an early Mass, but the Presbyterians, the Methodists, the Baptists, and the Pentecostals were making their way to their respective churches.

When she got to the Baptist church, Lanie had to park a block away. Everyone got out, and they walked toward the church, joining others from their congregation.

Reverend Colin Ryan stood at the door, greeting his flock. He was the interim pastor of the Fairhope Baptist Church, and many said with his black hair and dark blue eyes he was too good-looking to be a preacher. Besides that, Colin rode a motorcycle, rarely wore a tie, and broke most of the conventions that Baptists usually expected their pastors to follow. Those who didn't like his ways comforted themselves by saying, "He'll soon be gone from here." But Lanie hoped he'd stay a good long time.

Colin shook their hands warmly as they passed through the doorway into the church. "Well, here's my favorite folks."

Lanie smiled. "You say that to everyone."

"Well, I guess they're all my favorites. How you doing, Cody? Still preaching the Word?"

"Every chance I get, Brother Colin." Since he had been converted recently and baptized in the Singing River, Cody idolized the pastor.

"Better get in. It's crowded this morning." He smiled, showing his cleft chin to its fullest.

Lanie went inside and deposited Corliss in the nursery, where she at once began playing with the alphabet blocks. She had already learned her letters, which delighted the other Freemans.

As she left the nursery, Lanie encountered Louise Langley, which gave her more than a moment's worth of discomfort. The history of the Langleys and the Freemans had not been congenial. Otis Langley, the patriarch of the clan, had been furious when Lanie won an academic prize he felt should go to his son, Roger. Then later, when Louise had been engaged to Doctor Owen Merritt, the whole family had been jealous of the attention Owen paid to the Freemans—especially to Lanie.

Now, however, Louise was smiling. "Hello, Lanie, it's good to see you. What a pretty dress."

"Hello, Louise. It's cold out today."

"Yes." There was a moment's silence, and Lanie wondered whether she should say something about the broken engagement. Finally she said, "I ... was surprised to hear about your breaking your engagement to Doctor Merritt."

Louise's face changed momentarily, but then she smiled. "It was hard, but it was the right thing to do."

"I haven't seen Owen lately."

"No. He's keeping to himself. I suppose he's hurt by my decision not to marry, but he'll thank me for it some day." Lanie noticed there was no sign of regret on Louise's face.

"I must get back to the choir room," Lanie said. "We're singing a special today, so we need extra practice."

Leaving Louise, she went to the choir room, where the practice was being led by the choir director, Dempsey Wilson. Wilson was the high school football coach and was almost as attractive as Colin Ryan. Lanie was amused at how the women in the choir could not keep their eyes off him. He was single, and those who had no ambitions for him themselves had daughters they wanted to promote.

Loreen Parks leaned forward and said, "Why don't you set your cap for Dempsey? He likes you. I can tell."

"Oh, hush! Dempsey likes everyone."

⚬══⟨⊷

As soon as the choir filed into the loft, Lanie's heart warmed, for she saw that Colin Ryan had gone over and squatted down beside Cass, who was sitting at the end of the row toward the back of the sanctuary. The young girl's face was usually tight with tension, but something Colin said amused her, and she was smiling. It struck

Lanie that she was indeed an attractive girl, but a girl with lots of troubles.

She watched the little drama of the church from her place in the choir loft. *Why, this church is like a cosmos, a little world of its own—or maybe like one of the old English sailing ships. It has a captain—that's the pastor—and the deacons are the officers. Everyone has to do their job at the church, just like sailors on a ship . . .*

Lanie rebuked herself for her wandering thoughts, but church *was* a good place to observe what was happening. She noticed, for example, that Louise Langley did not seem particularly distraught about her broken engagement. Her gaze was firmly fixed on Colin, and Lanie remembered that Aunt Kezia had once observed, "That woman can't keep her eyes off the preacher. She's looking at him like he's a piece of caramel cake!"

Finally the song service began, and when the choir special was over, Colin came around and stood before the choir, his back to the congregation. "That was what music in heaven must sound like." He smiled, showing off the cleft in his chin. "Thank you, choir." As he turned back to the congregation and began to preach, Lanie's gaze went over to Louise, who still watched Colin intently.

She's not grieving over Owen, that's for sure!

Lanie settled back with a secret little smile.

CHAPTER 2

The following Saturday afternoon, Lanie bustled around the kitchen, gathering towels and soap for baths. Hot water bubbled on the stove, and the kitchen was filled with a warm glow. The cookstove, Warm Morning, was the pride of Lanie's heart. The bottom of the stove contained a wood box, which heated the oven, and at eye level were two warming bins. Everyone had crowded into the kitchen, for the arrival of January had brought with it freezing blasts.

"Davis, you go get the wash tub. We're going to have to take baths in the kitchen tonight."

Cody spoke up at once. "I don't need a bath." He was sitting at the table playing dominoes with Corliss. "Elijah never took no baths," he said as if that settled the argument.

"How do you know?" Lanie said. "The Bible doesn't say that."

"Well, it ort to! The body's got natural oils. When you wash 'em off, germs can get in and kill you."

Maeva laughed. She was sitting on the other side of the table reading a library book. She glanced at him over the top. "You're as dirty as a pig, Cody."

"I'm not neither. You just don't understand the scientific way dirt works. You see, when dirt gets on you, it stays a while and then it falls off. Can't stay on you forever. If it did, you'd be a mud ball. So I just let it fall off."

"You're going to take a bath. I don't care what you say." Lanie was accustomed to Cody's high-flying explanations, most of which made as little sense as this one.

Cody would have defended his thesis more vociferously, but a sudden sound of footsteps on the back porch made them all turn to look. "Who can that be?" Lanie said.

She went at once to the door, opened it, and found a man standing there, soft cap in hand. He looked to be in his mid-fifties, and sadness hung over him. "Hello, ma'am," he said. "Can I cut wood in exchange for something to eat?"

Lanie was accustomed to the hoboes, for the Freemans lived close to the railroad watering stop. Many would get off the train here and wander through town, and for the most part, she had stopped being afraid of them. She hesitated for a moment, wondering what to do, then nodded. "We'll find something. Come on in."

"My name's John Simmons," he said.

"Well, Mr. Simmons, this is our family." She introduced everyone and said, "You sit down here while I fix you a plate."

Her eyes big, Corliss watched the hobo. "Hello," she said. "My name is Corliss. I'm three years old."

The man suddenly smiled, and his whole face lit up. "Well, hello, Corliss, three years old. My name is John Simmons, and I'm fifty-three years old."

"That's pretty old."

"It is, for a fact."

Lanie quickly fried up three eggs and ham. She added some biscuits left over from breakfast and set a plateful before Simmons. He stared at it, then said, "This looks mighty good. I'm thankful to the Lord for it."

"Where are you from, Mr. Simmons?"

"Detroit, Michigan. I came down here to escape the cold weather." He began to eat, and they all noticed that he did not gobble his food as many would but ate in a rather refined fashion. "It looks like you folks have cold weather here too."

"Unusual for this time of the year. Now, Davis, you mind what I said about getting the tub in. Everybody's got to be washed off." She spoke mainly to turn the attention of the youngsters away from John Simmons. She knew their curious stares must be embarrassing, and she did her best to keep them occupied until he had finished.

"I'd like to have a shot at that woodpile." He looked over at Davis and Cody. "But that's not my real kind of work. I was a barber for a lot of years."

"A barber!" Lanie exclaimed. "We've got two prime candidates here. Get the high stool, Cody. You're about to get shorn."

"Aw, I don't need no haircut. Look at the trouble ol' Samson got into when that Delilah cut his hair."

"Just stop arguing. I declare. You'd argue with an anvil!"

Ten minutes later Cody was in the chair, and John Simmons was performing a beautiful haircut on him. "You've got a well-shaped head, son," Simmons said, cheerfully snipping and then brushing it back. "Some people have odd-shaped heads, and you can't do much with 'em."

"Yes, I sure do have a good-shaped head," Cody agreed. "You take old Robert Flyer at school, he's got a head shaped like a square box. And Minnie Dixon, her head's shaped like an egg. Couldn't do much for them."

Lanie smiled. "Well, that's a beautiful haircut. Davis, you get up there."

Davis got onto the stool, and Simmons put the cloth around his neck and tied it. "My head's not as beautiful as my brother's — " he winked at the newfound barber — "but just do the best you can."

They all watched as the barber cut Davis's hair with quiet efficiency. He was peppered with questions, mostly by Cody, with a few thrown in by Corliss. Finally, Lanie said, "My land, you kids would drive a body crazy. When you finish there, I'll fix you up with some food to take with you, Mr. Simmons."

"Mighty kind of you, miss."

Lanie filled an enormous sack with as much nonperishable food as she could. Then she added bologna sandwiches, two hardboiled eggs, and two fried apple pies. When she opened the door for the man, she put her hand out. "May God bless you, my dear friend, and go before you."

John Simmons swallowed hard. "I wish there were more folks like you in the world," he said, then turned and left. He did not look back once.

Lanie closed the door and sighed. "It makes me sad to see all those men out in the world with no place to go and no work to do."

⊜⊶

Baths were over and the sun was going down in a rosy haze when Lanie opened the door and found Roger grinning at her. "Roger," she exclaimed. "What are you doing here?"

"Just finished packing for college and I decided I had to see my best girl once more before I left."

As Roger followed Lanie into the house, she said, "Why, Roger, you got rid of your crutch!"

"Right. Just a cane now. Pretty soon I'll even get rid of that." He came forward and pulled Lanie into a bear hug.

"Roger, you're squashing me," she cried out.

"Well, you shouldn't smell so good." Roger was a tall young man of twenty. With his blonde hair and bright blue eyes, he was considered quite a catch in the Fairhope circle. True, he'd had trouble with his father, Otis. He also had broken his leg at Thanksgiving when he'd fallen into a deep canyon while hunting alone. He'd been found only by the efforts of Lanie and Booger, a bloodhound she had nursed back to life—or some said, prayed back to life. Lanie and the hound, along with Doctor Owen Merritt, had tracked Roger, an act that saved his life.

"Come on into the kitchen. Have you had supper?"

"Yes. I've already eaten."

"We've got something you're going to like."

Roger winked and squeezed Lanie's arm. "I found something I already like."

"Now you stop that, Roger." Lanie smiled. She could not help but enjoy the young man. He was imminently likeable and had already given an indication he had fallen in love with her. She was not sure how she felt about him, but she knew she would not fit into his family if she were to marry him. But he had been good to the Freemans, and when they entered the kitchen, they greeted him riotously.

"Some people will do anything to get sympathy." Davis grinned as he walked over to shake hands. "Falling down a mountain and breaking a leg is going a bit too far."

Corliss held up her arms. "Hello, Roger."

With one arm, Roger picked her up and said, "How's my best girl?"

"Who is she?"

"Why, you are. Now give me a kiss." He took the kiss on his cheek and said, "Now, don't you be giving any kisses away. They all belong to me." He turned to Cody and said, "What's the latest invention, Cody?"

"Whatever it is, it doesn't work," Maeva said. "You look good, Roger. It always hurts my feelings when you come to see Lanie and never me. Everybody knows I'm better-looking than she is. I can dance better too."

"Well, when Lanie throws me out, you'll be first on my list, Maeva."

Aunt Kezia was sitting on a tall stool watching Roger. She liked him a great deal but would never let it be known. "Well, if it isn't Roger Langley himself," Kezia said. "Good to see you ain't broke any more legs."

"Hello, Aunt Kezia. You're looking beautiful, as usual."

Kezia made a face at him. "Don't be trying any of your wiles on me. I'm past that stage."

"Try your wiles on me," Corliss piped up and then frowned. "What's a *wile*, anyway?"

"Never you mind." Roger grinned. "You'll find out soon enough. Learn any new songs?"

"Yes. I know lots of them."

"She knows too many of them." Lanie shook her head with wonder. "She hears a song one time and it's in her head for good."

"You want to hear a song about a chigger?" Corliss demanded.

"I sure do, honey."

As she sang, her eyes were alive with pleasure. The others smiled, clapping their hands in time, and occasionally Booger lifted his head and howled in a high-pitched moaning fashion.

There was a little chigger
And he wasn't any bigger
Than the wee small head of a pin.

But the bump that he raises
Well, it itches like blazes
And that's where the rub comes in.

Roger laughed and said, "That's a beautiful song. I'll have to learn that one for sure." He took a chair and pulled Corliss up in his lap.

Aunt Kezia announced, "I'm fixing to make something good. You can watch, all of you, but keep your hands off."

"This some kind of a secret formula?" Roger teased. "Maybe a potion to make all the girls fall in love with me?"

"Never you mind about that."

They all watched as Aunt Kezia moved around the kitchen, gathering ingredients. She put in a cup of sugar, a third of a cup of water, a pinch of salt, and then held up a jug of sorghum. It glugged three times, and she said, "That'll be about right. Three glugs usually does it." She added a cup of butter, some vanilla, and then stirred it thoroughly. "Now, Lanie," she said, "get that popcorn started."

Everyone knew how to make popcorn, so it wasn't long before the kitchen was filled with the sounds of pops and bangs and the heavenly scent of the exploding kernels.

While all this was happening, Davis picked his fiddle up and started to play and sing. Before he reached the end of the first verse of the old tune "Sourwood Mountain," Maeva joined in, blending her voice with his.

Aunt Kezia tapped her foot to the music while she stirred the syrup. After a few minutes, she said, "Come over here, honey." Corliss stood beside her, and Kezia poured a cup of cold water. "Now, you just put a drop of that syrup in there. If it makes a ball, we'll know it's ready."

"All right, Aunt Kezia." Corliss took the spoon and carefully tilted it until a dollop of syrup fell into the water. "Look," she said, "it's all ready! See? It's got a ball."

"All right. We're going to make popcorn balls now."

The children had not done anything like this before, but they all threw themselves into the task. Lanie poured the popcorn out on a piece of oilcloth, and then Aunt Kezia ladled syrup over it. The rest crowded in, buttered their fingers, and started forming the sticky popcorn into balls.

"You make 'em as big or as little as you want," Aunt Kezia said. "I like 'em little myself."

"Where'd you learn to do this, Aunt Kezia?" Lanie asked.

"Oh, my law. I was no older than Corliss here when I learned how to make popcorn balls."

"These are good!" Roger said, munching into one. "Couldn't find anything better than this at a carnival."

The rest of the evening was spent filling up on popcorn balls and playing music and checkers—which turned into a tournament that Davis won without trying. *He can do anything better than anyone,* Lanie thought sadly, *as long as it doesn't involve reading. He's so smart, but why can't he read?*

As Roger put on his coat and scarf, he winked at Corliss. "You going to marry me when you grow up, good-looking?"

"Yes," Corliss said at once. "Do you like kissing?"

"You bet!"

Maeva, who was standing nearby, laughed. "I like it too," she said. "I'll come along while you say good-bye to Roger, Lanie, to see that you do it right."

"You stay right here, Maeva," Lanie said. She put on a sweater and walked outside with Roger. "Not much privacy in our house."

"I like it though. Something's always going on." They stood on the front porch, looking out at the starry night, then he turned to her. "I hate to leave and go back to school."

"It's too bad the college isn't here in Fairhope."

Roger reached for her suddenly, pulled her close, and kissed her warmly. "Your nose is cold."

"So is yours." She put her hand on his cheek. "Write to me, will you?"

"Yes. And you can write a poem to me about how wonderful I am and how much you love me."

"You go along now. You're supposed to write the poems."

"All right. Maybe I will. When are you going to see your father?"

"Day after tomorrow."

"Tell him I wish him well and that I'm praying for him."

"Good night, Roger." She watched as Roger walked back to his father's car, got in awkwardly, and pulled away from the curb. He waved to her, and she waved back, thinking, *He's the best young man I know. Why can't I fall desperately in love with him?*

There was no answer to this, so she turned and went back into the house.

❦

Early the following week Lanie went alone to visit her father. The trip to see him was always bittersweet. She was always eager to see her dad, but the circumstances were almost too much to bear. As she approached Cummings Prison Farm, a pall seemed to descend on her.

The prison farm was surrounded by barbed wire and there was nothing attractive about it. It had not been built for architectural beauty but to contain criminals.

Lanie presented her pass to the guards at the gate and then repeated the process as she encountered still other guards inside, until at last she was permitted to continue on to the warden's house. At each checkpoint, the contents of the bag she carried were examined.

At last she saw her father. He was outside the warden's house walking a rawboned gelding back and forth. The horse's breath rose like steam in the cold air, and his eyes looked wild.

"Hello, Daddy, that's a bad horse you got there."

Forrest turned and suddenly his whole face lit up. He was a handsome man of six feet with crisp brown hair and blue eyes. After tying the horse up, he wrapped his arms around her, holding her tight. She clung to him and said, "I'm so glad to see you, Daddy. I brought you lots of good things to eat." She pulled back and smiled up at him, trying not to worry over the new lines in his face, the sad slope of his shoulders.

"Well, it's about dinnertime here, and we're going to eat first class. I made it all right with the warden. We can eat in the kitchen."

The two went in the kitchen and sat down across from each other at a small, scarred table. Lanie spoke rapidly, bringing Forrest up to date on the news of the family and the town. Her father leaned forward, the look in his eyes telling her how hungry he was for such news. It hurt her to see what prison had done to him.

The dinner was excellent. A black cook named Malachi served them fried pork chops, fried potatoes, and greens. "I growed them greens in our own greenhouse, missy," he said. "The warden, he got to have his greens."

"I probably eat better than any inmate in this whole place." Forrest smiled. "Gonna get fat if I keep on eating Malachi's cooking."

Lanie tried to return the smile, but it was a forced effort. Her father did not look well. He had lost weight. She could tell from the hollows in his cheeks, and there were lines around his eyes that she had never noticed before today. She did not mention it. Instead, she gave him news of Booger. "You'd be so proud of him, Daddy. He looks so good."

"Don't tell the warden that. He'd want him back. He says that bloodhound was the best this place ever had."

They talked for a while about the dogs and the animals, and then Forrest said, "How's the girl doing? Cass, I mean."

"Well, she has real good times and real bad times. She's had such a hard life, Daddy, and now here she is, just a child really, going to have a baby."

"That's always hard to hear. But you're doing the right thing, taking care of her."

Lanie had formed a habit of making a list of things to talk to her father about. She wanted to bring him as much of home as she could. "A funny thing happened just a few days ago. Aunt Kezia was making a cake, and Cass sat on a stool watching her. Cass had been telling her how sad she was and how there wasn't much hope for her. She was about to start crying when Aunt Kezia said, 'You love cake?'

" 'Why, yes, I love cake,' Cass said.

" 'Well, here. Have some cooking oil.' Aunt Kezia poured some cooking oil out into a glass and handed it to her.

" 'Ooh, I can't drink that,' Cass said. 'It's awful.'

" 'Well, here. Try a couple of raw eggs.'

" 'Why, that's terrible! Nobody could eat raw eggs.'

" 'Well, how about some flour then, or maybe you would like some baking soda?'

"She kept shoving all the ingredients of the cake toward Cass, and Cass just sat there making faces and saying no.

"Finally Aunt Kezia said, 'Girl, all these things seem bad by themselves, but when they're put together in the right way, they make a wonderful cake.' "

Lanie smiled. "Then Aunt Kezia went on to say, 'God works the same way. He lets us go through hard times, but He knows how to put all these things in order. And when He puts all the ingredients together, He's going to give you a cake.' That's what she said to Cass. It made Cass feel good too. She laughed and put her arms around Aunt Kezia and told her she wanted to make cakes."

"That's a wonderful story, daughter."

The two continued talking, and suddenly Warden Potter Gladden came in. He was a short, stocky man with intent gray eyes, and although he had a difficult job, he always had a warm smile for Lanie or for any of Forrest's relatives. "Hello. How's my favorite girl doing?"

"I'll bet you say that to all the girls, Warden."

"Did Malachi fix you up with a good dinner?"

"Wonderful."

"Best cook I ever had. He'll be out next month. I find myself halfway hoping he'll run a stoplight or something and get sent back here."

Malachi, who had been listening, said, "No, suh, Warden, you do your own cooking. When I get out of here you seen the last of me."

"I hope I have seen the last of him. He's a good man. I'll see you before you leave."

"All right, Warden."

⊂━━━⊹⊱

The warden was waiting for Lanie as she walked down the long hall to exit the building. "Lanie, I don't think your dad's doing too well."

Lanie stared at the warden, feeling a cold chill overtake her. "You mean he's been into trouble?"

"No. Nothing like that. He's a model prisoner. But he's not eating right and he's losing weight."

"Has he seen the doctor?"

"Well, he went once, but there wasn't much the doctor could tell. Forrest is like a lot of men. He doesn't like to talk about his ailments. But I thought you ought to know."

"Thank you, Warden. I'll have the church pray for him."

Lanie made her way out to her car, and as she started back to Fairhope, she found herself fighting off her fears. *Please, God, don't let anything happen to Daddy. Let him be healthy and strong.*

⌾═⊷

The cold weather continued, and with the holidays over, the early days of January seemed to drag. One morning when school had been cancelled because of a broken boiler, Maeva roamed around the house, restless and bored from being cooped up. "Come on, Cass, let's go to town." Maeva winked at Cass. "Maybe we can find some trouble to get into."

Cass seemed to be getting used to Maeva's teasing. "What are we going to town for?"

"Just to get out of the house. We'll have to walk though, so put on your warmest clothes."

The two girls dressed and headed downtown. Maeva had saved some change, and they bought a candy bar apiece. They were coming out of the grocery store when Alvin Biggins and one of his friends accosted them. "Well, if it ain't the Freeman girls, one of them anyhow. How you doin', Maeva?"

"Get out of the way, Alvin."

Maeva could not bear Alvin Biggins. He had been one of the witnesses against her father in the trial that had sent him to the penitentiary. Almost everyone knew that Biggins had lied about the way the shooting had happened, but the jury had no choice but to take his testimony.

Alvin winked at his friend. "Now, George, look. We got two good-looking girls here, but one of them done got a cake in the oven. Ain't that so?"

Cass flushed and turned her head down, which made Alvin's lip curl up in a sneer. "Yep, don't know which one of them boys is responsible, but bound to be one of them. Which one of them made up to you first? Davis, or was it Cody?"

"You shut your foul mouth, Alvin Biggins!" Maeva cried, anger rising up inside her.

Biggins barked out a coarse laugh. "You ain't got nothing to be proud of. Everybody knows you're wild as a buck anyway. You'll be just like her. You'll have a young 'un before you're a year older."

Maeva was anything but a gentle, peaceable girl. Impulsively, she plucked an ax handle out of the barrel that stood on the porch of the store. She gripped it and swung it like a baseball bat. It caught Alvin Biggins on the top of his head, making a clunking sound. He went down bonelessly, and the man called George said, "You done kilt him!"

"No such luck. Can't kill a Biggins by hitting 'em in the head."

Ed Hathcock, the chief of police, had been strolling down the street looking in the windows. He scurried over and stammered, "What'd you hit him fer, Maeva?"

"He used rude language. I can't abide rude language, Chief."

"Well, I'm going to have to arrest you."

"You mean it's against the law to hit scum like that? I thought this was America." She turned and said, "Cass, you better go tell Lanie I'm in jail maybe for murder."

"Oh, no. Don't tell her that. He's all right. See?" Hathcock reached down and pulled Alvin to his feet. "What was this all about, Biggins? Was you using vile language?"

"No. I wasn't doing nothing. She just cracked me over the head for nothing!"

"Well, get out of here."

"No, I ain't. I'm bringing charges against her." The blood was running down his ear, and he wiped it off with his sleeve. "Hey, look at that! I'm bleeding to death! Now you arrest her. I'm bringing charges!"

Just around the corner from where her sister had driven Alvin Biggins to the ground with an ax handle, Lanie was coming out of Pink's Drugstore. She heard her name called and turned to see a woman she had met in church the week before. "Well, it's Mrs. Wright, isn't it?"

"That's right. And your name is Lanie Freeman. I remember you from church."

"We were very glad you came to visit with us, Mrs. Wright. I hope you come back."

Amelia Wright was in her late twenties, a well-shaped woman with a wealth of strawberry blonde hair and rather striking green eyes. She had a full lower lip, and her smile exposed perfect teeth. "I wanted to ask you something, Lanie. I've been coming down with something, and I need to go to a doctor. Can you recommend one?"

"I surely can, and here he comes right now." Lanie smiled. She nodded to Owen Merritt, who was walking toward them. He saw Lanie and gave a small wave. "Doctor Merritt, have you met the newest member of our community?"

"I don't believe so."

"This is Mrs. Amelia Wright. She came to our church last Sunday. She needs to see a doctor."

Amelia Wright smiled. "You know how it is, Doctor. When you go to a new town, you don't know anybody. When you go to a repairman, you're liable to get the worst one in the country."

"Or the worst doctor?"

"I don't think that'll be the case."

"Well, I'm on my way to make some house calls right now, but if you'd like to come to the office at the end of the day, say 5:30, I'll be glad to see you then."

"I would like that." Amelia turned to Lanie. "Thank you. I enjoyed your singing in church Sunday."

"Maybe you'd like to join our choir."

"How nice of you to say so. Well, I will see you later, Doctor."

"Certainly," Owen nodded and headed for his car.

Lanie watched Amelia Wright walk away. Amelia was an attractive woman, and Lanie wondered for a moment if Owen had noticed. Lanie shrugged. At least Amelia would be a welcome member to the choir.

Lanie had just turned to get in the old Ford pickup when Cass came running down the street. "Lanie! Lanie! Maeva's been arrested for assault!"

~☜ CHAPTER 3 ☞~

There were those who believed Judge Phineas Aldridge came into the world with a flyswatter in his hand. He was never seen without one, whether he was fishing in the Singing River or handing out sentences in his courtroom, and he even swung it around in the wintertime when there was no fly to be seen. A great curiosity among the citizens of Fairhope centered on whether he slept with the flyswatter, but since his wife had been dead for ten years and he was not known for sleeping with anybody else, there was no way to find this out.

The flyswatter that he held right now in his right hand was green, made up with a green wooden handle with a piece of screening on the end. The words *Peaceful Rest Funeral Home* on the handle were faded to obscurity. He held it limply in his right hand as he tilted back from his desk and, from time to time, lashed out at an imaginary fly.

The judge was an extremely fat man with a series of chins that quivered when he spoke and a pair of pallid blue eyes, one of which was slightly cast so it was impossible to tell whether he was looking at you. He wore the same suit every day of his life, a worn dark blue serge garment with sleeves that came down almost to the tip of his fingers. From time to time he would reach over and hitch the sleeves up to his wrists, but they inevitably worked their way down again. Once Dorsey Pender asked, "Judge, why don't you wear a black robe, like them judges in the movies?" Aldridge put one of his eyes on Pender for a moment, then spat into the spittoon he kept at his feet. "Robes is for angels, not judges," he had replied.

It was late in the afternoon, and Judge Aldridge stared with distaste at the group that had gathered before him, including Alvin Biggins, Maeva and Lanie Freeman, Cass Johnson, Ed Hathcock, the chief of police, and Orrin Pierce, a distinguished-looking attorney whose face was flushed from frequent visits to a bottle. The group had crowded into his office and now stood arranged before him, awaiting his dispensation.

Judge Aldridge's chin trembled as he spoke. "So, the way you're telling it is that you, Alvin Biggins, did apply profane and blasphemous language to these two young ladies."

"That's a lie," Biggins yelped. "I didn't say nothing bad."

"He's a bald-faced liar!" Maeva broke out, glaring at Biggins. She repeated word for word what he had said, then added, "That's why I hit him with an ax handle. It was because he used rude language."

"And you consider that justifiable violence, Miss Freeman?"

"I sure do, Judge. Wouldn't you hit somebody that used vile language to you?"

Aldridge suddenly laughed, which made his body jiggle. He swiped at a nonexistent fly and then looked over at Orrin Pierce. "Well, Counselor, what is your defense going to be for your client?"

"Justifiable ax-handle hitting, I'd call it, Judge."

Biggins had a bandage on his head and according to his information had been forced to get six stitches put in by Doctor Givens. "Who's going to pay for these here stitches, Judge?"

"I expect you are, Alvin."

"Me!" Biggins yelled. "She's the one who did it."

"She wouldn't have hit you if you hadn't used vile language. I can't abide vile language, Alvin. Case dismissed." Judge Aldridge slapped his flyswatter down in lieu of a gavel and then waved it at them. "Now clear out of my courtroom, hear?" He brandished the flyswatter once more, then said, "Just a minute, Miss Freeman. I'm letting you off with a warning this time. You can't bust the head of every loudmouth who says something you don't like." He grinned. "Now, what would you say if I sentenced you to jail?"

Maeva smiled broadly. "Well, I'd say I was sent to jail by a mighty fine judge."

Aldridge liked this and laughed out loud. "You're right about that. Now, keep your hand off them ax handles, you hear me? And get out of my courtroom. I've got important criminals to see to."

Owen put the stethoscope on the right side of Amelia Wright's chest, listened carefully, then moved it several times. It was impossible not to notice the curves of her figure, although he tried always not to notice such things about his patients. He placed the stethoscope on her back and said, "Breathe deeply," and listened several times from different positions. Finally he removed the earpieces, stepped back around, and said, "Well, I don't find anything seriously wrong. Your lungs are clear. I don't see any infection in your throat."

"Maybe I'm a hypochondriac." Amelia smiled.

Owen noticed she had full lips with a pronounced sensual lower lip, and her eyes were a shade of green he had never noticed before. "I wouldn't say that. Better to come in early just to keep an eye on yourself. If you develop a cough or a fever, come back and you'll give me something to work with."

"All right, Doctor. As I said, it's so hard to get settled in a new town. Usually I have to go through two or three doctors before I find a good one."

"Well, you won't have a lot of choice here. It's either me or Doctor Givens. Otherwise you have to go to Fort Smith."

"I'm sure that won't be necessary." She looked down at the watch fastened over her breast. "My, it's getting late. You keep late office hours."

"Even later than this sometimes."

"I suppose your wife just has to accept things as that."

"Oh, I'm not married. But," he said with a sudden twist of his lips, "you'll hear about my love life soon enough if you haven't already."

"No, I haven't, but I'd love to hear it." She leaned forward. "Tell me about it."

Owen was aware of the fragrance of her perfume and the satin silkiness of her skin. He cleared his throat. "Well, nothing very dramatic, I'm afraid. I was engaged to a young woman up until recently, and she broke the engagement."

"Well, she's a foolish woman."

Owen suddenly laughed. "She didn't think so, and she told me I'd appreciate it in years to come."

"That's a line women always use when they want to do something a man doesn't want them to. They say something like, 'Oh, it's for your own good,' or, as you just said, 'Later on you'll find it was the wise thing to do.' I suppose I'll get all the details soon enough."

"I think you have them, Mrs. Wright."

"Oh, just call me Amelia."

"What does your husband do?"

"Nothing," she said. "He died two years ago." She laughed at his expression. "That sounded awful. I didn't mean it like that. He was killed in a train wreck in Minnesota."

Owen was interested. She had a rather exotic look about her. At least for Fairhope, Arkansas. "I don't want to wait for the gossip mills to get the news, Amelia. How did you wind up in an awful, out-of-the-way place like Fairhope, Arkansas?"

Amanda suddenly reached up and stretched, which threw her bosom into full effect. "I had an uncle who died recently. George McAfee."

"Oh, yes. I knew Mr. McAfee, though not well."

"I was the only family he had. It took the attorney some time to trace me down. He left all he had to me, which really means the house over on Longstreet Avenue and the income from some bonds that he had. Not enough to get by on."

"And you came from ...?"

"Oh, we moved quite a bit, my husband and I, when he was alive. Our last home was in Chicago."

Owen grinned. "Quite a switch from Chicago to Fairhope. I hope your heart can stand the excitement."

Amelia laughed. She had a rich, full laugh, and her eyes danced. "It's not very lively, is it?"

"Well, Fort Smith sometimes has a concert, and there was a circus over at Baker last week. You just missed it."

"Just my luck." Amelia snapped her fingers in mock despair. "What do eligible young doctors do for excitement?"

"Prescribe pills and listen to little old ladies tell me about their ailments."

"You sound bored, Doctor."

"No. Not really. I came from Memphis. It took some adjusting, but I made it. I'm sure you will." He stood up, signaling the end of the visit. "Well, I'm sure I'll be seeing you again. Everybody in Fairhope comes to this office sooner or later."

Amelia slid off the table and started for her coat, but Owen picked it up and held it for her. "Let me help you." When she slid into it, once again he caught the fragrance of her hair. "You know. I've heard of strawberry blondes all my life and there was a song, 'Casey Would Waltz with a Strawberry Blonde,' but you're the first one I've ever actually seen."

"It's my one claim to fame, and it didn't come out of a bottle either. What you see is me."

"Very attractive."

Her lips made a small change at the corners. "Why, thank you, Doctor. What's your fee?"

"First visit's always on the house."

"You're not going to get rich like that."

"I'm not going to get rich here in Fairhope anyway. Here, let me walk you to the door."

He walked with her out of the examination room and saw his nurse, Bertha Pickens, waiting. She was sitting at the desk and very obviously not looking at them, but he wondered if she had had her ear pressed to the door.

"I'm glad it's nothing serious," Amelia said. "Thank you, Doctor."

"Stop by anytime. We never close."

As soon as Amelia Wright was out the door, Nurse Pickens said, "What was wrong with her?"

"Nothing. She thought maybe a cold was coming on, but she's all right."

"Where's she from?"

"Chicago. She's inherited George McAfee's place."

"The old buzzard," Nurse Pickens snorted. "He was the tightest man I ever saw in my life. I declare, he breathed through his nose to keep from wearing out his false teeth! What kin is she to him?"

"Niece, I gather. Now, let's go home. It's getting late."

"You should've left the door to your office open."

"What in the world for?"

"So that I could testify in the trial that there wasn't nothing going on between you two."

"My heavens, Bertha, I can't open the door every time I have a patient in the examination room." Bertha's ways irritated him, but she had been with Doctor Givens for years. She was a genuine, certified, leather-bound Pentecostal with her hair tied in a bun so tight it seemed to pull her eyes into a slant. She wore no rings, and he had never seen any part of her arms above her wrist, for she always wore sleeves down at least that far. She wore heavy black shoes and skirts that nearly brushed the top. "Have a little charity, Bertha. She's all alone in the world."

Bertha Pickens stared at Owen. "Eve was all alone in the world, except for that fool Adam. You got no sense at all about women, Owen Merritt. She won't be alone long. Men will be buzzing around her like honey bees."

"Well, let 'em buzz. Give 'em something to do. Good night. I'll see you in the morning."

"Whatcha doing, Lanie?" Maeva asked, bursting into where Lanie was sitting at her desk. It was Sunday evening, and she'd just sat down to have some time alone and write.

Lanie put her pen down and looked up. "Maeva, make a fist with your right hand."

Maeva made a fist and looked at it. "What for?"

"You see those knuckles there, all four of them?"

"'Course I see 'em."

"They are useful for such things as knocking on doors before you come bursting in."

Maeva snorted. "You're afraid I'll catch you doing something evil, aren't you?"

"Oh, yes, Maeva. I'm making dope that I'm going to peddle out at Shantytown. Besides that, I have lewd pictures hidden under my mattress. Don't ever look under there. You'd be shocked."

Maeva grinned. "The only pictures you'd have would be of Owen Merritt. You still got that one you clipped out of the paper?"

"No, I haven't!"

"I caught you with it one time."

"You didn't *catch* me. I was interested in it because he is our friend, and I thought I'd put it in my scrapbook."

"Yeah, sure you were. Did you see he was sitting by that new lady in church today, what's-her-name?"

"Amelia Wright. Yes, I know."

"I think she's got her hooks in him."

"Don't be ridiculous. He just broke off his engagement."

"No, he didn't. Louise Langley broke it off."

"How do you know?"

"I just do. I wonder if she's rich."

"I don't know. I doubt it. She doesn't wear any expensive rings or jewelry. She seems nice."

Still sitting at her desk, Lanie tapped her foot, waiting impatiently for Maeva to leave. Her sister was in no hurry. After a few minutes, she said, "By the way, Cody's got another great idea—as in capital *G*, capital *I*."

"Oh, no! What is it this time?"

"He's keeping mum this time," Maeva said. "But he says it's sure-fire. It's going to make us all rich as Henry Ford." She sighed. "I get downright tired of his dumb inventions."

"Be patient with him, Maeva. He's got an active brain."

"He drives me crazy! You know he's still tearing pages out of his Bible and handing them to sinners."

"I know. He says he can't afford tracts. That's harmless enough."

"He handed a page out of his Bible to Billy Lassiter."

"Well, Lassiter probably needs some of the Bible. He's been the town drunk for as long as I can remember."

"Sure he needs it, but the page Cody handed him was one of the maps in the back. Now what good under heaven would a map do the town drunk?" Maeva snorted. "You've got to talk to him. He's your responsibility."

"You are my responsibility too," Lanie said.

"Well, talk to me then." Maeva laughed, her eyes dancing. "I've been good for a whole day now. I don't think I can stand it much longer." She left, slamming the door behind her. It was a known fact that Maeva could not pass through a door without slamming it. It seemed to be a prerequisite.

Lanie sighed and went back to her writing, picking up where she had left off:

> *I'm worried about Daddy. He didn't look good, and Warden Gladden said that he hasn't been eating right. So I'm going to the pastor, and at prayer meeting I'm going to get the whole church to pray for him.*

She wrote on for some time, detailing Maeva's escapade with the ax handle and the humiliating visit to Judge Aldridge's courtroom. Finally, she put the journal away and pulled her notebook out containing the poems about the life of Jesus. She had been working hard on one she called "Storm Tamer." It was about the incident in the boat when Jesus had been asleep and a storm had taken the disciples by surprise. He had commanded the storm to stop, and it had at once ceased. In her poem, she wanted to capture Simon Peter speaking to John about the experience. She wrote a verse of Scripture above the title and whispered the poem aloud:

But as they sailed he fell asleep: and there came down a storm of wind on the lake; and they were filled with water, and were in jeopardy. And they came to him, and awoke him, saying, Master, master, we perish. Then he arose, and rebuked the wind and the raging of the water: and they ceased, and there was a calm. (Luke 8:23 – 24)

Storm Tamer

Man and boy I've fished this sea;
All weathers, foul and fair, I've known,
That storm tonight on Galilee
I say, was of the devil blown!

It came too quick. Like a pack
Of howling desert dogs it slashed
Our sails to threads and then attacked
The ship as pale-green lightning flashed!

Look you at this hand that still
Is trembling like a wind-blown feather!
But yet, I did not shake until
The Master spoke — and calmed the weather.

Tell me, John, what manner of man
Is this, that howling winds grow mild,
and raging waves, at His command
Quiet as a sleepy child?

And see how restfully He lies:
More placid than the chastened sea

His face; cloudless as the skies
  Above — but who and what is He?

This storm, I'd say, is not the last
  We'll know — that's if we follow Him —
He's one who draws every lightning's blast:
  Dark His path, and very grim.

But though my hands are shaking yet,
  (And may shake more another day)
this Jesus has me in His net —
  I'll follow in the Master's way!

Lanie ran her fingers over the lines she had just written, and then shook her head. She loved to write poetry, but except for winning one contest she had not won anything else. It was difficult to send poems out. She sent them out to various magazines, but instead of using her street address, she simply put her name, general delivery, Fairhope, Arkansas. If she had put her own address, Dorsey Pender, the mailman, would know, and then all of her siblings would find out, and she would have to listen to more talk about it. "I feel like I'm leading a secret life," she said. "Or worse, like I'm in a birdcage with everybody looking in."

⊶⋆⊷

It was Monday afternoon. Maeva had complained bitterly about having to walk to the grocery store, but there was no money for gas. She was struggling along with a heavy sack, and the wind had turned her face red with the cold. She heard the sound of hoofbeats and turned to see a lithe young man riding toward her, his hat pushed back. He had very black hair and eyes so dark they seemed made of obsidian.

"Seems like you've got a load there, Missy. You need some help?"

"I can walk."

"Why, sure you can." The young man slipped off the horse and led him over. It was a beautiful animal, a shiny chestnut quarter horse. "But it's nicer to ride, don't you think?"

Maeva studied the young man, who was at least six-feet-two and good-looking enough to turn heads. She had seen him before, but she could not remember when. His face was wedge-shaped, and he had a broad mobile mouth.

"I don't ride horses with strange men," she said.

"Well, think what you're missing!" When she did not respond, he said, "Since you won't ride with a stranger, I'll remedy that by telling you my name. It's Logan Satterfield." The young man saw her reaction and grinned. "I see you've heard of me."

"You're mighty right I've heard of you. From what I've heard I don't need to be riding any horse with you."

"Well, I admit my reputation's a little bit tarnished." He fell into step with her, the shiny chestnut trailing slightly behind.

"A little bit tarnished? From what I've heard you've tried everything at least once."

"I'm a bad fellow all right. Women scream and babies cry the minute I show my face."

Maeva Freeman had heard the Satterfields were a wild bunch, but Logan Satterfield didn't look evil. She had also heard about his good looks and, seeing him now, knew the rumors in this case were true. "What's the other side of the picture?"

"Isn't any."

"Just as well you should think so."

"Well, missy, I can't blame you for being afraid of me."

Maeva suddenly stopped. Her arms were getting tired from the groceries. "I'm not afraid of any man, but I can't ride a horse in this dress. And don't call me missy. My name's Maeva Freeman."

Logan Satterfield grinned down at her. "The way I heard it—it's your sister, the straitlaced one, who's the good sister."

"Meaning I'm the bad sister?" Behind her, the horse nickered.

"Well, you know how rumors get started. I hear you went out to see the phantom brakeman once and got drunker than Cooter Brown."

"That's right, I did." This incident happened when Maeva sneaked out of the house with two boys to see if the legend about the brakeman was true. It was said a light would appear on the Mopac Railroad track at midnight, carried by the dead brakeman who had been killed in an accident. While they waited for the phantom to appear, she had taken a drink or two of whiskey. It was not long before she was caught and brought back home.

"Had a great time that night," Maeva said.

"You see the phantom brakeman?"

"No such thing as that. Anyway, my sister Lanie—the good one!—did ride on a motorcycle all the way to Cummings Farm where my pa's in prison. I guess you knew that."

"I heard about it. She's pretty nervy."

For some reason this irritated Maeva. She was the one who people said was nervy. "I'll ride sidesaddle. Here. Hold this sack while I get on." She forced the sack into Satterfield's arm, stepped into the stirrup, and plunked herself down sideways. "Now give me the sack."

"Here you go. But this horse is a little bit feisty. I better get on behind you." He leaped on with an athletic bounce and then put his arms around her on each side so he could hold the reins. "Better hold you on, don't you think?" he said, tightening his grasp.

"I'm not going to fall off."

Suddenly the horse gave a nervous bolt, and Logan Satterfield's arms closed around her. "See there. I told you. This horse is just plum mean."

Maeva laughed. "The fact you kicked her in the side, that didn't make her buck?"

"Aw, she's jealous of good-looking females. Her name is Cherry Pie."

Maeva enjoyed the ride home. When they pulled up in front of the house, she saw that Aunt Kezia was sweeping off the front porch. "And now we're caught," she said. "When they hear I've been running around with the notorious Logan Satterfield, I'll get it."

"Well, who paddles you now that your pa's in the pen?"

"Nobody paddles me!"

"I'll explain things." Logan slipped off the saddle, reached up and took the bag of groceries, and dropped the reins.

"Won't that horse run away?"

"No. She's trained to stop wherever I drop these reins. She obeys better than most of my lady friends do."

"Well, you better bet I wouldn't stop just because you drop reins on me."

Logan threw back his head and laughed.

Maeva was delighted with the encounter. As she walked up on the porch, she said, "Aunt Kezia, this is Logan Satterfield. He drinks whiskey, his family are moonshiners, and he ruins young women every chance he gets."

Logan Satterfield stopped dead still, stared at Maeva, and swallowed hard. She figured that a woman rarely got the best of him, so she gave him a sly wink.

"Wait a minute now, ma'am, that's going it a little bit strong."

"Which part of it?" Aunt Kezia said.

"Well, shucks, that takes a little explanation."

"Then you come in the house for some sassafras tea and a piece of caramel cake."

"Well, I don't see anything wrong with that—" Logan grinned — "as long as no women and children are around."

The three went into the house, and Logan ate two pieces of the cake and washed it down with sassafras tea. "You make that cake, Miss Kezia?"

"You reckon I found it out in the road? Of course I made it."

"That was prime. I tell you what. You could win the prize at the county fair with that." At that moment Davis and Cody came in and Aunt Kezia said, "These are some more Freemans. This is Cody. He invents things. And this is Davis."

"I saw you pitch against the Fort Smith team last summer, Davis. You're a great ball player. Gonna be better than your dad."

Davis's eyes shone with pleasure.

Corliss came in and was introduced to the tall, dark stranger. "You like little girls?"

Logan looked over at Maeva and grinned. "I like little girls and big girls too."

"Do you know any stories?"

"Hundreds of 'em! I can sing and play the fiddle too."

"Can you really!"

"Sure can. I play at dances. In fact, there's a dance over in Brandon Hill next week."

Lanie had come in by this time. All of them had heard stories about this young man all of their lives, and when she was introduced Lanie looked suspicious. She said only, "Thank you for bringing Maeva home."

"Why, it was my pleasure."

"That's a fine horse you've got," Maeva said.

"She's a rodeo horse."

"A rodeo horse?" Cody said. "What does she do?"

"Well, you can bulldog off of her. You can rope calves off of her. Valuable animal, that."

"Do you rodeo some?" Davis asked.

"Oh, yeah. I do. As soon as it gets spring, you'll all have to come out and see me get throwed off."

Somehow the visit was extended, and although Lanie never knew how it happened, they wound up in the parlor with their instruments. They quickly discovered that Logan Satterfield was a fine fiddle player. He stayed over an hour and ate more of the caramel cake.

It was getting dark when he finally said, "Well, I guess I'd better not wear my welcome out." He went around and shook hands with everybody, smiled at Maeva, then left the house.

"Charms the birds out of the trees, don't he?" Kezia shrugged. "He reminds me of Bat Masterson."

"You mean the gunfighter?"

"Yeah. Bat had that same kind of charm. One thing you have to say about old Bat. When he wasn't killing people, he was being charming."

Lanie started to say something to Maeva about staying away from Logan Satterfield, but she saw that Maeva was waiting for exactly that. Hard as it was, she bit back her words. *Better to say nothing at all and just pray.*

·⇒ CHAPTER 4 ⇐·

Snow started to fall the following evening. At first just a few flakes scurried across a gray sky almost invisibly driven by a cold wind. As the afternoon advanced, the flakes grew bigger, some of them as large as quarters. They came floating softly down and coated the landscape with a smooth, soft carpet of pristine whiteness. Lanie was watching out the kitchen window, admiring the artistry of the snow. Even something as plain and raw as a new post stuck in the ground achieved a sort of beauty as the snow put a rounded cap on it.

Little Orphan Annie was just beginning on the radio, and everyone had gathered in the kitchen for the warmth of the stove. The whole house smelled of bread baking in the oven and spicy applesauce bubbling in an iron pot on the stove.

Beau, who had been sleeping for most of the day, got to his feet, stretched and yawned, and came over to look up at Lanie. She smiled, reached down and patted his head, then went to the stove, opening the warmer at the top. She pulled out a biscuit and fed it to him a little bit at a time. When it was gone, she said, "No more," and Beau gave her a reproachful look. As usual, he went back to the wall and seemed to collapse. He always lay down this way, not gracefully, but just falling as if his backbone had been unstrung.

Over in the middle of the floor Cody and Corliss played with a set of wooden blocks. Corliss identified the letters as Cody attempted to build an intricate sort of shape with them. Booger, the big bloodhound, was sitting as close as he could get to Corliss. The hero's medal the hound had been awarded for finding Roger hung around his neck. Cody made a sudden move, and the structure came tumbling down. "Dadgum it! See what you done, Booger!"

Booger, who had not been within two feet of the structure, said, "Woof!" and licked Corliss on the ear.

"Dog," Corliss said and, picking out the blocks, spelled it. "D-o-g-g."

"There ain't but one *g* in dog, Corliss," Cody admonished and removed one letter.

"She spells better than you do," Davis said. He was at the kitchen table struggling with a book.

Across from him Maeva worked on a crossword puzzle. "She spells better than you do too."

Little Orphan Annie played out her adventure, and the announcer offered the Little Orphan Annie decoder ring to anyone who would send in two Ovaltine caps.

"I'd like to have one of those rings," Cody said.

"You're too old for that kind of stuff," Maeva said.

Cody began building another structure. "If I had some money, I'd buy some licorice sticks."

Davis looked up from his book and grinned at him. "If a toady frog had wings, he wouldn't bump his rear."

Aunt Kezia shook her head and snorted. "I wish there was some place to go where the conversation was a little bit more genteel." She winked at Cass, who was sitting next to Maeva. "This bunch must bore you to death. Tell you what let's do. Let's make some ice cream."

"Make ice cream?" Cass's eyes grew large. "Do you know how to make ice cream?"

"I purely do. Cody, you and Maeva go outside and get some fresh snow. Scrape it right off the top."

"It's too cold out there, Aunt Kezia," Maeva whined.

"It won't hurt you none. Now you git!"

Ten minutes later Cody and Maeva brought in two buckets full of snow, and everyone gathered around the table. Aunt Kezia divided it up into cups, and when everybody had one, she said, "Now, the thing to do is to pour some of that good, rich jersey cream over it like this." She got the cream out of the icebox and drizzled some on the snow. She took a spoonful and with a look of pure delight, said, "This is about right."

"I'm going to have maple syrup on mine," Maeva said. "It's better than cream, Cass. You'd better try it."

Cass was agreeable, and the two girls were soon eating the maple-flavored snow.

"I'm going to have ketchup on mine," Cody announced.

Davis gave a groan. "That's plum disgusting!"

But Cody would not be discouraged. He got the bottle of ketchup out, dumped it on the snow, and began eating it, a heavenly expression on his face.

For a time it was quiet until the snow cream was all eaten, and then Maeva, who was watching Cody, said, "What's all that stuff you been writing lately? You're getting to be quite a scholar."

"I've been writing tracts."

"What do you mean tracts? Like railroad tracks?"

"No, dopey. I mean tracts like you hand out with the gospel on them."

Everyone was staring at Cody with surprise. "Well, that's a fine thing to do," Lanie said. "Let me see one of them."

"Okay." Cody leaped up, left the room, and soon returned with a sheaf of papers. He handed one to Lanie, who stared at it while Cody passed out samples to the others.

"You can't hand these things out!" Lanie exclaimed.

Davis burst out laughing. "Well, it says what it means, don't it now."

Lanie stared at the tract. It was simple enough, for Cody had written in large capital letters with a red crayon, "TURN OR BURN!!!"

Maeva was tickled. "Oh, this is wonderful," she laughed. "Look at this, Cass. Don't you think this is going to make a lot of sinners give up their evil ways?"

Cass, who knew nothing at all about tracts, did not respond. She was staring at Cody, who was not at all upset about the criticism.

Cody said, "You got to say what you mean. Can't stand preachers that fool around not telling sinners where they're headed if they don't turn. So this is a good tract."

Everyone except Cass and Corliss began at once trying to convince Cody that it would be useless to hand out such things. Davis said, "Why, it'd make people mad."

"Let 'em get mad! They got to get the gospel."

For some time the argument went on, and finally Cody gathered up all of the tracts. "Well, I'm not going to argue about this. It's something I'm going to do."

"We'll have to leave the country." Davis grinned. "Everybody already thinks we're living with a crazy boy."

Aunt Kezia finally said, "Well, I got to admit I never saw a tracts that got right down to business as much as that."

"You're right, Aunt Kezia. Just say it right out." He riffled the tracts with his thumb. "I got an idea about how to make some money."

Maeva snorted. "What is this, idea number five hundred and six?"

"You go ahead and laugh, but this is going to make us a lot of money."

"Everybody get ready," Davis said. "We're going to be rich. I don't know if I can take all this money rolling in at once. I'll probably get proud and lifted up."

Lanie smiled. She was well accustomed to Cody's wild ideas. "What is it this time, Cody?"

"I've been thinking a lot about this." Cody was so serious he squeezed his eyes close together. "What we've got to do is start a rolling store."

Silence reigned for a moment, then Corliss said, "What's that, Cody?"

"Why, Corliss, it's the simplest thing in the world. I don't know why somebody hasn't thought of it." Cody's eyes brightened, and he waved his hands around, the tracts fluttering. "We got to get us an old truck and build a special bed on it, all covered, don't you see. Like a big bus. And inside it, we put shelves. Then on the shelves we put all kinds of groceries. Even other stuff like needles and threads and pens and nails. Stuff people want. Then we go around from door to door selling it. Why, it'll make us a fortune."

As was not too unusual, after one of Cody's proclamations, a silence fell across all of the listeners. Finally it was Lanie who expressed some doubt. "But they can buy those things at the grocery store. Why would they have to buy it off of a thing like you're talking about?"

"Because we're going to learn how to buy it and sell it cheaper than the grocery store. I've been studying this. There's such a thing called maintenance. Grocery store owners have to pay for their building, their lights, and all that stuff. We don't have to pay nothing."

"You have to have a truck, and trucks take gas." Davis shook his head. "We don't have a truck."

"You weren't thinking of using the truck we've got now?" Lanie asked.

"Aw, it's too little. We've got to have something bigger than that. I admit I ain't got all of it figured out yet, but it's a great idea."

Suddenly Davis gave Cody a look of astonishment. "You know, for almost fifteen years I've been waiting for you to come up with a good idea, and this may be it."

"Do you really think so, Davis?" Cass always looked to Davis for information. Ever since he had come to her rescue and brought her to live with the Freemans, she looked on him with something like awe.

"Well, not all of Cody's ideas are this good. If we could get some kind of a truck, it wouldn't be hard to convert it to a rolling store. A lot of the stuff we wouldn't have to buy like poke salad and dandelion greens and sassafras roots, stuff we can come up with ourselves, and then with a big garden we'd have all that. Not everybody has gardens. I think it might work." His shoulders slumped and he said, "But we'd never get enough money ahead to buy any kind of a truck."

Aunt Kezia snorted. "If God owns the cattle on a thousand hills, I reckon he owns the trucks on a thousand car lots!"

For the next twenty minutes they were all speaking excitedly. Finally Davis said, "Cody and me will draw a plan for our store. Then we'll start getting the wood for the shelves." He suddenly laughed and went over and rubbed Cody's head. "Wouldn't it be something if this knucklehead here came up with an idea that put us in the black."

Cody flushed with pleasure. His ideas usually weren't so well received. "Well, I could have told you that a long time ago," he said modestly. "Now I figure we can paint it purple so it'll catch everybody's eye."

⌁

The Dew Drop Inn was full of customers at noon, as was usual, especially on a Friday. Nellie Prather sat at the counter staring up at the menu that Sister Myrtle had printed by hand and put on the wall. Sister Myrtle came from behind the counter to stand in front of Nellie Prather. She had a ketchup stain on her bosom, and, as usual, she wore no makeup and her hair was tied back in a tight bun. She said in a loud voice, "Well, Brother Prather, I'm glad you come in."

"Always good to see you, Pastor." Prather was a faithful member of the Fire Baptized Pentecostal Church, and Sister Myrtle was his pastor.

"You missed prayer meeting Wednesday night. You got to fight to get your way to heaven, my brother."

Prather, a tall, good-looking man of thirty, flushed. He had blonde hair and very fair skin, and he always dressed neatly, even when farming. "I'm right sorry about that, Sister Myrtle," he said, "but I just couldn't come."

"Was you sick?"

"No, but I was shaving just before I got ready to come, and I dropped the mirror and it broke. Well, of course, you know what that means."

Almost everyone in the diner grinned with expectation, for they knew Nelson Prather was the most superstitious human being on the face of the earth.

"It was just a mirror. You should've come on anyhow."

"Oh no, Pastor, I couldn't do that. When you break a mirror that's real trouble," Nellie said quickly. "Of course there is a way to reverse the bad luck." He leaned forward. "You got to gather up all the broken pieces. Then you go out and find the clearest stream and throw them in there. Of course," he explained earnestly, "you got to be careful not to fall in love with your image in the stream."

"What if there's not a stream close by?" Pardue Jessup called out from the far end of the room. He was sitting across from Reverend Colin Ryan, both of them working on the liver and onion special.

"Well, I guess if a fellow lived out in the Sahara Desert that could be so," Nellie said. "But if that happens, you just have to pound that glass into pieces so fine ain't no mortals will ever see into it as a mirror."

"That's foolishness and downright superstitious!" Ed Hathcock said. His uniform hung on him, for he was short and thin, and he always ate so fast his face got red. "You ought to get rid of those superstitions, Nellie. They don't mean nothing."

"That's what you think, Chief," Nellie said with a decisive nod. "Well, I had a friend once who broke a mirror on New Year's Day, and he didn't pay no attention to it. Just throwed it out in big pieces, and wouldn't you know it, two years later he got throwed from a horse and broke both legs. Couldn't walk for a long time. I don't hold with mirrors. As a matter of fact, there's one that belonged to my mama in the bedroom where I sleep. Every night the last thing I do is hang a cloth over that mirror. If you don't, your soul can get caught in it while you sleep. Always best to keep your soul in bed with you, now."

"If you'd a come on to church, we'd a prayed that broken mirror away," Sister Myrtle snorted. "Now what do you want to eat?"

"I reckon I'll have the liver and onion special. Well done like always, Pastor."

"All right." She lifted her voice and cried out in a stentorian tone, "One special well done, Charley!" Sister Myrtle's volume was such that the windows rattled, and when they settled, she turned around and said, "I've got some things for you to do, Brother Prather. You've got to go by and chop Widow Mason some wood. She's plum out. After that you buy some grub and take it over to the Henderson house. Miz Henderson's sick, and I don't reckon they's a bite to eat in that house. You can cook supper and tell her I'll be there soon as I can get there."

Nelson Prather sat there meekly nodding and agreeing to the list of his pastor's demands.

Finally Colin Ryan said, "You know, Sister, I wish our church members would mind their pastor like yours mind you."

"You got them Baptists spoiled, that's what. It's that blamed vote that's got you in trouble. You Baptists are all alike. Got to vote on everything! I swan, you vote every time somebody wants to spit!"

Laugher filled the Dew Drop Inn, and for some time Colin had to endure the teasing that always came when a non-Pentecostal dared to speak his mind in Sister Myrtle's domain. Sister Myrtle, however, was not through with Nellie. After his liver was done, she put it down in front of him and prayed over it. Then she said, "Now I been meaning to talk to you about something. It's a little bit more personal than broken mirrors."

Phineas Delaughter, the mayor, was sitting in one of the booths with his wife, Geraldine. "Sister Myrtle," he said with a frown, "did it ever occur to you that the rest of us might not want to hear all these personal things about other folks?"

"Then stay home and eat a sandwich, Mayor. And before you leave I've got a few things I want to take up with you." She turned and leaned toward Nellie, who had taken a bite of steak. "You need to get married, Brother Prather."

Nellie was the shyest of all men, and to be getting such counsel in front of a room full of people brought a flush to his cheeks. "Reckon I will some day," he muttered, and stuffed his mouth with another huge piece of meat.

"You been saying that for ten years. Now, I been thinking about it. There's Sister Ona Mae Dickerson. She'd do you fine."

"Why, she's a widow with four children, Sister Myrtle."

"That's all right, Nellie," Jessup spoke up, winking at Ryan. "It'll save you the bother of siring all those kids. You know having kids is a time-consuming affair anyway. Now you'd get four ready-made."

"You hush your mouth, Pardue Jessup! You're a fine one to talk. You're depriving some woman of a husband."

Charley came out of the kitchen and laughed at Pardue. "I guess you'll keep your mouth shut, Sheriff, the way I learned to do. How you making out with that new filly that moved to town?"

"You mean Amelia Wright?"

"Sure. I seen you chasing around after her." Charley grinned. "Any luck?"

"Not a bit," Pardue said cheerfully. "She's aiming a little bit higher than a sheriff. She's got her sights set on Doc Merritt."

Ed Hathcock giggled. "I would have to say that woman's got more curves than a barrel of snakes."

It was the wrong thing to say in the Dew Drop Inn. Sister Myrtle marched over and stuck her face directly in front of the chief. "You hush up that sort of worldly talk, Ed Hathcock, or leave!"

Hathcock visibly shrunk in his seat. He was a mild enough fellow anyway, and Sister Myrtle Poindexter could intimidate a raging bull. "I didn't mean nothing, Sister. I apologize."

Pardue laughed. "Well, I got plans to beat Owen's time with that woman."

"How you going to do that?" Ryan grinned.

"I'll dazzle her with my wit and charm and sophistication."

Charley looked at Pardue, whom he admired and felt could do anything he set his mind to. "Well, if that don't take the rag off the bush," he breathed with admiration.

⌐══≺⌐

Indeed, Amelia Wright had attracted many of the single men in Fairhope—and the secret admiration of a few who were not single. She had gone out with two or three, but it was Owen Merritt who interested her. He had taken her to church a few times, aware that the eyes of the whole congregation were upon them.

On this Sunday, when they came out into the dazzling winter sun, she said, "Owen, I get tired of just cooking for myself. Why don't you come by tomorrow night? I'll fix you a meal."

"Let's make it Friday night, Amelia," Owen agreed at once. "There's a dance over at Brandon Hill. I'll eat your cooking and then we'll go to the dance."

"Well, that would be fun."

Owen smiled. "I'll get the best of the deal. I know you're a better cook than I am a dancer."

⌐══≺⌐

Monday evening Logan Satterfield pulled up in front of the Freeman place in a three-year-old Oldsmobile. He jumped out and, whistling, loped up to the front porch. When he knocked on the door and it opened, he said at once, "Well, hello, Miss Kezia. Do you reckon I could speak to Miss Maeva?"

"What do you want to speak to her about?"

Logan grinned. He liked the old lady a great deal. "I was thinking about asking her to a dance Friday night."

At that moment Maeva, who had seen Logan drive up, came around the corner. "You want me to go to a dance with you?"

"I think it'd be real nice. We'd be the best-looking couple there." Logan's black hair was carefully cut and trimmed, and he was wearing what appeared to be a new pair of pants and a new shirt. The Satterfields had plenty of money, but everybody knew their income came mostly from bootlegging.

Maeva smiled sweetly. "I'd be glad to go with you if you'd go somewhere with me."

"Well, you just name it, Miss Maeva," Logan said without hesitation.

"Good. I'll go to the dance with you on Friday if you go to church with me on Sunday morning."

Logan Satterfield was a young man of some poise. His good looks and musical ability had given him an edge over most young men in the county. This offer of Maeva's, however, took him off guard. He gasped like a fish that had been thrown on the bank, and then suddenly the idea tickled him. "I think that'd be outstanding." He winked at her. "Dance on Friday and go to church on Sunday. I'll be here at six o'clock. Wear your dancing shoes." It seemed he was unable to stop smiling at Maeva as he backed away from the front door. At last he nodded to Aunt Kezia, who was still standing next to Maeva. "Good to see you too, Miss Kezia," he said.

As soon as Maeva closed the door, she found herself confronted by Cody. "You can't go to one of those sinful dances with a bootlegger!" he said, almost shouting.

"Why, Cody, I thought you'd be happy." Maeva turned her head so he would not see her wink at Lanie. "Here I'm doing my best to evangelize the poor fellow."

Cody could not take this in. "You're going to evangelize him by going to a dance?"

"Didn't you hear what I said to him? He's going to go to church with me Sunday morning." Maeva laughed with delight. "Get some of your tracts ready. You can hand him a half a dozen of them when he comes in."

"Aunt Kezia," Lanie said, "I don't like this."

"I was just like her when I was sixteen years old, but I got it all figured out, honey. You don't have to worry."

"I do have to worry. You know what those dances are like."

"I know what they used to be like, and I reckon they ain't changed much. And I'll tell you what. We'll all go to that dance, every Freeman in the house. When he drives up, we'll load in there with him, and he'll wish he never heard of Maeva Freeman."

Maeva laughed aloud. "That's a great idea, Aunt Kezia! That'll take some of the starch out of that jellybean!"

Cody liked this idea. "Good. I'll take some of the tracts to the dance with me."

"Oh, that'll make you popular." Lanie smiled but shook her head.

"All right. We'll try it, but I still worry. Anything can happen."

Maeva did not look one bit worried. "He'll run like a rabbit when he finds out this whole bunch is on his hands," she said. "No man would put up with all of us!"

⇀ CHAPTER 5 ⇀

Lanie hurried getting ready for the dance, but she had some reservations. Cass came in to watch her, and the young woman said, "It doesn't seem fair, Lanie, not at all."

"What do you mean, Cass?"

"Oh, you know what I mean." Cass was wearing a light green dress that set off her eyes. Her pregnancy was plainly evident, and she had tried to beg off from going to the dance, but Lanie had insisted that she must go. "It just don't seem right for all of us to be going. Logan Satterfield wanted to take Maeva, not the whole family."

"He may get his feelings hurt a little bit, but he'll get over it. He's got a pretty bad reputation. I wouldn't want to trust Maeva with him alone."

Cass was sitting down in the chair beside the desk where Lanie did her writing. There was a poignant look in her eyes, and she said almost in a whisper, "I wish I had things like this happen to me."

Lanie, surprised, turned to look at the young girl. "Things like what, Cass?"

"Young men coming by, meeting my family, and being nice. Taking me places."

"You didn't have anything like that?"

"No. I never did."

Lanie moved across the room, picked up her hairbrush, and began brushing Cass's hair. "You're such a pretty young woman," she said. "You're going to have lots of gentlemen callers."

"Not with this." Cass put her hand on her stomach. "Nobody would want me, Lanie. You know it."

"I don't know any such thing," Lanie said. "A lot of women with children get married. True, most of them have lost a husband, but so have you in a way." Cass's fiancé had died in an accident in the steel mill where he'd worked.

Lanie took Cass's hand. "Now, I want you to have a good time tonight."

"I haven't had much experience with that."

"Well, it's time you started. Come along now. Let's see if the thundering herd is ready to go."

The two young women went downstairs and found that indeed everyone was ready to go. Corliss was wearing a new dress made from flour sacks. This one was blue with tiny cornflowers on it. "Will I get to dance with someone, Lanie?"

"Sure you will," Davis said. "You can dance with me. You're too pretty to let the rest of the fellows have a shot at you." Davis was wearing his father's only good suit. It was still a little loose, but the pants were just the right length.

For a moment, Lanie could not speak. "You look just like Daddy, Davis."

Davis gave her an odd look. "Well, I wish I were like him inside as well as outside."

"You are," Maeva said. She came over and put her hand on Davis's cheek. "Now, I want you to find the prettiest girl at that dance and take her away from whoever brought her."

"That probably means a fight," Cody said. "It ain't right to fight. It ain't even right to go to dances."

"There's nothing wrong with going to dances, Cody," Aunt Kezia said sharply.

"There is too!" Cody said, his voice rising. "A praying knee and a dancing foot don't go on the same leg."

"Where'd you hear that?"

"I made it up all by myself. Ain't it elegant?" Cody said, looking proud.

Suddenly Davis turned to the window. "Well, here comes your fellow, Maeva." A wide grin spread across his face. "I don't know Logan Satterfield much, but I'd venture to guess he's about to get the surprise of his life."

"Let me answer the door and break the news to him," Maeva said. She was wearing a dress of her mother's that she had cut down. She had done a fine job. It fit her snugly.

As she passed by, Corliss said, "You smell good, Maeva."

"That's some of Ma's perfume."

Maeva opened the door, and halfway up the steps, Logan stopped in his tracks. "Why, you're like a rosebush in full bloom. Better be careful some young feller don't come along and pick the flowers!"

"I think you're prettier than I am, Logan."

Indeed, Logan Satterfield did look beautiful, if such a word could be attached to a man. His suit was new, gray with a tiny stripe that matched his blue eyes. The coat had three buttons, and underneath, a six-button vest was fastened neatly. A striped red and white necktie completed his outfit.

As he stepped inside Maeva said, "You look just absolutely delicious. Why, if you had to go to your own funeral, the undertaker wouldn't have to do a thing to you. Just lay you in the casket and cross your hands."

Logan laughed, and humor danced in his dark eyes. "Well, always good to have a compliment. But you ought not to look so good, Maeva. I'll have to fight every young fellow in the world to keep them away from you. But don't worry, if any of them fellers even looks at you out of the corners of his eye, I'll threaten him with bodily harm."

"Oh, I don't think you'll have to do all the fighting."

"Sure I will."

"No, Davis here can handle some of it."

Logan suddenly noticed that the entire Freeman family stood waiting by the front door, all dressed with their heavy coats on. He could not speak for a moment but tried to put all this together. "What do you mean? Is Davis going to the dance?"

"Why, we're all going, sonny boy," Aunt Kezia said. "A man with your reputation's got to have somebody to watch him, so that's what we plan to do. That big car of yours will hold all of us, won't it?"

Logan Satterfield's face was a study. His mouth hung open as he tried to think of a reply. His gaze darted from one Freeman to another, but disbelief was in his eyes.

"Don't just stand there with your mouth open, Logan," Maeva said. "Will your car hold us all?"

"They—you mean—*all* of you are going?" Logan finally managed to ask.

"Every one of us," Cody said. "We aim to ride herd on you. There won't be any funny business going on with my sister."

Logan's gaze darted to the door as if measuring the distance it would take to turn and flee, but then suddenly he grinned. The grin turned into a laugh, and finally he shook his head with admiration. "Well, I've been to three county fairs and two snake stompings, but I ain't seen nothing like this."

"I knew you wouldn't mind, Logan," Maeva said, smiling up at him.

"Not a bit. Come on. That big Oldsmobile will hold every one of us. Let's get going, and we'll show the folks at the dance where the bear sat in the buckwheat!"

They filed out to the car, and Davis whispered to Aunt Kezia, "I didn't think he'd put up with it."

"A fellow will put up with almost anything to get to go to a dance with a pretty young girl. You need one yourself."

"I don't have time or money for that, Aunt Kezia."

"Don't take money for such a thing to happen. Just takes time and a little nerve. Tell you what, I'll look over the crop at church and see which ones you're fit to go with. I've already had my eye on Emmy Simpson."

Davis laughed. "Why, half the fellows in Stone County are after her—and she knows it. She's proud as a cat with two tails!"

"You can catch her eye, Davis. Just fly right at it!"

The dance was held in the Legion Hall. All the tables, which held the refreshments, had been pushed to the back wall in one long line to clear the floor for dancing. The refreshments were somewhat bland, but with Prohibition, lemonade was just about all that was legally allowed. Anyone interested, however, soon found that more potent refreshments were available outside behind the hall.

The room was filled with sound, for musicians were plentiful and as varied as their instruments. The plinking of five-string banjoes rose above the guitars, and two bass fiddles made their low-pitched *thump-thump-thump*. Jerry Watkins, the barber, played a dulcimer, and Kyle Satterfield added to the rhythm section with a washboard, his fingers capped in thimbles. Otis Bench blew into a jug, and Mozell French's fingers flew as he played a banjo.

Many of the folk songs were of the purest variety, some going all the way back to England. Some folks requested some newfangled country western songs, and someone even called out they wanted something akin to the songs sung by the Singing Brakeman, who yodeled as he sang. The evening wore on, and the dance floor filled with music and laughter, as folks trotted and whirled through square dances, waltzes, hoedowns, and the Texas two-step.

Lanie danced with several young men, enjoying herself more than she could have imagined. Her only discomfort came when one young man tried to hold her too close during a waltz. She routed him in short order by pushing him away and smiling him out of his intentions. All the while she kept her eye on Logan Satterfield. Finally, when she got a break between dances, she crossed the dance floor to stand beside Aunt Kezia.

Kezia said, "Don't worry, honey. I'm watching Maeva. She's having the time of her life. I don't know about that young Satterfield buck, though. He don't look too happy."

"It was a mean trick, Aunt Kezia."

"Well, that feller's too good-looking to be turned loose. Good-looking men ain't to be trusted."

"Oh, Aunt Kezia, I've seen a picture of Mr. Butterworth, your second husband. He was fine-looking."

Kezia tried to find an argument, but finally she had to nod reluctantly. "Well, Mr. Butterworth was an exception."

"What about Owen? He's nice-looking."

"Why do you always go around picking out exceptions? Look at that Rudolph Valentino. A man with slick black hair like that ain't to be trusted."

Lanie suddenly laughed. "I don't know anything about him, and besides, I don't think he's all that good-looking."

The door to the hall opened, and Lanie turned to see Owen and Amelia Wright enter. "Look," she said. "There's Owen."

"He is a good-looking fellow, and for a doctor he ain't bad. Yes, I'd have to say Merritt breaks the rule." Aunt Kezia narrowed her eyes and peered more closely. "That's the woman he's been dragging to church."

"I don't know if he's been dragging her or not, but he's brought her several times."

"She's got a look about her."

"What do you mean by that?"

"You just watch. Merritt will have a hard time hanging onto her."

Indeed, this proved to be the case. It was the custom at these dances to cut in on couples, and the other young men, and some not so young, found opportunity to cut in on Owen time and time again.

Pardue Jessup was not as fine-looking as Logan Satterfield, but he was strong, tall, and had a masculine attractiveness. He never missed a dance, and usually he brought someone like Mamie Dorr with him. Mamie, whose reputation was not any too good to begin with, was not with him tonight. So when he asked Lanie to dance, she said, "Why didn't you bring Mamie?"

"She's gone to visit her cousin over in Ellisville. You sure are a good dancer. Me and you might go on stage like that Vernon and Irene

Castle. I seen them in the newsreel down at the Rialto. They sure can hoof it."

"I don't think we're in their class, Pardue."

Pardue glanced over her shoulder. "Looky there at that doctor and Amelia Wright. Ain't they a sight? That's a good-looking woman. She beats hens a'pacing!"

Despite herself, when they turned, Lanie did watch Owen and Amelia. Pardue was right. They made a fine-looking couple. "I guess Owen's gotten over his broken engagement," she said.

"Didn't appear to hurt him much for a fact—which meant it wasn't too deep. You know what?"

"What, Pardue?"

"I'm gonna take that filly away from Owen. She's too good-looking to waste on a sawbones."

Lanie laughed aloud. "What I don't like about you is your lack of confidence. Aside from Cody, you got more brass than any male I've ever seen."

The dance came to an end. Logan, who had played his fiddle for several dances, stood up and began to sing "Red River Valley." After a while the band joined in, playing softly in the background. It was a plaintive song of lost love and sorrow. The words seemed to touch everybody, for a silence fell over the hall. Logan had a pleasant baritone voice. He sang easily without strain and put into the words some of the heartache the songwriter had intended.

"He sure can pull the chain on tears and squalling," Pardue whispered to Lanie. "Look at the women crying. I'm a little bit teared up myself."

Lanie did not answer, for she was struggling to keep the tears from her own eyes. "Red River Valley" was one of her father's favorite songs. She had heard him sing it a hundred times and even better than Logan.

Finally the song was over, and Pardue said, "I'm gonna grab that Amelia gal before somebody else gets her."

Lanie watched as Pardue Jessup make straight for the pair and swung Amelia out immediately. Owen's eyes met hers, and he came over, his smile wide. "It looks like I lost my girl to that no-good sheriff." He studied her face and leaned closer, his expression worried. "What's wrong?"

"Nothing's wrong, Owen."

"Why, sure there is," he said. "You're about to cry."

"It was just that song. It's one of Daddy's favorites. I've heard him sing it all my life. It made me a little sad."

"Well, tell you what. Let's go over and sit this one out. I'm tired of dancing anyway." He took her arm and led her over to the row of chairs, got her a lemonade, and then sat down next to her. They listened to the music, commenting on the various instruments and those who played them. Owen finally said, "Does this happen to you often, Lanie? But then I know it does. You worry about your dad all the time."

"I try not to, Owen, but it's so hard."

Owen reached over, took her hand, and squeezed it. "I know it's hard," he said quietly.

She turned to face him and saw the concern in his fine eyes. "You better not hold my hand. That'll give the gossips something else to talk about."

"If they're talking about us, they'll be letting someone else alone," he said, but he turned loose of her hand, which disappointed her a little.

⚬══⚬

Logan Satterfield was a good tactician. He had made no attempt to get Maeva alone during the evening, but finally as the hour grew late, he had somehow maneuvered her outside. "Too hot in here," he had said. "Let's get a breath of fresh air."

Maeva gave him an annoyed look but said, "That's all we're going for, Logan, just fresh air?"

"Why, certainly it is! You don't think I'd have any other notion, do you?"

Maeva laughed. "I know you got notions. Those things are bad for a young fellow."

Throwing a coat around her shoulders, she went outside with him. The area around the Legion Hall was filled with cars, pickups, and quite a few wagons and saddle horses. Logan said, "They ought to have more of these dances. Gives people a chance to let off steam."

"They're fun. I don't see any harm in them."

The two of them stopped beside a large wagon. It cut off the view of the Legion Hall, and they were isolated. Logan looked up and said, "Look at that moon. Ain't it pretty? Looks like a big silver dollar up there."

"I love it when it's cold and clear like this. Look. The moon's all speckled just like someone took target practice at it."

Logan leaned against the wagon and studied her. "You gonna make me go through with my part of the deal by going to church Sunday?"

"I can't make you do anything, Logan Satterfield."

"Why, that ain't true," Logan said without hesitation. "I reckon you could make me do just about anything, a pretty girl like you."

They stood there talking in the moonlight. The sound of the music was muffled but drifted over to them, making a pleasant harmony with the sounds of the night. "I feel like a wicked girl coming out here with you."

"Why, we ain't doing nothing."

"Good. I'm surprised at your gentlemanly behavior. I'll give a good report to your family."

"My family don't care much what I do. As a matter of fact, we ain't close like your family."

Maeva knew that this was true if she could count on what she had heard. The Satterfields lived far off the beaten track in the center of deep woods. It was well known, but never proven, that they made moonshine whiskey. They often got into fights and had carried on long feuds with their neighbors. One of the older Satterfield boys was in the pen for holding up a bank, and the reputation of the others was not much better.

"You know," Logan said, "you ought to be grateful for having a family like you got. Oh, I know you lost your mama and your daddy's in jail, but I ain't never seen people in a family hang together like you and your brothers and sisters."

"I'm the worst of them, Logan."

Logan suddenly stared at her. "Why, that ain't no way to talk about yourself."

Maeva was given to bouts of unpleasant introspection. She knew that she was the black sheep of the Freeman children, but she could not understand why she often got into trouble and gave the rest such difficult times. She said quietly, "I wish I could be good like Lanie or Davis. They're all better than I am."

The sound of the music seemed far away, and the light of the moon played upon Maeva's face. Logan leaned over for a closer look and what he saw made him whisper, "Don't be sad, Maeva." He reached out and put his arms around her. She tilted her face up toward his. He waited but she made no move so he kissed her. He held her tight, aware of the hungers that surged through him. He wondered if she was just as aware of her own. He had kissed many young women in settings like this, but somehow there was a sweetness in this one that caught him off guard.

Maeva was the first to break away. "I wondered when that was coming."

"Don't be mad."

"I'm not mad. I just don't like who I am."

"Well, I don't like who I am either. Everybody knows all the Satterfields are a worthless lot."

"Then why don't we change? Why don't we do better, Logan?"

Logan Satterfield had no answer. He struggled to find words, but they would not come. Finally he shook his head. "I don't know, but there's a better way to live than the way I'm doing it."

"We'd better go back inside. Lanie will be sending the army out to get me. My brothers will want to beat you up."

They walked back toward the Legion Hall, both troubled in a strange way by what they had experienced. It was not the kiss so much as the confessions they had made to one another. Neither of them was really happy, and now as they went back inside, the fun of the dance had vanished.

Amelia giggled as she ascended the steps to her home. "I didn't know doctors were so humorous."

Owen had just told Amelia a story about one of his patients. It was a trifle risqué, and he had been afraid he might offend her, but she was still laughing. When she turned, he saw by the light of the moon that her eyes danced. "Well," he said, "not all my experiences with patients are that amusing."

The two had left the dance early, and now they stood outside Amelia's house. She said suddenly, "I haven't had as much fun in I don't know when, Owen."

"Me too. I guess we need to do more things like this."

"There aren't that many dances, are there?"

"Not enough, I don't guess."

"Come in. I'll make us some coffee."

"Why, it's pretty late, Amelia."

"I'm wide awake. I won't sleep for hours. I get lonesome. Come on in."

"The neighbors might notice."

Amelia said, "Well, you can sneak around to the back door, if you'd like. But I'm going to fix some coffee."

Owen suddenly laughed. "Well, maybe Dorsey Pender won't see us — or Henrietta Green."

"I take it they're the chief purveyors of gossip in Fairhope."

"The mailman and the telephone operator—yup, they're the experts."

Amelia opened the door, and they stepped inside. The house was cold, but when they went in the kitchen, she stirred up the fire and soon had coffee boiling on the stove. They sat opposite each other at the table, and at her insistence, he began to tell her more about himself.

"... so that's about it," he concluded a few minutes later. "When Doctor Givens broke his leg, he had to have a replacement. I came to help out and never left."

Amelia held the coffee cup in one hand. "Do you think you'll stay here always?"

Owen leaned back. "I don't know about that. As a matter of fact, I don't know much about anything. I just live one day at a time."

Amelia had been studying Owen as he talked. There was a masculinity about him that drew her. There was no doubt that he was attractive to women. She had seen their glances when he took her to church, and she felt proud that he chose her.

"There's something I've wanted to ask you," she said. "Have you had a hard time since your engagement was broken?"

He looked down at his cup, studied it as if there were some meaning in it, then took a swallow. "I can't tell you, Amelia. I guess I was kind of shell-shocked. I've heard on the battlefield when a soldier almost gets killed and then doesn't, he's just out of it for a while. I've been going through the motions in much the same way."

"That's what I've been doing since I lost my husband, Owen. I've had a hard time." She fell silent for a moment, then said softly, "I suppose we're both walking wounded."

They sat there talking quietly and drinking coffee, and after a time he said, "I've got to go now. It's late."

She walked with him to the door, and after he put on his coat and turned to her, she put her hand on his chest. "It was a wonderful evening, Owen." Her voice was little more than a whisper, and she looked up at him with an odd expression. "I get lonely sometimes, and I suppose you do too."

Owen said, "I think most people are lonely, but maybe we can help each other." He hesitated, and then a smile turned up the corners of his lips. "You know, I made my mother a promise once that I'm going to break."

Seeing a smile, Amelia said, "I think I can guess what promise you made."

"I bet you can't."

"You promised her you'd never kiss a girl on the first date."

"That's right. I hate to be unfaithful to my promises to my mother, but, well—" He leaned forward, put his arms around her, and kissed her. He was surprised at the fervency with which she returned his caress. Her lips were eager and soft under his, and after a time he was the one who pulled back. Huskily, he said, "I'd better go before I break some more promises. It was a wonderful evening."

"Good night, Owen."

Amelia watched as he went out and got into the car. He waved as he drove away. She closed the door, leaned back against it, and a smile came to her lips. "Owen Merritt," she whispered. "Owen Merritt, the physician who makes promises to his mother—and then breaks them."

She laughed, feeling better than she had in months.

⇒ CHAPTER 6 ⇐

I don't think Logan's going to come," Maeva said. She was sitting in the pew beside Davis, who held Corliss on his lap. "He never intended to come in the first place."

Davis looked over his shoulder and then shook his head. "I don't know. He told me at the dance that he'd come. He seemed to make kind of a joke out of it."

Cody had been listening and now looked up from the Bible that he had been marking carefully. His Bible was marked up with *amens* and *hallelujahs* written in the margins, and he had practically every verse underlined, Old Testament and New. "He told me he'd come too. Of course, he's a sinner and you can't depend on sinners."

The choir came marching in to take their seats, and Brother Pink stood up to lead in the opening prayer. Just as he did, Cody whispered to Maeva, "Look. There he is."

Maeva turned quickly and saw that Logan Satterfield had indeed entered. Surprised and pleased, she smiled and lifted her hand to catch Logan's attention. He met her smile with one of his own, and she motioned him over. As he came down the aisle, a murmur seemed to follow him. A Satterfield in church!

"Sorry to be late," he said, sliding in to sit beside Maeva. "Did I miss anything?"

"No, you didn't. I'm surprised to see you here. I didn't think you'd come."

"Why, I told you I'd be here."

"Men have told me things before that weren't true."

"Now, Miss Maeva," Logan said, "you've got to learn to be more generous in your feelings toward men."

There was no time for further discussion, for Brother Pink prayed a brief prayer and then Dempsey Wilson said, "For our first hymn this morning we'll sing the old favorite, 'What a Friend We Have in Jesus.'"

Everyone stood, and Maeva was very much conscious of the curious glances toward Logan, and she well understood the whisperings caused by Logan choosing to sit beside her. They sang the first verse of the hymn, and she noticed that Logan did not sing but mouthed the words and kept his eyes on it. On the second verse, however, he sang along keeping perfect time but not loudly. On the third verse, his clear voice lifted above those around him, and she marveled at the beauty of his singing voice. Others also took notice.

"Do you know this song?" she said.

"I learned it in the first verse." He smiled down at her, and she was aware of the male handsomeness of his features. He had a tapered face, tanned and smooth, and his eyes were so black she could hardly see the pupils. His lips were broad and strong, and his features were cleanly cut. "That's a good song," he said. "I never heard it before. Of course, I haven't been in church more than once or twice. Both times for funerals."

The song service continued, and for each hymn Logan simply listened to the first verse and then sang the second verse as if he had been singing it all his life. He scanned the congregation more than once, and after about the third time he leaned down and whispered, "I see some of our customers are here."

Maeva knew he meant those who bought the homemade whiskey the Satterfields made. She said, "Not everybody is a drinker here. Just some."

"I reckon that's right."

Finally the offering was taken and the choir sang their special, then Colin Ryan stood up to preach. He wore a pair of dark blue trousers instead of the blue jeans he usually sported and a shirt with no tie. As usual, he did not stay long on the pulpit.

"I'm going to call your attention this morning to something the Lord revealed to me last night. It's in the eleventh chapter of the book of Matthew in verse nineteen. Jesus had been made the target of considerable talk by a group called the Pharisees, and in this verse they had accused Him of eating with sinners, publicans, and tax collectors. In other words," Colin said clearly, "He had been making friends of people who weren't members of the church. He said, 'The Son of man came eating and drinking, and they say, Behold a man gluttonous, and a winebibber, a friend of publicans and sinners.'

"I'd like to speak to you this morning on that phrase. Jesus, a friend of sinners. This verse struck me as being one of the most wonderful things that's in the whole Bible. I know it's simple and oftentimes we read right over it, but just think of it, friends. You all know what a friend is. It's someone that you love and trust and respect, one you lean on, one you go to in time of trouble. And here is Jesus Christ, who made the heavens and the earth, saying, in effect, 'I'm going to be friends with sinners.'"

Colin put his finger in the Bible and walked first to one side of the pulpit and then the other as he continued. "We get the idea," he said, "that religious people are the friends of God. Abraham was called a friend of God because he believed Him. But here in Matthew, Jesus has identified Himself as being one who is a friend, not just of the church folks, but of sinners. That's what I'm going to speak to you about this morning. You're here this morning. Some of you are not saved. You think God is your enemy, but this verse says that He's not. And I want to convince you, if I can, how the great God who made heaven and earth is your friend and how He wants you to become His friend."

In the sermon that followed it was clear that Colin had a heart for those who did not know God. He preached as though he would like to come out and wrap his arms around those who were not saved.

From time to time Maeva turned to watch Logan's face, and she saw he kept his eyes fixed on the preacher. Not once did he turn to look at her. She had expected he would misbehave somehow, but he did not.

Finally Colin said, "It's one thing for Jesus to be your friend, but let me ask you this. Are you willing to be His friend? That's the question, isn't it? I realize that some of you have never thought about this, but He says in the Book of Revelation, 'Behold, I stand at the door, and knock: if any man hear my voice, and open the door, I will come in.' Wouldn't that be a great thing, friend, for you to have Jesus Christ come into your life?

"I know it would make a difference. Some of you would have to quit your jobs. Some of you would have to go back to your families and start all over again because you haven't been a friend of Jesus. But I'm going to give you a few Scriptures now. They'll open the door for you. First is simply, 'Whosoever shall call upon the name of the Lord shall be saved.' That's simple. So we're going to pause for a moment here and I'm going to pray. And I hope you'll pray too. Ask Jesus to come in, and your life will be different."

This was all very familiar to Maeva. She had heard it many times before, but somehow, today was different. A hush fell over the room, and a sense of God's strength and power fell upon the congregation. As Colin prayed, she kept her head bowed and her eyes closed, but after a time she could not suppress her curiosity. Opening her eyes to a mere slit, she glanced at Logan. His face was pale, his lips were pressed tightly together, and he clenched the back of the pew in front of him with white knuckles.

After the prayer, Colin said, "We're going to sing an invitation hymn. If you want to become a friend of Jesus, as He became your friend at the cross, you need to make it plain. If you've called upon the Lord or if you want to come as we sing, then you'll find a friend such as you've never known before."

Maeva opened the hymnal to the invitation hymn, though she knew it by heart. She held it out so that Logan could see, but he clung to the back of the bench and did not move. The invitation was rather long. Several went forward, and Colin talked with each one. Twice he knelt down with people who came. Finally he said, "We rejoice over those who have come to accept Jesus as their Savior, but I know that there are others. I'm going to pray that even after you leave this place you will listen as God speaks to your heart. And I beg you, wherever you are, whether you're fishing or working or in bed at night, when you hear Jesus call, make Him your friend."

Colin asked one of the deacons to close in prayer, then he came down to stand beside Logan. As soon as the amen was said, he smiled and said, "I'm glad to see you. I'm Colin Ryan."

"This is Logan Satterfield, Pastor," Maeva said.

"We haven't met before, but I'm glad to see you. Come back when you can."

Logan did not answer. He said nothing, but when Maeva stepped into the aisle, he followed her.

Lanie came down from the choir loft and joined them. "I'm glad to see you, Logan." Logan muttered something, and she said, "We would love to have you come home and take dinner with us today."

Logan blinked, seeming shocked. "You don't know what you're talking about, Miss Freeman. We Satterfields are not the kind of people who want to take Sunday dinner." He turned suddenly and, without another word, pushed his way out of church.

Lanie stood there, frowning as she watched him go. "What happened, Maeva? Is he mad?"

"I don't think so. I think he's thinking about religion. Probably never has before."

"When he comes back, you try to get him to come and eat with us."

"I'll try," Maeva said doubtfully, "but I don't think he's the kind of fellow you can force into doing anything."

❦

Monday afternoon the kitchen was rich with the aroma of fresh-baked biscuits. Rays of pale winter sunshine slanted through the windows, filled with multitudes of dust motes. From far away came the sound of mocking birds, their cries floating into the room like a distant symphony.

Cody was teasing Booger with a biscuit. He broke off a chunk of it, said, "Here, Booger," and pretended to toss it. He made a motion with his hand, and Booger snapped at where a part of the biscuit should be but wasn't.

Finally Corliss came over and said, "Don't tease Booger. That's mean."

"Well, I'll tease you instead." Cody picked up Corliss and spun her around the room. She squealed with delight.

"You two are making so much noise I can't work." Davis was sitting at the table going over his homework with Lanie beside him. Maeva was reading a romance, as usual, and Aunt Kezia was teaching Cass how to crochet.

Cody put Corliss down and stood up. "I have an announcement to make."

"Heaven help us," Davis said with a grin. "Another announcement? What is it this time?"

"I've been thinking," Cody said, "and I've got the solution to our problem."

"Solution number five hundred and twenty-six," Maeva said wearily. "I get tired of all your schemes, Cody."

"Now just wait a minute," Cody said, his tone serious. "You all said my idea was good—the one about the rolling grocery store, didn't you?"

"Sure, Cody, but we'll never get enough money for a truck," Davis said.

Cody seemed to swell up, and his face beamed with pleasure. "I've taken care of that," he said proudly.

Lanie stared at him in disbelief. "What do you mean by that?"

"You know that old truck that's been up on blocks at the old Simmons place? Been there ever since Mr. Simmons died. I put on my thinking cap, and it came to me that Mrs. Simmons would never use that old truck. I went by and talked to her. Offered to get it out of her way. She tried to bargain with me, but I got it for twenty dollars."

"You don't have twenty dollars," Maeva said.

"No, but Pardue has."

"You borrowed money from Pardue?" Lanie exclaimed.

"Sure, but that ain't all. He checked the engine out and said it runs fine." Cody began pacing back and forth, his face wreathed in smiles. "Now, all we got to do is modify that ol' truck, put in some shelves, and we're all set."

Lanie ran over and hugged Cody. "I'll never make fun of your inventions again, Cody!" she cried. A hope was born in her at that instant, a hope of a small but steady income. It was like a vision of heaven. "When can we start?" she asked Cody, her eyes shining.

Tuesday after lunch, Lanie walked to the town library to save on gasoline, then decided to take a shortcut back alongside the Singing River. As always, she carried her notebook and pencil in case she found a good time to write a poem. The air was cold and crisp, for winter had not turned its grip loose on the country yet, but Lanie breathed deeply, enjoying its freshness.

Suddenly she saw a man who stood looking out over the river. She studied him and realized she hadn't seen him before. Better dressed than most people in Fairhope, he wore tan trousers and a leather jacket, and because he wore no hat, she could see the red glint in his chestnut hair. He turned, and she saw that his eyes were kind.

"Hello there," he said, smiling. "A little nippy out today."

"Yes. It's pretty cool."

"I take it you're from Fairhope?"

Lanie ordinarily would not have stopped to talk to a stranger, but there was something about the man that drew her. His smile broadened when he removed the pipe he had been smoking. "I've been admiring the river. What's the name of it?"

"It's called the Singing River."

Lanie had remarked long ago that there was a sibilant sound to the waters of the Singing River. Mostly it was caused by the water in the shallows flowing on the smooth stone, but since she was a girl she had pretended the river sang real songs.

"Well, that's poetic enough. It does sing a little bit, doesn't it?" He cocked his head as if to listen better. "I'm a visitor here, as you see. I just got off the bus. It crossed over this river and I doubled back to have a closer look at it."

"You're from the north, aren't you?"

"My speech does betray me. I'm mostly from New York."

Lanie was impressed. "I'd love to see New York."

"Well, New York would love to see you. Why don't you come for a visit?"

"Oh, that wouldn't be possible."

"Anything's possible. My full name is Brent Hayden."

Lanie started. "Not the writer!" she exclaimed.

"Well, I am impressed! A young woman here in the wilds of Arkansas knows something about a writer who hasn't got much of a reputation."

"You *do* have a reputation. Your book was nominated for the American Book Award."

"How in the world did you know that? How did word get from New York to Fairhope?"

"I read the New York paper sometimes at the library, especially anything about writing."

Brent Hayden suddenly smiled again. "Don't tell me you're a writer too."

Lanie shook her head. "I like to write, but I'm not a writer like you are, Mr. Hayden."

"Please. Just Brent. And what's your name?"

"Lanie Freeman."

"What do you write, Lanie?"

"Mostly poetry, but some day I'm going to write a book like you did."

"A novel? That's a big chore. Maybe you could start with short stories. I'd like to see what you've written."

"Oh, it's not worth showing to you."

Hayden picked up a rock and threw it out at the river. He watched the splash it made and then said, "Don't ever put yourself down, Miss Lanie." He stood looking at the river, and he seemed to have forgotten her. Lanie was about ready to move on, thinking he had finished with her, but then he turned, and she noticed his eyes were blue gray, a color she had never seen in a man's eyes.

"I've been looking for a place to work on my next book. New York's too noisy. I want a quiet place, so I've been just wandering around. I like this river. I will probably like Fairhope. Do you know of a place that could be rented cheaply? Just a single room."

"There's a cabin about half a mile down the river here. It belongs to a family named Harrison. They moved to town, so they keep it locked up. I think they'd be glad to make a little money from it."

"Right on the river, is it?"

"Yes, sir. Right on the river."

"Would you show it to me, Lanie?"

"Yes. It's on the way to my house. Come along and I'll show it to you."

⚬━⟨⟩━

"This is just the thing!" Brent Hayden exclaimed. "What a view of the river."

"The water gets high sometimes but never this high. You can fish right down there where that deep pool is. I caught a six-pound bass there once."

"I don't know how to fish." Lanie started to offer to teach him but felt shy. He said, "Maybe you could put me in the way of it."

"There's not much to it. My brothers and I fish all the time."

"This will be just what I need."

"It might be a little lonesome for you after New York, I would think."

"That's what I want. Lonesome. How do I get in touch with the Harrisons?"

"They have a house in town. I don't know the street address, but I could show it to you."

"Good. If you're not doing anything else, I'd appreciate it."

"I'd be glad to, Mr. Hayden."

"No, not Mr. Hayden," he said again. "Call me Brent. We writers have to be on a first-name basis. Come along now, and you can point out the sights of Fairhope."

Lanie listened with fascination as Brent Hayden spoke on the way to town. It was actually only a quarter of a mile, so it did not take long. She took him to the Harrison house, knocked on the door, and Mrs. Harrison opened to them. She introduced Brent Hayden, and then said, "It's good to have met you, Brent."

"Don't run off. I want to say thank you after I settle the terms with Mrs. Harrison here."

Lanie went outside to wait. Just imagine! A New York writer! Right here in Fairhope! She had read his first book and had never imagined she might meet an author she liked so much. As she stood waiting for him, her thoughts took wing.

Maybe I will let him see some of my poems.

She leaned back against the huge walnut tree that spread its bulk, blotting out the sky. The branches, once clothed in riotous color, were bare now, stripped by the winter cold, and it seemed to Lanie that the naked limbs were lifted up as if in prayer.

PART TWO

The Freeman Rolling Emporium

← CHAPTER 7 →

The old barn on the Freeman homeplace had long ago ceased to be used for anything much. It had, however, proved to be an excellent place to convert a truck to a rolling store. It had been Cody's idea to use the barn, and to make things even better, he had salvaged an old wooden stove, set it up in the barn, and run a pipe out through the ceiling. He had stoked it up until its sides glowed a cherry red.

Davis, who had worn his heavy coat, quickly removed it and shook his head. "You're gonna burn the barn down getting the stove that hot." Lanie and Maeva, who were sanding shelves nearby, agreed.

"No, I'm not!" Cody argued. He stepped back to admire the progress that had been made on the project. He let out a low whistle of admiration. "I wish you'd look at that! You know," he said with a sage nod, "if it wasn't for me, there wouldn't be no thinking done around here."

Davis threw up his hands. "I wish you would *think* all these shelves into this truck."

Pardue Jessup had taken a great interest in their venture, coming over in his spare time to work on Freeman's Rolling Emporium. He had used his welding machine to do the necessary metalwork, welding a framework on the bed after extending it an extra four feet. Davis and Cody had then covered the entire bed with thin plywood.

Lanie and Maeva had been working for days on the shelves that Davis had made. Maeva complained, "All I can see here is a lot of work for nothing."

"Well, that's where you're wrong, Maeva," Cody said. "It's all pre-destined that it's going to work."

"Don't get him started on that," Davis moaned. "You'll never get any sense out of him about predestination."

"Why, it's all in the Bible," Cody said. "Everything we do is meant to happen. This here project of mine, shucks, the Lord figured it out before the earth was even made."

Lanie could not help smiling. She loved Cody, but his theology sometimes made her want to pinch his head off. "It's a beautiful piece of work, and I'm proud of you, Cody."

Indeed, Freeman's Rolling Emporium, as the family referred to it, was in the last stages of completion. Davis had obtained a set of tires with the treads hardly worn. The framework was made of cedar, which they had obtained at the local sawmill. Cody and Davis had done a good job fashioning the ribbed sides and covering the exterior with thin-sawn cedar to keep the weight as light as possible. The cedar also smelled heavenly and was weather resistant.

The back of Freeman's Rolling Emporium was composed of two hinged doors that swung open. On the inside were other shelves: one side for hardware, nails, string, tacks, and a few tools, while the other side was packed into compartments with all sorts of sewing materials, needles, thread, and scissors. A pair of steps unfolded so that customers could step up and walk the length of Freeman's Rolling Emporium.

To complete the project, Davis had made a flat roof with a three-inch high lip all the way around the top. He had explained, "We can put brooms and mops and any oversized stuff over it and make a canvas to fit over the top in case it rains."

"When do you think we can go out on the road, Cody?" Lanie asked.

"Well, she's got to be painted and decorated. I'll take care of that myself."

"Why, I wouldn't trust you to decorate my toenails," Maeva exclaimed.

"You don't know what you're talking about, Maeva! That's going to be my big contribution."

Davis grinned and climbed inside, where he began installing another set of shelves. He listened as Cody explained his project, but mostly tuned him out. He turned to see Cass, who was struggling to get up into the back.

"Let me help you, Cass." Quickly he moved over, reached down, and pulled her up. Her figure revealed the child she was carrying, and Davis quickly looked away.

"Can I help you do something?" Cass asked.

"Why, sure. You can varnish these shelves."

"I'm not very good at painting."

"Well, varnish is different from paint. Look. You just slop it on like this and smooth it out." He gave her a quick demonstration, and soon she was painting away, intent upon the job. "That varnish brings out the pretty color of that red cedar."

"You sure are a good carpenter."

"Oh, just average, I guess." He thought about her struggle to get up into the bed of the truck and cleared his throat. "You know, Cass, you ought to be a mite more careful of yourself."

"What do you mean?"

"Well, I mean like getting up here into the truck. That was a little bit too much for you."

Cass turned to look at him. He noticed that she had large, well-shaped eyes. They were an unusual shade of blue, very dark with hardly any pupil. He noticed also how smooth her skin was. Except for Corliss he had never seen such smooth skin in all his life.

He backed off a bit. "Well, I mean women having babies need to be careful."

Cass did not reply but turned her head away and continued to apply the varnish. "When do you reckon the baby will come?" Davis finally asked.

"I think sometime in April." She quickly changed the subject. "What are you going to do when you get out of school, Davis?"

"Get a job, I guess. But I don't think I'll ever graduate."

Cass turned to face him. "Why not?"

"I'm just too dumb."

"You're not dumb! Look at how you made these shelves and made this old truck into a rolling store. And you're always helping the others with their arithmetic."

"That doesn't help much if you can't read."

Cass was well aware of Davis's inability to read. She understood it no more than did the others. It was a great mystery. But she said, "There are lots of jobs you can do without knowing how to read." She continued to apply the varnish and finally said in a wistful voice, "I didn't get to go to school much, but I liked it when I went. I wish I could have finished."

"Maybe you can go later."

"No. That's all over for me."

"What are you going to name your baby, Cass?"

"Davis."

Surprise washed across Davis's face. "You mean after me?"

"Of course after you. I don't know anybody else named Davis, and you're the one that took care of me."

Davis scratched his chin and said, "Well, there'll be two Davises here. I guess we'll have to be Big Davis and Little Davis. What if it's a girl?"

"I'll name her Davis."

"Why, you can't do that," Davis shook his head. "Whoever heard of a girl called Davis?"

"Oh, I don't know." Cass dipped the brush into the varnish and applied it carefully, but she said no more.

Finally Davis said, "What's the matter, Cass? Don't you feel well?"

"I feel all right, but I – I get worried."

"About what?"

"You know what." She turned to him, and again he noted the beauty of her eyes. "I don't know what I'm going to do when the baby comes. I can't hardly take care of myself. How am I going to take care of a baby? What's going to become of us, Davis?"

Davis reached out and took Cass's hand. It was the first time he had ever touched her. He held it and squeezed it and said, "You don't have to worry about that. You're part of our family. That's all there is to it."

Tears welled up in Cass's eyes, and she whispered, "Nobody was ever as good to me as you folks!"

⌖

February 16, 1932

The papers say there's some kind of a war going on with Japan fighting the Chinese. I don't know why people have to fight. I hope nothing like that ever comes to this country.

The Freeman Rolling Emporium is almost ready. The shelves are in, and Davis and Cody have done a beautiful job. All we're waiting for now is for Cody to finish the painting and decoration. He won't let any of us go to the barn and see it, so who knows what he'll come up with. But I will have to say, this idea of his is better than most.

One good thing happened. We've all been trying to get things together to sell, and, of course, some of it came from our place. Like we can take some of the eggs the hens lay and the sassafras root that we dug up last spring. Things like that. But the big thing that happened was that Owen came and took Davis and Cody to Fort Smith two days ago. He had heard of a big grocery store going out of business, so the three of them went over, and when they came back the truck was loaded down. The stuff was so cheap. Of course I was worried, but when I told Owen we didn't have the money to pay for it, he just laughed at me like he does. He patted me on the shoulder and said, "Don't you worry about that. I'll take it out in trade." He never will, of course, but we're going to pay him back.

He sits with Amelia Wright in church all the time now. I guess they're courting. Lots of the men have tried to date Amelia, but she only goes with Owen now. I don't know what will happen to them, if they'll get married or not.

I said when I started this journal I'd always be honest, but it's hard to say what you feel even if you know nobody will ever see it. Well — here it is. I'm jealous of Amelia Wright. I don't know if I'm in love with Owen or not. He's been so good to us, and he thinks of me more as the little girl that he first knew than as a woman. I wouldn't want anybody to know it, but I sit around sometimes and daydream. I pretend that we're married and I'm Mrs. Lanie Merritt, wife of the doctor in Fairhope. I dream about keeping a house for him, and when he comes home from work I have him a nice meal cooked — I'm ashamed to write this and I've got to stop it. It's just too —

Suddenly Lanie broke off, for she heard dogs barking and the yells of Davis, Cody, and Maeva as they came down the road after school. She closed the journal, put it back in the drawer, and left the room. When she got downstairs, she found Cody and Maeva in the kitchen. As always, they had brought Beau and Booger in with them. Beau was still barking and Booger was pushing at people with his head. He was a big dog and quite capable of pushing people down, especially Corliss, who loved it.

Davis was the last one in, and as soon as Lanie saw his face she knew that something was wrong. She said nothing to him then, but as soon as the others left the kitchen and they were alone, she said, "Did you have a good day at school?"

"Not really, Lanie." Davis dropped his head and stared at the floor. When he looked up, she saw that his eyes were troubled. "Mr. Pringle called me into his office. He told me he doesn't think I'll graduate unless I pull up my grades."

"Oh, I'm sure you will. You'll just have to work harder."

"I don't know, Lanie. What I'd like to do is quit and get a job."

"You can't do that. Think how disappointed Daddy would be. And Mama, she would have been disappointed too."

"But I just can't do it. I try as hard as I can, but I just can't read."

Without another word Davis, who never sought sympathy for himself, whirled and ran out of the kitchen.

Worried, Lanie watched him go. Tomorrow she would talk to Mr. Pringle and try to convince him that he just had to let Davis graduate. She hoped he would listen.

☞↤

Lanie's interview with Silas Pringle, the principal of Fairhope High School, did not go well. Pringle was a fair man, rather slight and bald-headed. He sat across from her at his desk, fiddling nervously with his watch chain while he explained the problem to Lanie.

"Davis's grades are good in any kind of science, but as you know, Lanie, he just can't read. Nobody knows why. Me, least of all."

"But won't his grades average out?"

"I'm not sure they will. That's why I talked to Davis. I'd hate for him to be disappointed, but unless something is done, I just don't see how we can let him graduate with the others."

"It'll break his heart, Mr. Pringle."

Pringle dropped his head. "I know it, and I don't like it any more than you do. But we have to keep our standards up."

A sudden anger overtook Lanie. She was a mild-mannered young woman, but occasionally circumstances ignited a spark in her she could not contain. "Standards are more important than people?" she demanded. "Davis works harder than anybody in this school in his reading. There's just something wrong, but he's smart at everything else, and you know it." She stood, glowering down at him, thinking only of Davis and his hopes and dreams.

Pringle stood with her, his face flushed. It was obvious he did not like confrontation. "Well, we'll see what can be done. Perhaps if he got a tutor it might help."

As soon as she left the high school, Lanie went at once to the church to talk with Colin. She found the pastor and Louise Langley loading her big Oldsmobile with groceries. Louise was in charge of the welfare committee, and she and the pastor saw to it that those who were destitute had food on the table. It was the first time in her life that Louise Langley had shown any interest in poor people. There were those who said she was more interested in Reverend Colin Ryan than in poor people.

But at first she wasn't at all interested in him. As a matter of fact, Louise had disliked Colin intensely when he first arrived in Fairhope. He broke all the rules she had in her mind about pastors, how they should speak, how they should dress, and how they should behave. All that had changed now, and it was clear to any careful observer that Louise Langley had more than a casual interest in the pastor.

"Hello, Lanie," Colin said. "What's happening?"

"I need to talk to you, Pastor."

"Why, sure. Come on in. Do you mind waiting, Louise?"

Louise smiled. "No. Not a bit. As a matter of fact, why don't I take the first load over to the Williams's house? Then I'll come back and pick you up for the rest?"

"That'll be fine." Colin turned and the two of them went back into the church. "Sit down, Lanie."

"No. I won't stay long. It's just that I'm so upset."

"What's the matter?"

"It's Davis. The principal says he's not going to graduate if his grades don't come up, and he just can't bring them up. I'm so worried about him."

"I know the problem. I can't understand it. He's so smart in every other way, but somehow he just can't read well. Have you had his eyes checked?"

"Twice. Both times the doctors said his eyes are perfect. It's something else."

"Well, if it's not his eyes and it's something else, we'll just have to ask God to fix the something else."

"That's why I came by to ask you to pray with me."

"Well, that's what we'll do right now."

The two bowed their heads and committed Davis to the Lord. Colin prayed fervently and at times even loudly. He seemed to be demanding something from God in a way that rather frightened Lanie.

"Well, amen," Colin said when he had finished. "Now. We've called on God, and all we can do now is trust Him. Would you trust Him even to the very last night of graduation even if everybody says Davis won't graduate?"

"I–I'll try, Pastor."

"That's what faith is. Believing what you can't see. I've got a friend in St. Louis who has done a lot of work with young people who have had problems in school. I don't know if he's ever run across this particular one, but I'll write him tomorrow and see what he says."

"Thank you, Pastor."

"Say, I've heard about that store business that you're going to start. Be sure to drop by the parsonage. I'm always in need of eggs and other things."

"Yes. We'll do that."

As they walked outside, Lanie saw Louise in the car, waiting.

Colin said, "By the way, I've noticed that Amelia Wright has been a regular at church."

"Yes, she has."

"I think she and the doctor are getting pretty close. Wouldn't it be something if they made a match out of it?" Colin started to speak, but he saw something pass across the young woman's features. He quickly added, "Of course, it probably won't happen."

They approached the car, and when they said good-bye, he got into the car beside Louise.

"I think I just made a mistake, Louise."

"What's that?"

"I said something about Amelia and Owen Merritt getting pretty thick, and it bothered Lanie."

"Why, of course it did. She's been in love with him ever since she was fourteen years old."

"I guess I'm a little bit thickheaded."

Louise smiled and reached over and patted him on the arm. "Men are rather dense about things like that. Now, where do we go next?"

On her way back home, Lanie saw the solitary figure on the road ahead of her and recognized Brent Hayden. She slowed down at once, and he came over to the truck, his face pale from the cold. He shivered and said, "I didn't know it was this chilly out here."

"Get in. I'll give you a ride."

"Thanks. I could use it."

As soon as Hayden was inside, Lanie urged the truck forward. "Do you usually walk to town?"

"Yes. I'm going to have to get a bicycle or something."

"Why don't you buy a car?"

"Don't have the money."

Lanie turned to stare at him. "I thought writers made lots of money."

"Some do. My first book was well received critically, but the sales were only fair and I had a lot of bills to pay." He laughed and shook his head. "Most people think writers are rich even if they're not."

He spoke of people's ideas about writers, and Lanie listened, fascinated. When she pulled up in front of his cabin, he said, "Come on in and I'll brew you a cup of tea."

Lanie hesitated, and he looked at her with surprise. "You're not afraid, are you?"

"No. I just—well, I just try to be careful."

"I'm harmless enough. Besides, I see you've got your folder with you. Is some of your work in there?"

"Well . . ." Lanie hesitated, then blurted out, "I thought you might read some of my poems and tell me if they're any good."

"Come on in, we'll have tea, and I'll give you a personal critique."

The two went inside, and Brent stirred up the fire. By the time it was blazing merrily he had heated the water for tea. "Let's sit at the table here," he said.

Lanie sat down across from him, feeling somewhat awkward.

"Let's see what you've written," he said. "I heard about you winning that contest. I think that's wonderful."

"I was very happy. But I've sent several other things off that haven't gotten published."

"Well, let me see some of it."

Hesitantly, Lanie opened the folder. "I've been working on a collection of poems about Jesus. They're all dramatic monologues, all people looking at Him and not quite understanding Him."

"Well, from my not very thorough reading of the New Testament, I think that's a fairly good description. But then there was never anybody else like Him, was there?"

"No, there wasn't. Anyway, I've tried different forms. This particular one is by the leper that got healed."

"Let me read it."

Lanie handed the poem to Hayden. He studied it for a moment and then began reading aloud. He had a marvelous reading voice and threw himself into the role of the leper who had been healed of his disease.

God in heaven!
What is this glow of blood I feel?
My hands tingle — look you here —
Fingers straight and long,
Not knobs of flaking flesh!

My face,
It burns — as flesh long frozen prickles into life!
Let me pull way these stiffened rags —
*   O Mighty God, I'm whole! whole!*

No more a dead and ravaged face
With bloody flap for a mouth
And ragged holes for eyes!
No more this carcass of a face
Nibbled and torn as if by vultures
No longer will it frighten children!

O Master
The others go without a word;
Forgive them, Lord;
So long they've tasted hate,
So long they've snatched for crumbs
That they forget to kneel to God who heals.

You give me life!
My flesh has long my coffin been,
Entombed by peeling walls;
But deeper than my flesh
Disease has cried
Sickness of my soul!
Unclean! Unclean! Unclean! Unclean!
I have cried of corrupted bone and flesh;
Unclean! Unclean! Unclean! Unclean! Cry I now to Him who sees
the heart.

Make now my soul as clear and pure
As you have made my flesh, O Lord;
If God Immanuel will touch the flesh
With healing hand,
Does He not yearn to heal the
Sickness of our broken hearts?
The hurt of every man?

"Why, Lanie, this is wonderful! I had no idea you were so accomplished."

"I'm not really."

"Now, now, never argue with the professionals! I'll tell you what. Why don't you let me make copies of these, say four or five, and send them to a friend of mine who runs a magazine? It's not a Christian magazine, but this might be a change for them."

"Why, that would be wonderful. I'll type them out for you."

He told her more about his friend and the magazine, and how he had come to be its editor. Curious and fascinated by the publishing business, Lanie thought of a dozen questions she wanted to ask. But she could tell by the slant of the sun that it was getting late, so she said, "Now, I really have to go."

She rose, gathered her materials, and went to the door. He stopped her there and said, "I never have thanked you for helping me find this place." He leaned forward and kissed her on the cheek. "There. There's your reward."

Lanie flushed, feeling both in awe of him and more than a little flustered. "You're—you're welcome, Brent."

Brent saw her discomfort and said, "Well, it's good to see one pure and innocent woman left in America after the Jazz Age. I hope you never change."

"Thanks for looking at my poem." Lanie hurried out the door to the truck. As she drove away, her face felt warm and she put her hand on her cheek. "He shouldn't have kissed me," she said. It bothered her that she had entered his house alone.

That same afternoon, Maeva had gone hunting for sassafras roots and had gathered a large sack full. She was headed back home on a shortcut through an old timber road.

Suddenly two men stepped out in front of her. She halted mid-step, fear prickling her spine.

"What are you doing here?" The man who spoke was tall, lanky, and badly needed a shave. He carried a shotgun under the crook of his arm.

"I'm just going home. I've been gathering sassafras roots."

"This is our land," the other man said. He was short and stocky, but there was a family resemblance. "We don't welcome strangers around here."

The taller of the two suddenly grinned. "Well, a pretty little thing like you we don't mind." He began moving toward her, his intention clear in his face.

"You stay away from me," Maeva said, backing up.

"Oh, come on now, sweetheart, be friendly."

"Frank, you and Ed light a shuck," another voice called out.

Maeva whirled around to see who was speaking.

Logan Satterfield stepped out of the dark woods to her right. He was wearing a plaid mackinaw jacket and a cap with fur earmuffs. His face was flushed as if he had been running, and he moved quickly to stand between Maeva and the two men.

"This ain't none of your put in, Logan," the taller man said.

"I'll just make it mine, Ed. Now, you two be on your way."

Maeva stared at the two and for a moment there seemed to be a distinct air of violence in both. Then finally the shorter man laughed. "Come on, Ed, looks like he's got this filly all staked out."

They turned and walked away laughing coarsely.

Logan shook his head. "Sorry about that. Ed and Frank don't have very good manners."

"Who are they?"

"My brothers."

"They don't look like you."

"Same mother, different father. What are you doing out here, Maeva?"

"I was gathering sassafras roots."

"Well, I'll help you."

"No. I've got enough. I've got to go."

"I'd better walk with you a ways."

They walked on, but neither seemed to find anything to say. Finally, when they emerged from the deep woods, Maeva said, "I can make it all right from here." She thought he had probably walked with her to see that she was not bothered any further. "Thanks for walking with me, Logan."

"I'm sorry about my brothers, but it'll be best if you didn't come here alone anymore."

Maeva stared at him and then gave him a quick nod. "All right. If you say so, Logan." She waited for him to say good-bye, but he seemed in no hurry to leave. So she smiled and said, "Come back to church sometime — or come by the house and I'll make you some biscuits."

The dark cast of his face suddenly brightened. "Well, I've never turned down an offer like that. I'll see you later."

As Maeva watched Logan Satterfield walk away from her, she thought about his brothers and wondered what the rest of the family was like. *I'd sure hate to be part of a family like that*, she thought.

◆ CHAPTER 8 ◆

W ell, folks, it's time for the great unveiling. Better get your
sunglasses on, because when you see what I've done to our
project it's going to sear your eyeballs." Cody grinned at the rest of the
family, just finishing up supper in the kitchen.

He had been working in the barn on the Rolling Emporium all
that Saturday, coming out only to get a sandwich at noon, and now
his eyes were glowing and his face was suffused with pride. "Come
along," he said, "and behold my masterpiece."

Lanie got to her feet and winked at Maeva. "Come along. I think
we're in for a spectacle."

The whole family traipsed out with her, Davis, Maeva, Cass, and
Aunt Kezia holding Corliss's hand.

Cass whispered to Davis, "He's worked so hard on it."

"Oh, Cody will work hard on something when he takes a notion.
He's just lazy when you need him to do something useful."

"Now, you stand right here," Cody said when they reached the
barn doors. "Everybody shut their eyes. I want you to get the full
beauty of this."

"Oh, come on, Cody, let us see it!" Maeva said. "It's cold out here."

"Just shut your eyes," Cody demanded.

"We'll have to do it," Davis sighed, "or we'll all freeze to death."
Everybody shut their eyes.

Cody looked to see that their eyes were tightly closed, then
quickly swung the barn doors open. "Now, come right along. Don't

open your eyes," he warned. He led them into the barn, and then he said proudly, "All right. Now everybody *look*!"

Lanie opened her eyes, and for a moment could not believe what she was seeing. She had known that Cody was going to paint the Rolling Emporium, but somehow she had gotten the idea he would paint it black just like most automobiles. Or maybe white with a black sign on it.

"Look at that!" Corliss yelped with delight. "Ain't it pretty!"

Lanie took a step forward and stared in disbelief. Freeman's Rolling Emporium was the most brilliant, blinding red she had ever seen in her life! Even the spokes of the wheels were painted red, and across the side, painted in purple letters, were the words:

FREEMAN'S ROLLING EMPORIUM

"That is the ugliest thing I have ever seen in my life!" Maeva whispered. "What in the world made you paint it red?"

"Why, I wanted to be seen, sister. Ain't she a certified sockdologer?"

Aunt Kezia walked around the vehicle shaking her head. For once she seemed to have lost all power of speech. Finally she said, "Well, I might have expected something like this from you, Cody Freeman."

"Of course you should. It's the kind of thing I do," Cody said.

Suddenly Lanie started laughing. It was either laugh or cry. She shook her head and joined Aunt Kezia as she circled their new store. "Once you get used to it, it's not so bad."

"I wanted everybody to see it coming," Cody said. "And looky here, I got a bell that we can ring when we go down the street. Everybody will hear it and come out and see us."

Davis went over and stood next to Cass. "What do you think of it, Cass?"

"Well, I never saw a redder wagon in my whole life. It's kind of loud."

"Cody's kind of loud," Davis said with a grin. "Where did you hear about an emporium?"

"Just one of them things I happen to know, Davis," Cody said with a sense of importance. "It really means a fine store, but I thought *emporium* would sound better than *store*."

For the next ten minutes they all walked around the wagon laughing and talking. Finally Cody said, "I reckon we'll be ready to pull out on Tuesday as soon as we get it loaded down with stuff."

"Stone County folks don't know what's coming at 'em," Davis said, "but I will say of all the red wagons I've ever seen in my life, Cody, this is sure one of them!"

On Monday after school the family gathered again around the emporium wagon and worked hard stocking the shelves. They were nearly finished when they heard the *clip-clop* of a horse coming near.

"Look, there comes Nellie," Maeva said. "I wonder what he's up to."

Nellie Prather was old-fashioned enough to prefer a horse and wagon for hauling things. He pulled the horse up and leaped down. "Well, howdy, folks." He took a look at the wagon and said, "Sure is red, ain't it now?"

"Red as I could make it," Cody said. "How do you like it?"

"Why, it's plum downright pretty, I think."

Cody showed him the finer points of the store by Cody. At the end of his tour, he said, "You know, I raise stuff in a greenhouse. I heard about your rolling store and thought you could use some fresh vegetables, so I went out and harvested a little. Got some squash, peppers, okra, and some fresh tomatoes."

"Gosh, nobody has fresh tomatoes this time of the year," Davis said in awe.

"Well, I just wanted to help the cause. Here. You fellows help me unload."

"After you finish come on in, Nellie, and we'll warm you up with some coffee and gingerbread," Lanie said.

Ten minutes later they were all in the kitchen. When Nellie finished his third piece of gingerbread, he said, "Why, this is downright good gingerbread. Did you make this, Miss Kezia?"

"No. Cass here made it," Aunt Kezia said. "She's getting to be a right good cook."

"Well, you'll have to come over and cook me a meal some day, Miss Cass."

"From what I hear you're a pretty good cook yourself," Maeva smiled. "You cooked for your family mostly, didn't you?"

"Well, I done my share of it, but I couldn't make gingerbread this good. You know what? I seen my first robin this morning, so I knew I'd have good luck."

"A robin brings good luck?"

"Well, this time of the year it does. I think this fellow was kind of ahead of the crowd. They're usually not back by this time. Come to think of it, I couldn't see him very good. It may not have been a robin. Maybe it was a cardinal. They usually hang around most of the winter."

Cass was sitting at the table between Davis and Cody. She very rarely offered anything, but now she smiled rather wanly and said, "I wish I could see a robin. I could use some good luck."

"Why, you don't have to see a robin. I got what you need right here, Miss Cass." Nellie reached in his pocket and pulled out an object. "You see this?"

"Why, it's a wishbone," Lanie said.

"Sure is. You know how to get your wish, don't you, Miss Cass?"

"No. How does it work?"

"Well, I grab hold of this part of the wishbone, and you take the other part. We pull, and the one that gets the biggest piece gets their wish. Go ahead and grab a hold there."

Cass smiled shyly at the big man, reached out, and laid hold on the wishbone. "Make your wish now, Cass," Nellie said.

Everyone watched as Cass closed her eyes. She made a rather appealing picture as she sat there. She was wearing a dress that mostly covered her condition. She had made it herself with considerable help from Lanie. Her skin seemed to glow with health, and her lips were pink as she whispered something under her breath. "All right. I made a wish."

"Well, you pull. Whoever gets the biggest piece wins. Pull."

The two pulled. "Well, looky there," Nellie said. "It looks like you're the one that gets your wish."

Maeva laughed. "Do you really believe that a bone of a chicken has anything to do with what we get?"

"Oh, yes, I do. I believe in dreams too. You know—" he leaned back, his eyes thoughtful—"I dreamed about this place three times in a row. I don't know what that means, but anytime you dream anything three times in a row it's plum serious."

Nellie got up and left shortly after that, and Aunt Kezia whispered to Lanie, "That's a good feller. You notice he broke that wishbone off short so Cass could get the biggest piece?"

"I saw that."

"We need more young fellers like that in the world."

"Well, we're all set." Tuesday after school, Cody climbed into the driver's seat of the Rolling Emporium for their maiden voyage. Lanie, nervous and excited, climbed in beside him. As they pulled away, they both waved at Davis and Maeva and Aunt Kezia, who was holding Corliss's hand on the porch.

Lanie turned back to her brother. "I'm scared to death, Cody."

"Scared? Why, what's to be scared of?"

"What if we don't sell anything?"

"We're gonna sell lots of stuff. You just wait and see." They had gone only a block down Jefferson Davis Avenue when Cody began to ring the bell.

"Why you ringing the bell now? We're not going to sell anything here."

"I bet you we do."

Sure enough a door or two opened, and two of the neighbor women hurried toward them. With a grin, Cody shot a look of triumph at Lanie and stopped the Emporium. "Howdy, ladies, here we are. Freeman's Rolling Emporium. No sense going down to the grocery store. We got what you need."

Mrs. Bell and Mrs. Hanley smiled. "We heard about this. Let's see what you've got."

For the next half hour the neighbors came out. Almost everyone bought something and wished Cody and Lanie well.

"What'd I tell you?" Cody said as they drove off. "You know what we're going to do?"

Lanie was counting the money before putting it in the cigar box they kept under the truck seat. "What?" she asked.

"We're going to go right smack dab down the middle of Main Street."

"We can't do that. We need to go where there are houses."

"There'll be people on Main Street." Cody refused to listen to any argument. He drove down Jefferson Davis and turned west on Main Street. They passed by businesses, and Cody started ringing the bell.

They got as far as Mamie D'Orr's beauty shop, then stopped when Mamie came out laughing, bringing all five of her customers with her.

"What in the world are you young 'uns doing?" Mamie's hair was dyed blonde, and she wore too much makeup, but she was a good-hearted woman. "Let's see what you've got."

"How about some fresh tomatoes?" Cody said.

"Fresh tomatoes in February? Impossible."

The women actually fought over the fresh vegetables, and within minutes the Emporium sold out. Mamie winked as she paid for the vegetables. "Go on down and park in front of the Dew Drop Inn or the courthouse. Lots of lazy loafers there. See what you can sell 'em."

"No. We need women folk," Cody said. "Men don't buy stuff as a rule."

Cody did drive right down the middle of Main Street so that cars and wagons had to swerve around him. He rang the bell constantly, and finally Lanie, who had been terribly embarrassed, grew amused. They stopped several times and made sales, and then she said, "Now let's go out to the outskirts. That's where our real customers will be."

While Cody and Lanie were out selling, Aunt Kezia started supper. As Kezia cooked, she talked without pause and loud enough to be heard above Corliss banging on the piano in the parlor.

"That young 'un can actually pick out a tune on a piano at her age. Ain't that a caution!" Aunt Kezia exclaimed.

"It sure is. I can't play anything," Cass said.

"All the Freemans can, but not when they're as young as Corliss. Go out and get that pot that's out on the back porch, will you?"

Cass went outside and brought in a pot that had been sitting out in the cold for three days. "What is it, Aunt Kezia?"

"Well, that's Glinny Ann's coleslaw. It's a right good coleslaw. You have to keep it cold for three days." She peered at the pot. "You better be careful when you take the lid off, Cass. Sometimes, if it don't go right, it smells like old feet."

But the coleslaw proved to have a good smell after all. "I'm gonna make me up some Mary Magdeline's Never Fail Potato Rolls."

"Why do your recipes always have names of people?"

"I put the names of the women I get the recipes from."

"I never heard of potato rolls before."

"Well, you'll hear of 'em again. First of all we got to cook up some potatoes."

Cass was a quick learner, and she watched carefully as Aunt Kezia made the potato rolls.

"I reckon we'll make some crackling corn bread. And then we'll have fried chicken with milk cream gravy. You know how to make milk cream gravy?"

"I don't know much about cooking, Aunt Kezia."

"Well, you'll get an education around this place. Lanie can cook about as good as I can, and Maeva can cook when she wants to. She'd rather be dancing or something frivolous."

Aunt Kezia whirled around the kitchen as she cooked the supper, talking all the while. She seemed to throw it together without aim. Once in a while when Cass would ask, "How much salt do you use?" she would answer, "Oh, a pinch." Or "A little bit." Or "Just a dab. A couple of glugs of milk." Which was about as scientific as she ever got.

"I won't ever learn to cook like this," Cass said with a sigh.

"I learned a lot of my cooking at home, but then when we married we went out to Oregon. I got with the women out there. It wasn't easy because we settled pretty far apart."

"You were all by yourself, you and your husband?"

"Sure. Most of us were. Cabins were pretty far apart."

"Did you ever see any Indians?"

Aunt Kezia suddenly cackled. "One of 'em come through the door one time. Just marched right in and made for me. I was boiling some water to make myself some mush. I picked it up and threw it right in his face. He took off like a scalded rat. Never did tell my husband about that. He had too much on his mind."

"Like what?"

"Well, he got sick."

Cass studied Aunt Kezia's lined face, thinking how her lively eyes made her look younger than her years. "What happened to him?"

"He died, child. That's when I went back to Texas. Had a sister to stay with there, and I married Mr. Butterworth. Then he died too."

Cass was very still. Aunt Kezia looked over and said, "What's wrong, child?"

"I thought I had trouble, but you had a lot more, Aunt Kezia."

Aunt Kezia went over and put her arm around the girl. "Don't ever worry about what's going to happen. God's going to take care of you."

"You really think God cares about people like me?"

"There's a verse in the Bible that says something like this, 'He will gather the lambs in his arms, and carry them in his bosom. And he'll gently lead those who are with young.' I don't remember the exact words, but I know that's how he feels about you, child. You and your little one. Of course he cares."

⌖

When the Rolling Emporium returned, the family sat down and ate Aunt Kezia's supper like there was no tomorrow, including something she called Goofy Balls. That particular confection was a mixture, as far as Cass could tell, of a little of everything in the larder: butter, brown sugar, chopped up pecans, eggs, and vanilla all rolled together in balls and baked in the oven.

"Why do you call them Goofy Balls?" Maeva demanded of Aunt Kezia.

"I disremember. I think I was just feeling goofy the day I made up this recipe. Anyway, they're pretty good, ain't they?"

Once dessert was finished, Lanie announced, "Listen, everyone, we're going to count the money." She retrieved the cigar box from the battered desk and upended it. The coins made a merry noise as they piled out upon the table.

"Let me count 'em," Corliss pleaded.

"You put all the pennies in a row, the nickels, dimes, and quarters in another row, and we'll let Cody count it," Lanie said.

Corliss separated the coins, stacked the few bills, and then Cody counted it quickly. "Why, we got seventeen dollars here! A full-grown man sometimes doesn't make any more than a couple of dollars in a whole day. Why, we're going to make enough money to burn a wet mule!"

"Wait a minute," Maeva said, frowning. "That's not all profit. We had to buy some of that stuff."

"That's right," Lanie said, "and besides, it was a novelty." She saw Cody's face fall, and her heart ached for him. She put her arm around him, grabbed him by the chin, and pulled him around. "But I say you did yourself proud, brother. Here's your reward." She gave him a kiss.

Aunt Kezia said, "I ain't kissing you, but I'll make you a pecan pie tomorrow just for you."

Everyone complimented Cody, and he began to swell up with pride. "Well," he said, "we're going to do real good."

"It'll be a lot of work," Davis warned, "but we'll all help. It's good to have a genius for a brother." He winked across Cody's head at Lanie, who returned the wink.

"Oh, shucks, I ain't no genius," Cody said with a shrug. "Not yet anyway, but I'm aiming to be some day."

CHAPTER 9

The small blaze licking at the apple wood in Lanie's fireplace gave the bedroom a cheerful note. She sat on a stool in front of the fire, soaking in its warmth and enjoying the snap and crackle of the wood. She saved the apple wood especially for fires in her room because it smelled mildly sweet like incense.

As she sat basking in the bright blaze of the fire, memories sweeter than the apple wood scent filled her heart. She remembered when she and her mother had put up the wallpaper. It was covered with small bluebirds, most of them babies, and around the top was a white border with lilacs that looked real enough to burst into bloom.

Lanie had a quick stab of memory as she looked at the furniture. She had never become accustomed to the loss of the antiques she'd grown up with in the old house. They had been forced to sell most of the pieces to an antique dealer to pay off the mortgage. It had been a miracle that saved the homeplace, but even now, months later, Lanie felt like a visitor when she walked into a room filled with cheaply made pieces.

Even so, this room was her citadel and had been since her mother died. She had it all to herself, and all her treasures were here, such as they were.

As she pulled the brush through her thick hair, a restlessness seized her, a stray current of something from her distant past, a tinge of regret and a pale longing for something she could not identify. Rising from the stool, she returned the brush to her dresser and stepped to the window. Across the road, Agnes Jinks was hanging clothes out. She had on the same oversized gray sweater she always wore for such a task. As Lanie watched, Mrs. Jinks turned toward the Freeman house. Because her red hair was tied back, Lanie could clearly see her face. It was filled with anxiety, almost desperation. Even as Agnes pinned her clothes to the line, something in her demeanor troubled Lanie.

She's worried about Max, Lanie thought. Max Jinks, the same age as her brother Cody, had been in trouble lately. He was running with a wild bunch, and they had been picked up by Ed Hathcock, the chief of police, only a week earlier. They had not been arrested, but all of them had been drinking. Max had been Cody's best friend all through school, and now he seemed to be going the wrong way.

Agnes Jinks turned back and hung the last of the washing on the line. Lanie knew their clothes almost as well as she knew her own family's. There was no privacy on a wash line! Underwear that no one ever saw when worn was now blazoned out for all to look upon. She could even see the red dress Alice Jinks had bought on her sixteenth birthday. Lanie had been with her that day, and she remembered how happy Alice had been.

"Only two years and now it seems an eternity," Lanie whispered.

She studied the houses up and down the street. Lanie knew some of the families, but others were a mystery to her. Still, every house in Fairhope had its trouble, its tragedy, and its good times too.

A tiny scratching at the door suddenly caught her attention. She turned as Cap'n Brown pranced into the room. She uttered a small cry of disgust when she looked down. "Cap'n Brown, you're a bad kitty!" She extracted a tiny wriggling mouse from Cap'n Brown's mouth. He often brought her "gifts," and Lanie had been the recipient of baby squirrels, tiny rabbits, shrews, mice, and grasshoppers—anything small enough for Cap'n Brown to carry.

Lanie cupped the tiny creature in her hand but noted the perfection of his shiny fur and the brightness of the bright, frightened eyes that looked up at her. She marveled at the perfection of the tiny whiskers and remembered a line of poetry she had read from Walt

Whitman: "A mouse is miracle enough to satisfy thousands of infidels." The words had always pleased her, for it seemed it did not take a great deal of wisdom to see that even a tiny creature such as a mouse was a miracle.

She put the little creature in a small box from her dresser and for a moment watched as he twitched his nose and raised himself up on his hind legs. A sudden strange thought came to her, and she looked down at Cap'n Brown. "Cap'n Brown, I don't know if there are animals in heaven or not, but if there are cats, they won't be able to catch mice."

Cap'n Brown looked up at her. He was a large cat, a Manx, with no tail and enormously strong hind legs. He reared up and dug his claws into her skirt and said, "Wow!" clearly.

"No. Even if there are lions, they'll have to eat whatever we eat in heaven. Manna, I guess — or milk and honey."

Suddenly Lanie laughed at herself. "Lanie Freeman, you have the craziest thoughts in the world! It's a wonder they don't lock you up in an institution."

She placed the lid on the box, put it down, and took her mother's coat off the peg on the wall. It was wool with a rabbit fur neckpiece and had been a gift from her father. She remembered the day he bought it. As she put it on, it gave her a warm sense of identifying with her mother. There were times when she felt her mother's presence as clearly as if she were in the room. At other times she missed her so much she had to bite her lip to keep from weeping.

She plucked her mother's cloth hat off of another peg, pulled it down over her head, and returned to the fireplace to place the screen in front of the still crackling fire. Cap'n Brown at once came over, curled up, and lay down with a sigh. His eyes closed as he purred with contentment.

"I wish I didn't have any more worries and troubles than you do, Cap'n Brown," Lanie whispered, and then she turned and left the room. Stepping to the door next to hers, she gave it a short knock. "Let's go, Cass. It's time."

The door opened after a pause, and Cass stood there. "Do I have to go?"

"Certainly you have to go. Doctor Merritt needs to look at you. Now put your coat on."

Cass turned and moved reluctantly across the room. She was seven months along now and her stomach plainly showed. She picked up a coat that had once belonged to Maeva, put it on, and then pulled a hat down over her ears.

"It's cold out there," Lanie said.

"I don't want to go. I hate to go to town."

"Why do you hate to go to town? You need to get out of the house, Cass."

"Everybody looks at me."

"No, they don't. That's your imagination. Come along now. We're going to have a good time. After you see Doctor Merritt, we'll go to the library and find something good to read. Come along now. We'll have a good time."

The two descended the stairs, and they found Aunt Kezia and Corliss seated at the kitchen table. They were playing a game of solitaire with a pack of Aunt Kezia's cards that looked as if they had been around for a hundred years. The edges were worn, and they were thickened with age, making them almost impossible to shuffle.

Aunt Kezia played solitaire as fiercely as some soldiers made war. Her games were accompanied by shouts of exaltation when she turned over a good card and howls of grief when she was beaten. She slammed the cards down and pushed them around with a fierce intensity. Corliss enjoyed howling and thumping the table along with her aunt.

"You enjoy solitaire better than anybody I ever saw, Aunt Kezia."

"Well, I'm losing this dratted game. Corliss here can play better than me."

"It's all a matter of luck. There's no skill involved in it," Lanie insisted. She knew this was a losing argument, for Aunt Kezia was convinced that intelligence had a lot to do with beating Old Sol, as she called it.

"I remember Wild Bill Hickok. He'd come into the Lady Gay Saloon and play solitaire. My husband, Mr. Butterworth, told me about it. He said he could win two times out of three. Nobody ever saw nothing like it. Mr. Butterworth always said he was such a no-good rascal he cheated even at solitaire when there wasn't no money involved."

Cass was staring at Aunt Kezia. "You actually saw Wild Bill Hickok?"

"Certainly did, the no-count varmint! Should have been shot a long time before he was."

"You're a bad influence on these girls," Lanie laughed despite herself. "We're going now, and we'll be late getting back."

"I want to go too," Corliss said.

"No, it's too cold for you. You stay here with Aunt Kezia."

Aunt Kezia nodded. "Right. Let 'em go on. Me and you will make popcorn, and we'll make hot chocolate. Then we'll listen to *Lum and Abner* on the radio."

This satisfied Corliss. She kissed both girls and then went back to watching the solitaire game.

The young women left the house and got into the pickup. It ground so slowly Lanie was afraid it wouldn't start. But it finally caught, and the engine clanked along merrily. "I've got to have Pardue do something with this old truck. It sounds like it's on its last leg."

As they made their way toward the doctor's office, Cass suddenly turned and said, "Lanie, I'm worried about Davis ... that he won't graduate."

"I know, Cass. I am too. We'll just have to trust God though. We've done everything we can do."

"You really think God will help him? God knows about little stuff like that?"

"Why, Cass, the Bible says He knows when a sparrow falls. Just one little sparrow. And in another place He says the hairs of our head are numbered." She reached over and playfully tugged at a wisp of hair that had escaped Cass's cap. She smiled and said, "I don't know how many hairs you got in your head, but God knows. If He knows that, He knows Davis needs Him. Now, don't worry."

Doctor Merritt's office had been half full when Lanie and Cass arrived. When the last patient left, Nurse Bertha Pickens said, "You can go in now, Miss Johnson."

Lanie watched as Cass, looking extremely nervous, moved across the room and entered the inner office. As soon as she was gone, Bertha Pickens turned to Lanie and said, "That's a shame about that girl being in her condition."

"I think she'll be all right. She's a healthy young woman."

"I didn't mean that. I mean her having a baby and not being married."

There was no answer to make to this, and Lanie just continued to look through the copy of *Liberty* that she had been reading.

But Nurse Pickens was not to be denied. "I suppose you heard about that Amelia Wright woman."

"She's been coming to our church," Lanie said.

"Well, I'm glad to hear she goes to church somewhere. I went by and invited her personal to come to our church, but she wouldn't even listen to me. She comes regular, does she?"

"She's there every Sunday."

"Bet I know why. She sits with Doctor Merritt, don't she?"

Lanie had no choice but to admit it, and when she did, Nurse Pickens sniffed. "I warned him about getting tied up with another woman. You know how it is when a man gets rejected by a woman. Men don't have much sense anyway, and she's just liable to get him on the rebound."

"Oh, I think Doctor Merritt is wise enough to be careful."

"Speaking of that, being wise and being careful, there's something I need to mention to you. Of course it's none of my business, but if I was doing something that wasn't wise, I'd want somebody to tell me about it."

Instantly Lanie stiffened. "What is it, Miss Pickens?"

"It's all over town about how you visit that writer fellow from New York, just you and him in the house alone." Nurse Pickens put the full force of her gaze on Lanie. "I've known you since you were a child, so I feel it's my duty to warn you that what you're doing ain't Christian."

"I just stopped in one time for a few minutes."

"The Bible says avoid the very appearance of evil. Well, I don't take no pleasure in delivering these messages, but since your mama's dead and your pa's in prison, somebody's got to look out for you."

Lanie wished desperately that Nurse Pickens would "look out for" somebody else. "Thank you for the warning. I'll be more careful," she said, and bit her tongue to keep from saying more. She turned the pages of the magazine, hoping the inquisition was over.

When the door opened and Cass came out with Doctor Merritt, she could have shouted with relief. She got up at once and smiled. "Hello, Doctor."

"Hello, Lanie." Owen returned her smile, then turned to Nurse Pickens. "I want you to go through our vitamin samples and see if you can't fish some out for Miss Johnson here. Lanie, come in for a moment. I've got something to tell you."

Lanie followed him into his office, and he shut the door. "I didn't want Nurse Pickens to hear this. Might as well put it on the front page of the *Sentinel*."

"Is it about Cass?"

"Cass? Oh, no. She's fine," Owen said with a slight surprise. "Never saw a healthier young woman. Of course it's too bad about the circumstances. I haven't had a chance to tell you how much I admire you for looking out for her."

Lanie basked in the warmth of the compliment and shrugged. "It's the least we can do."

"This is what I wanted to show you, Lanie." He marched over to his desk and pulled out an envelope. "I wrote to a friend of mine who practices in St. Louis. He's not an MD, but he and I got to be friends in college. He teaches at the university. I wrote him about Davis, and he said he had been doing some experimental work with young people who have exactly the same problem."

Hope sprang up at once in Lanie. "What did he say?"

"He said it would be good if he could examine Davis. I really think we ought to send him."

Instantly Lanie computed the cost. It irritated her that her first thought had to be about money, but even so she did not hesitate. "We'll find the means somehow."

"Of course you will. Just a matter of timing and getting an appointment with my friend. His name is Doctor Smith, by the way. John Smith. Isn't that an unusual, exotic name? I always called him Studs because I said his name was too common." He grinned. "I also called him that just to make him mad. You talk to Davis. Tell him Doctor Smith thinks he might be able to help. We'll get him there. Don't worry."

A feeling of warmth suddenly swept over Lanie. "You've done so much for us, Owen. I can never thank you enough."

"No trouble at all. You know how I feel about your whole family."

Lanie studied his face for a moment and then asked, "How are you doing, Owen?"

Owen smiled. "I suppose you're talking about my love life." He laughed. "Why, you're blushing, Lanie. That's good to see."

"I didn't mean to pry. I suppose you get enough of that from Nurse Pickens."

"That's for sure. Well, here's what's surprising. I thought that I'd really be shaken and emotionally damaged when Louise dumped me, but it never happened. I kept waiting for it. Every morning I'd wake up and I'd think, 'This is the day it'll hit me. I'll know how bad off I am.' But it never happened."

"I'm glad, Owen!"

"Well, it means one thing, Lanie." Owen shook his head in wonder. "It means I wasn't really in love with Louise Langley. It also means I fooled myself pretty badly—so I'll have to be more careful in the future."

It took all of Lanie's strength not to blurt out, *Then why are you hanging around Amelia Wright?* But she knew that would be exactly the wrong thing to say. "I'm sure you will," she said as she stood. "Will you let me pay you for this visit?"

Owen stood with her and walked her to the door. "You know I won't. As a matter of fact, not one person out of ten that comes through that door has the means to pay me. This Depression's that bad. Now, you scoot on out of here. I'll see you at prayer meeting."

Lanie left and, with Cass in tow, she headed to the library, and Lanie helped Cass pick out three books by Grace Livingston Hill, a woman who was writing fine Christian novels.

When they started toward home in the truck, Cass turned to Lanie. "Doctor Merritt says I'm fine. That my baby's going to be healthy."

"Of course it is."

"I like Doctor Merritt, don't you?"

Lanie smiled. "Yes. I like Doctor Owen Merritt very much indeed."

The weather had cleared up and the sun was shining bright in a cloudless blue sky. March sometimes brought such days when the warmth of the sun would touch the frozen earth of the Ozarks. It should have been a perfect day for Maeva and Lanie to take the Freeman's Rolling Emporium out, but they returned disappointed after only moderate success.

Maeva sat beside Lanie, hunched over with her hands in her pockets. "Things are going to have to be better than this, or we're not going to make it with this business."

"It'll be better when spring gets here, but I've got some good news." She then told Maeva about the man in St. Louis who might be able to help Davis.

"What good does that do? He might as well be on the moon. We don't have the money."

"No, Maeva, you know God can do it. He's done it before for us. Remember how, when we were about to lose our house, we thought an angel was leaving money, and all the time it was Annie?"

"Well, Annie doesn't have any money this time. I wish I could go to St. Louis or Little Rock or somewhere. I hate this town!"

"Maeva, don't say that! Fairhope's a fine town. There are good people here."

"Oh, I know it." Maeva shrugged. "I just get bored out of my skull. You know what I'd like to do?" She turned and her eyes were alight with hope. "I'd like to be a singer or maybe a movie star."

That was about the last hope Lanie would have for her sister, but she carefully did not argue with her. She knew better, for if anyone would argue more than Cody, it was Maeva. "Look. There's Brent's house. I'll bet he'll buy something," Maeva said.

Lanie said, "No. We can't impose on him." But at that moment Brent stepped out, called loudly, and motioned to them.

Lanie steered the Emporium toward his house, and when they stopped, Brent smiled at them. He was wearing a cardigan sweater and a pair of gray flannel slacks, and he looked very handsome. "Get out, ladies. I'll give you something to warm you up."

Instantly Maeva was off the seat onto the ground, and with a sigh, Lanie followed.

Ten minutes later they were drinking hot chocolate, and Brent pulled out a canister. "I got these things from the store. They're called moon pies."

"Ooh, I love moon pies!" Maeva said.

"Well, you can have them all. I hate them." Brent shook his head. "They taste like wax to me."

"How would you know what wax tastes like?" Maeva grinned mischievously. "Did you ever eat any?"

"No. But that's what I think they'd taste like. Hey, I got some new records I want to play for you. I ordered them from the store in Fort Smith."

Going over to the table, he wound a handle on a portable record player and carefully put a record on. "This one's by Bing Crosby, that singer everybody's going crazy about." He played the record and then several others while Maeva ate the moon pies and washed them down with hot chocolate. Finally she said, "Tell us about New York. What's it like, Brent?"

For the next thirty minutes Brent told them stories of living in New York. As Maeva listened, her eyes filled with envy. "I'd give anything," she sighed, "if I could go to New York where there's some life."

"Well, there's some life there, all right. But it's not all good." Brent shrugged.

"I want to be a movie star or a singer."

"You're pretty enough," Brent said.

Maeva perked up. "You really think so?"

"Yes. But there are probably fifty thousand more who are pretty enough. They go to New York or Hollywood, go on stage, or get in the movies, and they find out it's not the fairyland that they thought it would be. I've seen lots of young women have tragic experiences there. It's not really a nice place. Not nearly as nice as Fairhope."

Suddenly Brent turned to Lanie and said, "I'm glad you came by. Guess who's going to be in Fort Smith March 4?"

"I have no idea," Lanie said. "Who is it?"

"Robert Frost."

Lanie stared at him. "You mean Robert Frost the poet?"

"He's your favorite, isn't he?"

"Yes, he is. What's he doing in Fort Smith?"

"Some kind of a reading tour. You know, to publicize his books. I'm going to go, and I was going to come by your house tonight and ask you to go with me. A writer like you needs to hear men like that."

"Oh no, I couldn't possibly." Lanie's mind went at once to Nurse Bertha Pickens. If she had made so much of a quick visit in a house, what would she make of a trip all the way to Fort Smith with a man? "I don't think I could possibly go, but I appreciate your asking."

Brent stared at her. "Well, of course you've got to go."

"Yes, you do," Maeva said. "You don't have anything else to do, and it's something you really want to do. I'd go in a minute if it was Bing Crosby or Errol Flynn."

Lanie knew she was on dangerous ground, but the temptation was strong. "Wouldn't we get back awfully late?"

"Well, it's an early reading. I don't know why, but it starts at four o'clock. We'd have plenty of time to get home. You're invited too, Maeva," Brent said.

"Not me. It'd bore me out of my skull."

Lanie scarcely heard anything else that was said. The two left, and as soon as they were in the truck and rolling along, Maeva started, "You've got to go," she said. "You can't miss it."

"Maeva, I can't do it. It wouldn't look right."

"What do you mean *look right*? You're not going to do anything wrong."

Lanie wanted to remind Maeva how thick the gossip got in a small town, but she said simply, "Well, I'll think about it."

She did think about it all the rest of the day, and by the time she went to bed that night she knew she had to go.

The trip to Fort Smith was a delight for Lanie. Brent picked her up in a car he rented from Pardue Jessup's garage, and all the way to Fort Smith the two talked about writing. They arrived early enough to have a late lunch at a small diner.

When Robert Frost began reading his poetry, she sat back in awe, knowing these were moments she would never forget. The frosty-headed old man reminded her of an oak. His voice was rough and coarse, but somehow it resonated with power as he read. Lanie listened, spellbound, when at the completion of his poetry reading, he gave a lecture on writing.

Later, Brent escorted her to the front of the hall to meet Frost and buy one of his books. "Mr. Frost," he said with a broad smile, "Miss Freeman here is a poet too."

"Is that right?" Frost grinned, his eyes bright with amusement. "You better start writing novels. They pay better than poems. Most of the time you can't even give poems away."

She thanked him for his advice and he signed the book "To Lanie Freeman, a fellow poet," and dated it. Lanie was euphoric.

They stopped for a snack on the way home, and when they pulled up in front of her house, it was late. She said, "Thank you, Brent. I've never had such a wonderful time."

Brent suddenly leaned forward and rested his hand on her shoulder. "You should have good times like this all the time, Lanie." He drew her into his arms, and she knew he was going to kiss her. For a moment she struggled, but he simply laughed and said, "Don't be such a little puritan. It's only a kiss."

Lanie surrendered then, and he held her and kissed her firmly. She was so shocked she did not return the caress. Brent laughed and said, just as he had the first time he kissed her, "I didn't know there was such an innocent young woman left in America. Good night. We'll talk about Frost later."

Lanie got out and walked in the house. Everyone was asleep, but as soon as she closed the door to her room, the door opened again and Maeva came in, her eyes wide with interest. "Was it fun? What did you do?"

"I'll tell you about it some other time."

"No. Now." Maeva listened intently, then demanded, "Did he kiss you good night?"

"Well, yes."

"Did you enjoy it?" Maeva grinned wickedly. "I'll bet you did. He's a handsome fellow."

"It was just a friendly kiss."

"Well, it's a beginning. Now you've got Owen *and* Roger *and* Brent on a string. I can't wait to see which one you pick."

Chapter 10

Lanie drove up to the gate at Cummings Prison Farm. It had been two months since she'd last visited her father. She prayed he was doing better.

This time she'd taken her sister Corliss. The poor girl barely knew her father, so Lanie took her when she could. She turned to Corliss and said, "Now you must be on your very best behavior, Corliss."

Corliss turned her big eyes on Lanie. "Do I have to behave better here than I do at home?"

Lanie turned the engine off, set the brake, and smiled at Corliss. She did not want to frighten Corliss. The prison was frightening enough, so she said simply, "You don't get to see Daddy very often, and you want to make him happy, so you just be a good girl. But then you always are. Come along now."

The two got out of the truck and walked up to the gate. The guard smiled at her. His name was Hendrix and he knew Lanie well. "Well, who's this you got with you, Miss Lanie?"

"This is my younger sister, Corliss Jeanne. She's the beauty of the family."

"I should say she is. You come to see your daddy, did you, missy?"

"Yes, please. Where is he?"

Hendrix laughed. "I can see she's got some of you in her. Go ahead on in. I know your visit's already cleared."

Lanie walked slowly, holding Corliss's hand and talking with her constantly. Many of the guards smiled and spoke to her, and finally they entered a large room with tables and chairs. Over against one wall was a coffee pot. The room was only half full of visitors today, and Lanie thought the cold weather had probably kept some from making the trip.

"How long will we have to wait, Lanie?"

"Not long. Usually Daddy's up at the warden's place, but he said in his last letter he'd be here in the mornings. I don't know why."

Even as she spoke a tall, gray-haired man not wearing a uniform came through the door and headed straight toward them. "Is this Miss Freeman?" His gray eyes were steady and kind.

"Yes, it is."

"I'm Chaplain Jones. Most of the fellows here call me Brother Buck."

"You mean you're Buck Jones the cowboy?" Corliss's eyes grew large.

"No such luck." Chaplain Jones grinned. "I been called that most of my life. What's your name?"

"I'm Corliss, and I'll be four years old on July the Fourth."

"Well, you're a grown-up young lady. Your dad talks about you a lot."

"I don't remember him very much, but he'll remember me, I bet."

"I'll bet he will." Chaplain Jones turned to Lanie and said, "I don't know if you've heard from your father, but he's had a little setback physically, so we're keeping him here in the infirmary."

Lanie was suddenly afraid. "What's wrong with him, Chaplain?"

"I'm not quite sure. At first we thought it was the flu, then we thought it might be diabetes, but we tested and that's not it. He just seems weak and run-down. Men here get that way sometimes." Jones rubbed his chin thoughtfully. "But I didn't expect it of your dad. He's the healthy outdoor type. But even men like that get sick sometimes."

"What does the doctor say?"

"You can talk to him before you leave, but he'll probably tell you the same thing." He gave Lanie and Corliss a gentle smile. "Come along. I'll take you to the hospital. He's not in a bed, but he's in the ward."

Lanie stood, and holding Corliss's hand, followed the chaplain down the hall. They turned a corner, walked down another hall, and finally entered the infirmary.

Her father sat in a chair beside a window. He seemed to be half asleep, and when he turned she saw he had lost weight. He got up at once. "Lanie," he said, and then his gaze fell on Corliss. "There's my baby girl! Come here and give your daddy a hug."

Without hesitation Corliss ran forward and threw her arms around her father. He picked her up off the floor, and then suddenly backed up and sat down. "Wow, my goodness! You're such a big girl I can hardly hold you. Let me look at you."

Lanie stood back, letting the two have their time together. Corliss had visited her father at the prison once before, but she was too young to remember. Since then Lanie had debated bringing her, and finally decided it was the best thing to do.

Chaplain Jones touched her arm. "Let me get you a seat, and I'll go down to the cafeteria and rustle up some food."

"Oh, I brought all kinds of food. I left it at the check-in. Would you mind getting it and bringing it here?"

"I'll do that. I know your dad always shares what he gets with the other men."

Chaplain Jones left, and Lanie went over to her father, kissed him on the cheek, and hugged him. "How are you, Daddy?"

"Fair to middlin'."

"You've lost weight. I'm going to talk to the doctor. What has he told you?"

Forrest Freeman said, "You know doctors. They never tell you anything."

"Have you been eating well?"

"Oh, yes. Very well."

Lanie knew just by looking at him that this was wrong, but she let it go. She listened as Corliss told her father everything she could think of to tell—from Cap'n Brown's latest mouse offering to Aunt Kezia's bestest-ever popcorn balls. It was a good thing Corliss did most of the talking, for their father didn't look well at all. The nagging worry that had troubled Lanie since her last visit now became stronger. She said quickly, "I think I'll go help the chaplain bring the food in. Would you like coffee too?"

"That would be nice, daughter. You just leave this young lady here with me. Maybe she can sing some songs to me."

"I know lots of songs," Corliss said. "You want to hear one?"

"I certainly do."

As Lanie left, Corliss was singing the crawdad song at the top of her lungs:

"You get a line and I'll get a pole, honey
You get a line and I'll get a pole, babe.
You get a line and I'll get a pole.
We'll go down to the crawdad hole.
Honey, sugar baby mine."

Lanie had seen the doctor's office sign when they entered the building and headed toward it as soon as she left her father's room. She knocked and when a voice said, "Come in," she opened the door and stepped inside. She had met the doctor before on a previous visit. "Hello, Doctor Campbell."

Campbell got up at once. He was a short burly man of forty with mild blue eyes. He was balding and wore thick glasses that gave him a froglike appearance, but he had a good smile. "Why, Miss Freeman, I'm glad to see you. Here, sit down."

Lanie sat and at once said, "I'm worried about my daddy, Doctor. He doesn't look well."

Campbell drummed his fingers on the table. "I'm worried about him myself. He really needs to be in a good hospital where they can do more tests than we can afford here."

"What do you think it is?"

"I just can't say. It may be some form of anemia. That's what I've been thinking."

"Where would he have to go to get tests?"

"Well, Little Rock, I suppose."

"Is there any chance of getting him sent there?"

"I've tried, but the budget's tight. Though I may be able to persuade the warden with just a little more time."

Lanie looked down at her hands and saw that her fingers were twisting together nervously. "It scares me a little bit, Doctor. He's always been such a strong, healthy man."

"I know, Miss Freeman. I'm going to do the best I can. He's lost his appetite, which troubles me. But don't worry. I'll do my best to persuade the warden to have him sent to Little Rock for tests."

⚬══⚬

As they were leaving, Forrest hugged Corliss and then Lanie. His voice sounded husky. "It's always good to see you girls. You tell the rest of the kids I miss them."

"I'll bring them back next visiting day, the whole bunch—including Aunt Kezia. We'll bring you some of her Aunt Sara's blueberry shortcake like you like."

"That'll be good, daughter. Be careful now on the way back."

"I'll write you a letter, Daddy," Corliss said. "I can make my letters now. I just can't spell the words. But I can play 'O Susannah' on the piano."

"I'd love to hear that, darlin'."

Lanie knew better than to prolong their good-byes, so she pulled Corliss from the room. When they were out in the car, Corliss suddenly teared up and began to cry. "I don't want to leave my daddy in that place. I want him to come home with us."

Lanie had to blink her eyes to keep the tears back. She reached over with her right hand and pulled the child closer. "So do I, sweetheart, and some day he will."

While Lanie and Carliss visited their dad, the rest of the family went to school, as usual. American history class was almost finished when the substitute teacher, a tall angular woman named Miss Bell, called on Davis to read a paragraph. She had been choosing students to read at random, for she knew none of them personally.

"Let's see. Davis Freeman. Where are you? There you are, Davis. Will you read the next paragraph, please? The one that begins 'The generals of the revolution ...' Right there."

Suddenly the classroom became very quiet. Miss Bell looked from student to student, then shrugged. "Did you hear me, Davis?"

"Yes, ma'am, I heard you."

"Well then, please read the paragraph as I've asked you."

Suddenly Howard Oz, the son of Harry Oz who owned the local hardware and furniture store, snickered. "He ain't gonna read, Miss Bell," he said loudly. Howard was a year younger than Davis, a bulky boy like his dad. Davis had beaten him out as pitcher for the local baseball team, and Howard had resented him ever since.

"What do you mean? Of course he'll read."

Howard Oz laughed loudly. He turned around and sneered at Davis. "He can't read. He can't read a word. He's dumb as a tree."

At that point it might have been expected that Davis would jump up and defend himself, but he did not. Instead it was Maeva, who was seated three seats behind Howard Oz. She did not utter a word but got to her feet, her face crimson. She flung herself forward, grabbed two handfuls of Howard's hair, and jerked at it, trying desperately to tear it out. Howard yelled at the top of his lungs, and when he did his older sister Lolean and his younger brother Billy came to their brother's aid.

Billy swung his fist at Maeva, catching her high in the temple. The blow dazed her, but she hung on desperately, Howard screaming like a banshee. Lolean grabbed a ruler and began flailing at Maeva.

Davis flew out of his chair, grabbed her, and slung her across the room. Then he pulled Billy off and shoved him backwards.

"Turn him loose, Maeva," he said. But Maeva doubled up her fists and struck Howard right in the eye.

This brought Howard's best friend, Dale Jemison, into the fray, and soon the whole room, delighted at a little action to break up the boredom of history, joined in. It was a glorious fight, and there were bloody noses, black eyes, and sore muscles a plenty.

In the end, Mr. Pringle came in and settled the business by wading into the battle, yelling at the top of his lungs. As soon as Miss Bell, who had gone into hysterics at the first blow, calmed down, he pulled her aside and tried to get some sense out of her.

Soon after he called Maeva and Davis into his office. Staring at each in turn with unblinking eyes, he said, "As far as I can tell, you two are responsible for this."

Maeva flared out. "We're not either! It was Howard Oz. He called my brother a dummy. I'll whip anybody who does that."

"You're both suspended for a week," Mr. Pringle said sternly.

"What about them Oz kids?"

"That's none of your business. Leave the school now, and I don't want to see you back for one week. I'll be talking with your sister about this. Send her to see me tomorrow."

As Maeva and Davis left the school, Davis said, "I'm not going back, Maeva. There's no sense in it anyhow. I'll never graduate."

Maeva suddenly grabbed Davis by the lapels of his mackinaw. She shook him, shouting, "Yes, you are going back!" Her eyes flared. "You're going back, and we're going to make them Ozes eat dirt! You wait and see."

Davis shook his head, bitterness marring his mouth. "I know what Lanie will say about this."

"When she hears the truth of it, she'll be on our side."

When Lanie got back from the prison, they were waiting for her on the front porch. After sending Corliss inside, they told her what had happened. "I know you think it's all our fault, but it wasn't," Davis said.

"I know it wasn't and I wasn't even there."

"Why would they suspend us and not the Oz kids?"

"You don't know that they're not suspended."

"They won't be. Mr. Pringle's afraid to offend Mr. Oz. He's on the school board," Davis said.

Indeed, this proved to be prophetic. Lanie went to school the next day and argued long and hard for a different punishment, but Mr. Pringle refused to budge. Lanie left angry and bitter.

It so happened that that was prayer meeting night, and she was not in a good mood at all to go to prayer meeting. But she determined long ago that she would not let her emotions rule her duty. When the others complained, she said flatly, "We're going to prayer meeting, and that's all there is to it."

❦

The Wednesday night prayer meeting at the First Baptist Church was well attended, better than usual, for Colin had been teaching a series on the book of Revelation, and everyone was interested in prophecy. Maeva glared at the Oz family, but when she started to go for them, Lanie jerked her back and told her to keep her seat.

Colin must have heard some of the stories, but he did not refer to it. He taught the lesson and then said, "We'll now have our benediction." But before he could begin the closing prayer, Mrs. Maxine Oz rose and said, "I have a matter of business, Pastor."

"This is not a business meeting, sister."

"It doesn't make any difference. I'm going to ask the church to vote to discipline Maeva and Davis Freeman."

This was the beginning of one of the longest and most violent meetings that the Fairhope Baptist Church had ever seen. Though most people spoke against it, Maxine was determined to have Maeva and Davis disciplined. She did not define what "disciplined" meant.

Baptist churches are democratic and anyone who pleased could speak as long as they were a member. Colin did the best he could, and finally he said, "This meeting is out of order. I'm going to declare it closed. I'm also going to declare a prayer meeting. I would ask all of you to stay now and seek the Lord that this may be resolved."

The Ozes and their close friends stormed out, not interested in any such thing as prayer.

Lanie went forward at once and knelt at the altar. She sensed someone beside her, and she turned to see Owen. He nodded and smiled. "I know it seems bad, Lanie, but it'll be all right."

"Thank you, Owen," she said, and then bowed her head once more to pray.

"It was a fine dinner, Amelia," Owen said. He had come to her house Thursday evening after his office hours were over, and she had indeed fixed a fine supper. "You make a delicious roast. I don't get enough of that. Let me help you with the dishes."

"No. That's a woman's work. Let's go sit in the living room. I know you're tired. We'll listen to some music."

"Sounds good to me."

They went into the living room, and Amelia put on a Freddie Martin record. As the soft melody filled the room, Amelia sat down beside Owen. They listened to several records.

Finally Amelia said, "I almost feel like we're an old married couple. Here I've been doing the housework, and you come home tired from the office." She looked at Owen expectantly, but he only smiled.

Amelia waited for him to speak, and when he didn't, she said, "Did you hear about that writer from New York, Brent Hayden, taking Lanie to Fort Smith for a lecture?"

"No, I didn't," Owen said. "When did this happen?"

"Last week."

"Did somebody go with them?"

"No. They went alone," Amelia said. "But, after all, she's a grown woman. She can make those decisions. She's almost eighteen, isn't she? He might actually be a good match for her, Owen. They're both literary types."

"Nonsense! She's too young to be thinking of that, and besides—"

"And besides what?"

"Besides, she's got responsibilities."

The rest of the evening seemed to drag. Amelia tried to keep the conversation going, but Owen rose after a short time and said, "Been a long day, Amelia. Thanks for supper. It's my turn next time. I'll take you out for a meal. Good night."

He left her house, and both of them were dissatisfied, but for different reasons.

⚬══⟨⟩⟩

Owen was grumpy the next day all during his practice so that Nurse Pickens snapped at him. "You're getting to be a worse grouch than Doctor Givens! I'd be glad to have him back."

Owen did not even bother to apologize. He saw his patients, but after he left the office, instead of going to Doctor Givens's house for supper, he picked up some fresh vitamins and stuffed them in his pocket. He drove out to the Freeman place and when he knocked on the door, he was met by Cass. "Hello, Cass," he said.

"Why, Doctor, good to see you. Come on in. Lanie's teaching me how to make a buttermilk pie." Owen followed her into the kitchen.

Lanie looked up and smiled. "I saw you drive up, Owen. Who are you doctoring out here?"

"Just wanted to leave these pills with this young woman here." He fished them out of his pocket, gave them to Cass, and said, "Be sure you take them now."

Cass nodded, and then Lanie said, "Sit down and have a cup of coffee."

"I think I will." He sat down and after a time, when the pie was done, Cass left the room. At once Owen said, "Seems like the biggest industry in Fairhope is minding other people's business. I've had enough of it shoved at me."

Lanie stared at him. "Are you going to mind my business, Owen?"

"I heard about your going all the way to Fort Smith with Brent Hayden. Are you sure that's wise, Lanie?"

"Do you think I did something wrong?"

"I don't think you could."

"Then why are you talking to me like this?"

Owen twisted in his chair. "Well, he's an older man. Writers are romantic, especially to you, but he's not for you, Lanie."

"You need to start an advice to the lovelorn column in the *Sentinel*, Owen. What if I said it's not right for you to call on Amelia Wright, just you and her alone?"

Owen was stopped dead in his tracks. He dropped his head, unable to meet her gaze. "That's different," he said. Then abruptly he got to his feet and said, "Good night. I'll see you later."

Owen left the house feeling miserable and knowing he had made a fool out of himself. All the way back to Doctor Givens's house, he wished he had kept his nose out of this particular situation.

⤙⇒ CHAPTER 11 ⇐⤛

It was mid March. The first rays of spring sun had come to warm the earth, and the snows that had blanketed the Ozarks in February were gone except for tiny spots around fence posts and under trees. As Lanie drove Freeman's Rolling Emporium along the road toward home, she looked up to see Brent walking beside the road. He was wearing a lightweight brown jacket and a pair of dark blue trousers. As always, his clothes looked like they had just come out of the store window. Some men had that ability, while others could put on a new suit and look like they had just been to a rummage sale.

Brent turned, and when he saw her a smile lit his face. He stuck his hand up, fingers turned over and thumb pointed. Lanie pulled up and smiled. "Get in, Brent." She waited until he was seated and put his packages down on the floorboard. "Been shopping?"

"Just needed a few things. Mostly I needed to get out and clear my head. Too much writing makes me woolly brained. How about you?"

"Oh, I don't know," Lanie smiled. "I like to write awfully well."

Brent pulled a newspaper from a sack he was carrying and showed her the headline. LINDBERGH BABY STILL MISSING. "Did you hear about this?"

"It's all everybody's talking about. The poor Lindberghs! I feel so sorry for them."

Indeed, the kidnapping of the Lindbergh child twelve days ago had shaken the nation. Lindbergh had become a national hero through his flying exploits. He abhorred publicity, but now there was no avoiding it, for he and his wife were doing everything they could to get their baby back. They had promised the kidnappers immunity and a large sum of money.

"Do you think they'll get the baby back, Brent?"

"I doubt it. Kidnappers get capital punishment in this country. I hate to say it, but the child's probably dead."

Lanie didn't answer for a while, and Brent looked over and studied her profile. There was a calmness about this girl that he admired, and now he said gently, "You take things hard." He shifted his weight, turning toward her, and made an effort to get Lanie's mind off the tragedy. "Did you try that villanelle?"

Lanie at once brightened up. "Oh yes, I did, Brent. It was the hardest thing I've ever written."

"Villanelle's are hard. Not everyone can write them."

"I had fun with it, but most people would say why don't you just say what you mean."

"That's right, they would." Brent nodded. "But there's some kind of pleasure in putting things into form. You know my favorite chapter in the Bible?"

"What is it?" she said, intently curious, for he never mentioned his faith.

"The one hundred and nineteenth Psalm. It's a beautiful piece of work. You know the Psalm."

"It's divided up into small parts."

"That's right. Each section has a set number of lines, usually eight, and every one of those verses begin with the same letter. The first one is *aleph*, the first letter in the Hebrew alphabet. The second one is *beth*, and it goes all the way through the alphabet. Also, to make things even more difficult, every line has a word in it having to do with the law of God. The statutes, the law, the commandments, the testimonies. You know. I think it must have taken the psalmist a long time to write this psalm. I don't think he sat down and God just dictated it to him. I think he worked on it like a woman will work on a quilt or a piece of fine embroidery, every little stitch meaning something."

"I never thought of that, but people have loved the Psalms for thousands of years. There's something about the form of it that's pleasing, just like the villanelle. I brought it with me if you want to see it."

"I sure do."

Lanie reached down and picked up the folder that was beneath her feet. She extracted one sheet of paper, and for a moment she held it. "I don't know if I did it right or not. I wanted to write a poem about Jesus when He was in the Garden of Gethsemane."

"That must have been terrible," Brent said. "His sweat was like drops of blood, I think the Scripture says. It would be hard to capture that torment in a poem. Let's see what you've done."

Lanie handed the poem over almost reluctantly. Brent had taught her how to write it and told her it was a French poem composed of six stanzas. There were only two rhymes throughout the whole poem, and in addition to this, the first and the third lines had to be repeated throughout the poem and then end up as a couplet. He had given her several samples.

Brent took the sheet of paper, held it up and scanned it rapidly, then he read it aloud slowly:

> *Some deadly grief the heart cannot contain.*
> *See there — that bloody sweat on Jesus' face!*
> *Each man must taste a secret bitter pain.*
>
> *Why groans He so tonight? Is it not plain*
> *He's tormented by a fear He can't erase?*
> *Some deadly grief the heart cannot contain.*
>
> *From whence this sweat, these drops like bitter rain?*
> *Are we to learn (in this dark place)*
> *Each man must taste a secret bitter pain?*
>
> *Pale He is as one who has been slain;*
> *Wild His eyes as one by demons chased!*
> *Some deadly grief the heart cannot contain.*

He's loved too much, too much! Love has drained
Away His life, cut short his daring race.
Each man must taste a secret bitter pain.

His agonizing grief I can't explain.
What means these tears, these groans — from Him so chaste?
Some deadly grief the heart cannot contain.
Each man must taste a secret bitter pain.

After Brent had finished the poem, he sat there staring at it without speaking. She began to get nervous until finally he looked up and said, "Lanie, this is a wonderful poem. You've done a great job of capturing the sufferings of the Savior in these lines. I want a copy of this for myself."

"You can take that one, Brent. I have a copy at home."

Lanie waited for him to say something, but he was silent for so long that she asked rather timidly, "What's the matter, Brent?"

There was an expression on his face she did not often see. He was usually smiling, but now his mouth was drawn tight with a grave sobriety. "This is a sad poem, Lanie. I daresay you think I'm an irreligious dog, Lanie, and you wouldn't be far wrong."

"I know. I've thought about that and wished you were a believer."

"I hope I will be some day, but I'm troubled by what I see. It's such a terrible world. How could a good God be in charge of it?" He folded the paper, put it in his shirt pocket, and said, "Before I came here I made a tour of the big cities — Chicago, Pittsburgh, New York, and Birmingham. I wrote a piece about what this Depression's doing to the country."

A flock of blackbirds rose out of a field, their harsh cries breaking the silence. Brent looked up at them as he continued. "You don't see it so much in a small town like Fairhope. A few stores closed down, people aren't buying very much, but you see it in the big cities. The bread lines in the poor district break your heart, Lanie, and there are settlements outside most big cities called Hoovervilles—blaming the Depression on President Hoover. People are living under terrible circumstances. Worse than you can imagine. They are making crates out of whatever wood they can find and building fires in steel drums just to keep from freezing. In every city, I saw homeless people sleeping in alley doorways, and outside restaurants I saw people fighting like animals for scraps."

"I don't think I'll ever complain again, Brent," she said. "We have it so easy compared to those people."

Brent continued to speak of the conditions across the country. "It's not just the very poor. It's the middle class too. You see men without jobs leaving their homes and families, walking the streets looking for work when there's no work to be found. Even those who were well off have lost everything. They've let their servants go, and women who never cleaned in their lives are now scrubbing their own floors. When I was in Baltimore, a man killed himself. He and his family were living in a forty-thousand-dollar house, but they didn't have any food to eat and had exhausted all their resources. He just couldn't handle watching his family suffer."

Brent continued talking about the tragic circumstances he had seen until they reached his house. As she pulled over, he shook himself and tried to smile. "I sound like Job, don't I? Woe to me! But I'm worried about this country." He got out of the truck, picked up his sack, and managed a grin. "One bit of news you might be interested in—I'm beating the doctor's time."

"What do you mean, Brent?"

"I'm taking Amelia Wright to a concert tonight. That'll make the doctor mad, won't it? He's a good-looking chap, but he hasn't had much experience romancing widows. I think I can give him a run for his money. I like your poem," he said abruptly, then turned and walked into the house.

"Roger, how good to see you!"

Roger Langley was home from college for spring break. He had gotten rid of his cane and now walked with only a slight limp. His badly broken leg had healed, and now as he stepped inside, his face was suffused with a huge smile. "It's good to see you, Lanie. You look so good."

"So do you. Come on into the parlor where it's warm."

"Where is everybody?"

"Well, the kids are at school, and Aunt Kezia finally wore Corliss down. They're taking naps. On second thought, let's go into the kitchen. I'll find you something to eat."

Five minutes later Roger was sitting down with a cup of scalding black coffee in a large mug and a concoction he did not recognize on a saucer. "What is this?" he asked.

"It's one of Aunt Kezia's makings. You know she names every dish. This is what she calls Juliette Bingley's Easy Grasshopper Pie."

"It's got grasshoppers in it?"

"Oh, no. She just calls it that. It's mostly made up of cookies crushed up and mixed with melted butter and anything else sweet she can throw in there. Try it and see if you like it."

Roger cautiously bit into a fragment of the grasshopper pie. "This is good."

"Aunt Kezia can cook better than anybody I've ever seen, but she can't teach anybody. She doesn't ever know how much she puts into things. She just dumps it in."

As the two sat there talking, Roger reached for her hand. "I'm going to be working for my dad here in town this summer. I'll be underfoot all the time. You'll have to sweep me out with a broom."

"I won't do that," she said and smiled. She had had a schoolgirl crush on Roger when she was in the fifth grade—but then so had most of the young girls. He had been the star athlete and the best-looking boy in school as well as the son of the wealthiest man in Fairhope. It was only during his last year that he became aware of her at all.

She looked down. "Roger, you're holding my hand."

"Oh, was I? I didn't notice."

"I bet you didn't," Lanie laughed. She pulled her hand away and then a thought came to her. "I suppose you heard about this church fuss over the Oz family."

"Oh, yes. The gossips kept me well informed. Does it bother you, Lanie?"

"Well, of course it does. They come in church and just glare at us. I've talked and talked to Cody and Maeva. They've got hard feelings too. Davis doesn't, and he was the one that was involved. Anyway, it made it hard to go to church yesterday."

"We ought to turn Sister Myrtle loose on them." Roger grinned.

Lanie suddenly laughed. "I don't think she'd put up with that in her church. She'd singe their tail feathers."

Roger stayed for another half hour, and then she invited him for supper.

"I was going to sit here until you asked me," he said. "Now it's safe to go."

⊂═⟨⊶

Roger came out of his room to find his parents in the parlor talking. Louise was there also, and he said quickly, "I'm going over to have supper with the Freemans."

"You should have told us, Son," Otis Langley said. He spoke with great restraint, for his altercation last fall with Roger had hurt him. After Roger had almost died, Otis had taken a hard look at himself and discovered he hadn't been as good a father as he should have. He was a proud man and it was hard for him to admit it, but now he was very careful as he said, "How are the Freemans?"

"Lanie's upset about that ruckus they're having with Mrs. Oz."

"I guess the whole church is. Mrs. Oz is going around recruiting people. There is some talk of disciplining the Freeman children," Louise said, "but Colin put a stop to that."

"That's good. I was a little surprised that Colin's still the pastor. I thought you would have found a permanent one by now."

"We just can't seem to arrive at an agreement," Otis said.

"I hope we never do," Louise said pertly. "The church is doing better than ever under Colin's leadership."

Roger winked at his mother, then said, "Well, sis, I hear that you've hit the glory road now that you're running around with that preacher all over town—all over the county really."

"I'm chairman of the welfare committee," Louise said quickly, her face flushed. "It's a good work."

"I know it is, Sis, and I'm real proud of you." He stood to leave. "I may be a little bit late tonight. Don't wait up for me."

Otis waited until he heard the door slam. "I'm afraid he's serious about Lanie Freeman."

"Oh, I don't think so, dear," Martha said.

"I think Dad's right, Mother," Louise said. "Roger's pretty easy to read."

"Well, I'm not so worried about that as I am about you and that preacher. You know the talk's going around about you two. Oh, not that you're doing anything wrong," Otis added quickly. "Just that he spends more time with you than he should, that's what people are saying."

"It's all the welfare work. We help so many people, and the money's come in from everywhere to help those in need." She got up and left the room without another word.

Martha shook her head. "You can do a lot for a child, but when they reach a certain age, they're going to go their own way. What would you think about it, Otis, if she decided to marry Colin Ryan?"

"There's no chance of that," he said quickly. "He doesn't even know what he's going to do after he leaves here. I must admit I've changed my opinion of him. He's a better man than I thought, though he has some strange ways. But he's not for Louise. And as for that Freeman girl, why, Roger will get over her."

Martha stared at her husband and started to speak but then changed her mind. She rose, saying, "Well, I hope you're right."

Lanie went to extra pains to cook a good meal for Roger. She baked a country ham with candied yams and cracklin' cornbread. Aunt Kezia made what she called Hopping John, which was really black-eyed peas cooked with hog jowl and rice. For dessert they had apple cobbler made from dried apples.

During dinner, Roger was kept busy telling his experiences at college. When he questioned the others about school, he noticed that Davis said little. He was aware of Davis's reading problem, but now he saw that the young man was grieving over it.

After the dishes were all washed and put away, the Freemans pulled their instruments out and they all joined together to play and sing.

Roger stayed so late they wound up making popcorn balls. He endured until finally everyone but Lanie went to bed. They sat in the parlor, looking at an old photograph album. After a time he said, "I hear that writer's been courting you."

"Brent Hayden? No. Not really. I did go with him to hear Robert Frost give a lecture, but he's not courting me."

"I hear he's been squiring Amelia Wright around."

"I heard that too."

"You know, there's going to be a box supper over at Springdale on Saturday. Are you going?"

"Oh, yes. It's for a good cause."

Each year a box supper was held in one of the small communities. The young women in the area fixed a boxed lunch and then the men bid for the box. If a man wanted to eat supper with a girl, he attempted to buy her box, and the two would eat together. The profits went to the local orphanage.

"Maeva and I are both fixing boxes. Are you going?"

"You bet I'm going. I'm buying your box too. Be sure you let me know which one it is."

"Well, don't spend too much, Roger. You need your money."

"Why, I might go as high as fifty cents. You're worth that at least."

"Why, you're the last of the big spenders, Roger," Lanie laughed. She got up. "You shoo along home now. Your folks will think I've kidnapped you."

"I'd like to," he said. He leaned over and kissed her on the cheek. "I've missed you, Lanie, but I'll be around this summer."

⌖

When Roger got home, he found Louise was still up. He sat down with her and told her about the evening. When he mentioned the box supper, he said, "Why don't you go, Sis?"

"Oh, that's not for me."

"I know you like fancy things, but it'll be fun. Besides, I'll put a bug in that preacher's ear. You do your box up in red paper so he won't miss it."

Louise laughed. "You're getting to be quite a matchmaker."

"You're not serious about Brother Colin, are you?"

Louise did not answer. "I admire him more than any man I've ever seen. You know how I despised him when he first came." She laughed ruefully. "I've felt bad about that, Roger. He loves God more than anybody I know."

Roger studied his sister. She had never been particularly religious, though she was a Christian. Her variety of religion had been rather staid and safe. He did not question her any further, but he saw that she was indeed serious about a preacher who rode a motorcycle and possessed only one tie that he seldom wore. "He'll be leaving pretty soon, I suppose," he said carefully.

His sister's expression changed, and she said, "Good night, Roger. I'm glad you had a good time."

Rubbing his chin, Roger watched her go. "I'll have to put a bug in Colin's ear."

The next day Colin was surprised to see Roger come in. "Hello, Roger," he said. "Welcome back."

"Good to be here," Roger said. The two talked for a while, and then he said, "I have a favor to ask."

"Just name it."

"Louise has decided to go to that box supper on Saturday at Springdale, but she's nervous about it. She wants to help with the cause, but she's afraid somebody she'd be uncomfortable with might buy her box. She's comfortable with you though, isn't she?"

"Yes. We're very close. I don't have much money though."

"Do the best you can."

"Maybe I'll dip into my savings." Colin grinned. "I think I've got almost eleven dollars."

"Blow the whole wad. My sister's worth it."

"I think she is, Roger. Good to have you back again."

ᴄ CHAPTER 12 ᴄ

"... and going once, going twice—and three times for six dollars."

Jed Markham, who was conducting the sale of the box lunches, beamed at Logan Satterfield. "Logan, it looks like you done spent all your money on this pretty Freeman gal, but I reckon she's worth it."

Logan looked across at Maeva and winked at her. "I'm going through all the young ladies in the community. Trying out their cooking to see if they're good enough to qualify for matrimony. I've already eliminated about twenty-five of 'em, I think, so we'll see how Maeva Freeman qualifies."

Lanie, standing beside Maeva, whispered, "He's just awful, Maeva!"

"I'll get even with him for that," Maeva said. When Logan came over holding the box in his hands, she said, "You might as well have saved your money, Logan. I wouldn't marry you if you were the last man on earth."

"Stop playing hard to get, Maeva." Logan wore a white shirt, blue pants, and a string tie. He looked particularly handsome as he hefted the box in his hand. "I'm hungry. Let's start in and we'll see what kind of a cook you are."

Lanie smiled as the two walked away toward the benches that had been provided for the couples. They were already half filled, for the sale had been going on for thirty minutes. Lanie always enjoyed these box suppers. She saw her own box sitting on the table along with those that had not been sold, and her heart beat a little quicker as Jed Markham picked it up and started back to the front of the rostrum.

Lanie would have preferred not to have a box to sell, but it was for the good of the orphans. The dance had been fun. She had danced with Brent, Roger, and several others. The only one she had not danced with had been Owen. She had waited for him to come to her and had been disappointed when he had not. Now she saw him standing over against the wall talking to Amelia Wright. She wondered if Amelia had prepared a box supper and knew that, if so, Owen would bid for it. Amelia was looking well in what appeared to be a brand new white dress that made her stand out from the other young women.

"And now, folks, we've got a prize here. Everybody knows from past box suppers what a good cook Miss Lanie Freeman is, so we're going to expect you boys to step right up and have a spirited rivalry. Now, what am I bid for Miss Lanie Freeman's box?"

"One dollar," Terry Fuller said loudly.

"One dollar!" Markham stared at him. "Get out of here, Terry! You ain't getting this box for no dollar bill. Come on, boys. Don't embarrass the lady."

The bidding went on, increasing in increments of five or ten cents, and most boxes went for a dollar or at the most two. Sally Needham, a very popular girl, had been the prize so far with her box selling for nine dollars. Money was tight, and Lanie was surprised when a loud voice said, "I bid ten dollars for that there box."

Lanie—and everyone else—turned quickly. She saw Luke Satterfield grinning at her. He was Logan's brother, the son of old Caleb Satterfield, and a notorious bootlegger. He had not shaved, and his face was flushed with drink.

A chill went through Lanie. *I can't eat with that man*, she panicked. According to the rules, if no one outbid him, she would have to. Suddenly another voice rang out. "Eleven dollars." Lanie turned to see Roger Langley, who was staring at her with a grin.

"Twelve dollars," Satterfield said.

Whispers began to run through the crowd, and suddenly Owen, who was standing a few feet away from Roger, moved over and whispered, "Son, he'll outbid you. He's made enough money off of bootleg to do it."

"I can use my savings," Roger said.

"You don't want to do that. Let me take care of this fellow."

"Fourteen dollars," Owen called out.

Luke Satterfield was a notorious barroom fighter. He had huge, hamlike hands, and despite running to fat, was a man of immense power. He had been arrested often for brawling, and now he glared at Owen. "You Yankees better stay out of this. This is just for home folks."

"Never mind that," Jed Markham said, his annoyance evident. "You heard the bid."

Luke Satterfield, still glaring at Owen, said, "Fifteen, and you better not try to best me, Yankee."

"Twenty dollars," Owen said, meeting the big man's angry stare.

A gasp went around the room, followed by another flurry of whispers.

Jed said quickly, "Well, that's the most that's ever been bid for a box at one of our suppers. Any more bids? No. Going once, twice. Sold to Doctor Owen Merritt for twenty dollars. Come and get your box and then choose your lady, Doctor Merritt."

Lanie's eyes were fixed on Luke Satterfield. She saw him take a step forward, but his younger brother Ed took him by the arm, whispered something, and then pulled him away.

Owen was smiling as he bought the box. "Well, I didn't buy this for myself. I want you and Roger to have it."

"That's so sweet of you, Owen."

Owen suddenly turned and frowned. "Well, where is Roger? He was right there."

"I think he left," Lanie said. "He's so proud. I think it hurt his feelings that you had to help him, but I'm glad you did. It would have been awful to have to eat with that man."

"Well, sit down here with the box and I'll go find him." He placed the box on the table.

"I think Amelia's upset with you," Lanie said. She had noticed that Amelia Wright had been frowning at Owen throughout the bidding. "You'd better get back to her."

"I'll just find Roger first." Owen started for the door. Lanie had been right. It was obvious that Roger's feelings were hurt, but Owen was determined to put it right.

Maeva had been watching all of this, and now as Owen started for the door, Logan got up. "Where are you going?" she said.

Logan did not answer. Without a word he followed Owen through the door. Maeva stood and went over to where Lanie was watching. "There's going to be trouble, I think."

⚬══⚬

The cold air hit Owen as he stepped outside, but he saw Roger headed toward his dad's car. He called out, "Roger, wait a minute—" Suddenly a hand seized his arm and whirled him around. He found himself staring into Luke Satterfield's face. He could smell the raw alcohol on the man's breath, and when he tried to pull his arm away it was locked by an awesome strength. "Turn me loose, Satterfield," he said. "I don't want any trouble."

It was the last thing Owen Merritt remembered, for it was as if a light had been turned out. One moment he was standing there, staring into Luke Satterfield's face, and the next moment there was nothing.

Satterfield looked down at the fallen man and grinned. He held up his fist. He had struck Owen a terrible blow over the right eye, and blood now flowed down the man's face. "That'll teach you to try to mess with me," he said.

He was aware that others were watching, but he had a total disregard for the law and for anything like fair play. He swung his leg back to give greater power to the kick he intended in Owen's ribs. Suddenly, someone seized him violently and shoved him backwards. He almost cartwheeled, his arms flailing as he tried to catch his balance.

He was a man with a fiery temper, especially when drinking, and now his temper had reached the boiling point. He could not see who had grabbed him but doubled his fists and started forward. "I'll kill you," he yelled.

A sudden blow caught Luke in the chest. Big as he was, it stopped him dead, and still another blow on his jaw sent him sprawling flat on his back. He was tough as boot leather and came up as if from the dead. This time he stood ready to plunge into the battle.

Then he stopped, peering through his drunken haze. "Is that you, Logan?"

"It's me. Get out of here, Luke."

A crowd had gathered, and Lanie was one of them. She saw the two big men facing each other and could well believe that they had different mothers. Luke Satterfield had the big bulk of his father, Caleb, while Logan was lean but strong as a whip, just like his mother.

Blood ran from Satterfield's lip as he staggered toward Logan. He said hoarsely, "You'd take sides against your own kin with a stranger?"

Logan's voice was steady and even. "If my kin acts like a jackass, I would. You're drunk, Luke. Go home."

"I'll go home after I teach you who's the bull of the woods."

"You just fly right at it if you think you're man enough," Logan said.

"Just a minute." Everyone turned to see Caleb Satterfield, as big a man as his son, step out into the light. He turned to Logan and said, "What are you doing, boy?"

"I'm trying to make this family look halfway decent, Pa."

"You hit your brother, take up for a stranger?"

"You heard what I told him, Pa. Doctor Merritt hasn't done nothing to Luke."

Caleb Satterfield, like the rest of the men in his family, was backward and stubborn. There was little affection, if any, shown even among the family members. He stared at Logan. "I won't have a son under my roof that takes up with strangers. I want you out of my house."

"You mean that, Pa?"

"You know I mean it. I always mean what I say. You ain't a Satterfield. I won't have you on my place."

"Suits me fine," Logan said. "I'll get my things and get out tonight." He turned without another word and went back inside.

Logan put on his coat and tucked his fiddle under his arm. He stopped long enough to say to Maeva, "Sorry I won't get to eat that box supper, Miss Maeva. I know I'm missing a good one." He would have gone, but Maeva reached out and took his arm. When he turned, she looked up at him, and Lanie saw her lips were trembling and she had tears in her eyes. It shocked her, for Maeva was not easily moved.

"Th–that was noble what you did, Logan."

Logan Satterfield paused for one moment and looked down at the young woman. He did not speak for a time, then he nodded briefly, and a slight smile turned the corner of his lips upward. "Well," he said briefly, "that's the first noble thing any Satterfield ever did." He turned then and walked away without another word.

❦

Owen was aware of a pain in his head that felt like someone was pushing the point of an ice pick through it. He opened his eyes slightly, and his vision was blurred. "Where—?" he began, but then could not remember the question.

"Owen, are you all right?"

Owen looked up and saw Lanie bending over him with a cloth in her hand, which she placed on his forehead.

It came rushing back to Owen. "I remember talking to Satterfield, but nothing after that. What happened?" He touched his forehead and winced.

"You got hit."

"What with?"

"Luke Satterfield's fist."

Owen sat up. The dance was still going on inside the hall, but judging from the crowd that had gathered, he seemed to be the center of attention. He tried to grin. "Well, I guess I'll make the newspapers tomorrow. 'Local Physician Brawls at Dance.'"

"Don't be foolish. It wasn't your fault."

Owen touched his head again. "This might need some stitches."

"I don't think so, but I was terribly afraid."

"What kept him from kicking me to death? I understand that's his habit."

Lanie put the cold cloth back on Owen's forehead. "Let me just hold that here for a minute," she said. Then she added, "It was Logan. He stopped Luke from kicking you." She went on to tell the rest of the story.

When she finished Owen said, "I didn't know any of the Satterfields had that kind of kindness."

"Logan's different from the rest of them."

He stood up shakily and looked around. "Where's Amelia? I need to take her home."

"She's already gone, Owen."

"Well, I don't blame her." He managed a smile. "Instead of a lunch I paid twenty dollars for, I got a punch in the face. I don't feel much like eating that supper now anyway."

"I'll make it up to you, Owen. You come over for dinner Sunday. I'll fix you something better than I had in that box."

⇥ CHAPTER 13 ⇤

A throbbing headache troubled Owen all weekend, and on Monday he found it necessary to have Doctor Givens take three stitches above his eye. The doctor was of the old school opinion that people should be willing to suffer when they were fools, so he did not go easy on Owen. He also left the ends of the gut showing, which set off the delicate shades of lavender and purple on Owen's face.

By ten o'clock Owen had grown weary of people asking him about the fight. Some were a little bit sophisticated, going at the thing as tactfully as they could. Others simply blurted out, "How'd you get your face busted up, Doc?"

By noon the headache partly mitigated, and as he passed through the outer office he said, "I'm going to get a bite to eat, Bertha."

Bertha Pickens looked up and said without a change of expression, " 'Whatsoever a man soweth that shall he also reap.' "

"I didn't sow anything, Bertha. I've tried to explain to you it wasn't my fault."

Bertha had the irritating habit of answering with verses of Scripture. Without missing a beat, she said, " 'Why do the heathen rage and the people imagine a vain thing?' "

Owen tried to think what in the world that Scripture could have to do with his getting punched in the face. Sometimes Bertha simply quoted a Scripture that popped into her mind whether it had any relevance to the situation or not. "Thank you, Bertha. I'll remember that."

Leaving the office, he headed straight to the Dew Drop Inn. Before he went in he braced himself. Whatever he might find in the way of something to eat, he knew he would also find something else in a plentiful supply: the nosy curiosity of proprietors and customers. For a moment he considered going to the grocery store and getting some sardines and crackers, but given the way his head felt, the effort might take more starch than he could muster. Bracing himself, he entered. As usual, at noon, the Dew Drop Inn was full.

"Hey, you can come and sit by me, Doc."

Owen looked up to see Dorsey Pender in his postal uniform sitting at a booth with Pardue Jessup and Nelson Prather. Making his way to their table, he sat down heavily. "How are you fellows?"

"Better than you are, it looks like, Doc," Pardue said, grinning broadly.

"I hear you got your ticket punched by Luke Satterfield," Dorsey Pender said, his eyes bright with anticipation. "It ain't smart to mess with a fellow like that. How come you do it, Doc?"

"I was just out looking for trouble. I'd had too much to drink, and I wanted to get in a fight and get arrested," Owen said loudly.

Pardue laughed with delight. "Doc, you're not a truthful man at times, are you?"

"I just get tired of telling the same story, Pardue."

Sister Myrtle made her way to the table. As usual, she had a word of correction for Owen, but then she had instructions and warnings for practically everybody that entered the Dew Drop Inn.

"I guess you see now what comes of going to them dances, Doctor Owen Merritt. Nothing but sin, that's what it is."

"Lay it on me, Sister Myrtle," Owen said and suddenly found it amusing, which was good. He had found very little to be amusing since Luke Satterfield knocked him silly. "I'm just a sinner and need to repent. Get on with the sermon."

Sister Myrtle sniffed. "You can make fun all you want, but I'm downright disappointed in you."

"Well, the way I heard it," Nellie Prather said, "the doctor here didn't have no choice. He didn't even get a blow in."

"That's what you want to learn about fighting, Doc." Ed Hathcock, chief of police, looked up from his meal and grinned. "Always get the first blow in. Luke, he learned that lesson pretty good."

"Thanks for the advice, Chief. I'll remember that."

Owen sat there enduring the conversation until Dorsey Pender reached over and fished through his mailbag. "I got an important letter for you, Doc. Here it is. All the way from St. Louis." He handed it to Owen and waited.

"How do you know it's important?" Owen asked. "You don't know what's in there."

"Well, if it comes from St. Louis, it has to be important."

"That's the dumbest thing I ever heard," Nellie sniffed. "I don't know of anything important coming out of St. Louis." Nellie reached into his shirt pocket and pulled out a matchbox. He handed it over to Merritt and said, "Here, Doc. I found it this morning and I thought about you."

Owen took the box, opened it, and smiled at Nellie. "Four-leaf clover. Supposed to be good luck."

"Ain't no 'supposed to be' to it. Why, when Adam and Eve was kicked out of Eden, she grabbed a four-leaf clover."

"I never knew that," Owen said with a straight face. "It's not in any of the books of theology I've ever read."

"Well, it's so. Anyhow, let me tell you how to handle this. It ain't enough just to have a four-leaf clover. You got to do it right."

"How do I do it right?"

"Well, one way is to pin it over the door to your house. Don't use tape, Doc. That might break the charm. There's something about the clover touching metal," Nellie said earnestly, "that makes the charm work. Or you might put it in your shoe. There's some that say if you do that, the first unmarried person you meet the next day will be the one you marry. But that's kind of dangerous."

"Yeah, you might meet Minnie Hoffmeyer. That woman's so skinny she could take a bath in a gun barrel," Dorsey guffawed.

Owen was accustomed to Nellie Prather's fierce superstitions and liked the big man immensely. "Thank you, Nellie," he said. "I'll tack this to my door tonight."

"What about that letter?" Dorsey demanded. "It might be bad news." Somehow Dorsey Pender had come to the conclusion that the mail was his because he was the one who delivered it. He did everything but demand to see what was inside the letters he delivered.

"How could it be bad news when I just got a four-leaf clover?" Somehow Owen managed to fend off the mailman's questions, but when he left the Dew Drop Inn, the first thing he did was open the letter and read it.

His day suddenly brightened, and he almost shouted, "Good news!" as he ran to his car.

<hr />

"It's the doctor," Corliss cried, and she flew out the door to meet Owen.

Lanie watched through the window as Owen grabbed Corliss, kissed her on the cheek, and gave her a hug. It pleased her that he was so partial to Corliss, but he always had been. She ran her hand over her hair and thought, *Why does he always have to come when I'm at my worst?*

"Hello, Lanie. I'm about to spoil this young lady rotten."

"What's rotten?" Corliss wrinkled her nose.

"It means I'm about to take some candy out of my pocket and give it to you." Owen pulled out a Baby Ruth and handed it to her. "There. That'll spoil your appetite. Be good for you."

"And spoil me rotten?"

"I don't think that's possible after all," he said, ruffling her hair. Then he turned to Lanie. "I've got some real good news." He took a letter out of his pocket and said, "I've heard from John Smith, my friend in St. Louis. I want you to read it."

Lanie took the letter, her hands unsteady. Good news came rarely to her, it seemed, and when she read the letter suddenly tears filled her eyes. "This is wonderful, Owen. It's all your doing."

"Not at all. It's John's doing." He took the letter and read it aloud: "'I believe I can help the young man you spoke of. Why don't you send him here as quick as you can. I have a place for him to stay and there'll be no charges.'"

"He needs to go at once," Owen said.

"It'll be expensive. I'll have to see about the money." Owen started to speak, but she held up her hand. "No," she said, "I'm not going to let you pay for it."

"Well, I'll see about the fares. He can go on the train or on the bus."

"You're too good to us, Owen Merritt."

Owen was embarrassed by her words. "Not at all," he said and started toward the door. "I've got to go. There are still a few people who haven't asked me how I got my face bloodied. Maybe I ought to just put the story in the paper."

"I'm so sorry it happened."

"Have you heard about what Logan's doing?"

"He came by to see Maeva and said he was going to cut timber for George Meeny."

"That was terrible — that his father threw him out."

"I don't know. Maybe he's better off. He told Maeva he was sick of bootlegging anyway and wanted to be an honest man."

"Well, sometimes bad things turn out well. I've got to find him and thank him for saving me from some broken ribs."

"He's staying with his friend Neal Jamison."

"I'll go by and check on him." He hesitated for a moment, and then said, "I'll be praying that John will be able to help Davis. Somehow I think he will."

As soon as Maeva heard about Davis's trip to St. Louis, she began to scheme. She said nothing to Lanie, but she was determined to make the trip with Davis. Finally, after thinking hard about it, she came in late for supper on Tuesday to find the family already eating.

"Where have you been, Maeva?" Lanie said. "You were supposed to help me cook tonight."

Ignoring her sister, Maeva said, "I'm going to St. Louis with Davis."

Davis looked up, surprised. "Well, there's not even enough money for me to go."

"We don't have to worry about that," Maeva said. "I went down to talk to Walt Fletcher."

"The one that sells used cars?" Cody asked.

"That's right. I talked him into letting us use one of his cars. It's a nice one. All it'll cost us is the gas money, and we've got that much."

"You can't run off and go to St. Louis," Lanie said.

"I'm going, Lanie. That's all there is to it. This'll be the cheapest way for us to go."

Maeva argued her cause, but Lanie remained opposed to the idea. Finally Davis said, "Let her go, Lanie. It was her idea. Besides, I can use a little encouragement on the way."

Lanie had not thought of this. She hesitated and then said, "All right. Maybe it would be best."

"We'll leave Saturday morning," Maeva said, her face lighting up. "Next week is our spring break anyway, so we won't miss any school. After we see the doctor and get you all fixed up, maybe we can explore St. Louis a bit."

Davis shook his head. "We won't have any money for that."

"It doesn't cost anything to look."

The Wednesday night prayer meeting was abuzz with the news that Davis was going to St. Louis to see some specialist. The family filed down the aisle and sat in a row with Cody at one end. As soon as he was settled he looked over the congregation, a satisfied expression brightening his face.

Davis, who was sitting next to him, said, "Why you looking so funny?"

"I'm not looking funny. I just got a message from heaven."

Maeva, who was sitting on the other side of Davis, leaned forward and gave Cody a crooked grin. "I didn't hear anything."

"You don't understand things like this, Maeva. We've got to do something about Lanie."

"What do you mean?" Davis asked, looking puzzled.

"It's worrying her to death, this business with the Oz family."

"You're right about that," Maeva said. "But what are we going to do?"

"Here's what the Lord wants us to do. All three of us need to go over right now to the Oz family and tell 'em we're sorry for what happened."

"I think that's a good idea," Davis said at once.

Maeva frowned and started to argue, but Cody beat her to it. "I know it's hard for you to say you're sorry. It's hard for me too, but we're doing it for Lanie. Okay?"

Maeva swallowed hard, then shrugged her shoulders. "All right. Let's go get it done then."

The three got out of their seats, and everyone in the congregation stopped talking as they went over to where the Oz family was sitting. There was a stubborn look on each of their faces, but Cody took the lead. "Mr. and Mrs. Oz, I want to tell you I'm sorry about what happened. I really regret it."

Davis stepped up at once. "Me too. It was the wrong thing. I was wrong, and I apologize to you, Mr. Oz, Mrs. Oz, and to all three of you."

Maeva plunged in next. Her voice was loud and clear. "I don't apologize much," she said loudly, "but I think it's wrong for Christians to fuss in church. I was wrong to fight, and I'm sorry, and I hope you'll accept my apology."

At once a loud buzz carried through the church, and Lanie, who had watched this drama unfold, was shocked. She would never have dreamed Maeva would apologize to anyone ever.

Harry Oz jumped to his feet. "That's a handsome apology, and I'm proud of you kids."

Maxine Oz, Harry's wife, was flustered, but seemed relieved. "My husband's right. I'm sorry it all happened, and I'm glad it's over."

Lolean Oz was the same age as Cody. She had a wealth of auburn hair, large green eyes, and was just coming into young womanhood. Suddenly she stood up in front of Cody and said, "Cody Freeman, I'm tired of being mad. I always liked you." Without apology, she leaned over and kissed him on the cheek. "There," she said, laughing when Cody's face turned red, "the Bible says to greet the brethren with a holy kiss."

Laughter swept through the church, mixing with sighs of relief. Everyone, it seemed, was tired of the feud.

Now they waited to see Cody's response.

Not often was Cody Freeman struck speechless, but for this moment he was. He stared at the handsome young woman in front of him and tried to think of something profound to say. Finally he said, "Well, I'll be dipped in gravy!"

PART THREE

Lies and Scandal

⇒ CHAPTER 14 ⇐

The family gathered to see off Maeva and Davis early Saturday morning. As their car disappeared around the bend, Lanie sighed and headed for the barn. While her siblings traveled to St. Louis, she would spend the day restocking the Freeman Rolling Emporium.

Stocking the emporium had become a very trying labor. Lanie had discovered that people wanted all sorts of things, but it was not possible to carry them all. Now she stood in the aisle holding a box of salt in one hand and a box of starch in the other, trying to decide which one she would take.

"As sure as I take the starch, somebody will want the salt and I won't have it," she muttered. Finally she moved items around until she squeezed both into the small space and then stepped back and eyed the rows. A sense of pride came to her as she studied the arrangements. She knew where to find even the most obscure, tiny item whether it was on top, behind something else, or shoved into the small side pockets.

The emporium had not brought in as much money as she had hoped, but still she was optimistic. Now that winter was almost over, she planned to drive the route herself, or send someone, every day.

She stepped outside the emporium just as a noisy flock of crows wheeled across the blue skies. They rent the air with raucous voices then, as if they had a single mind, suddenly wheeled again and headed for the cornfields on the outskirts of town.

Cody had been splitting wood for the stove, and now he was just sitting there on the chopping block stump staring off into space.

She walked over to him. "What are you thinking about, Cody? You're sitting there still as a statue."

Cody sighed heavily and turned to face his sister. He was a fine-looking boy, growing taller, and getting to look more like his father every day. He would never be as tall as Davis, but there was some of Forrest Freeman in him, all right.

"I was just meditating."

"Meditating about what?"

"About life and stuff like that."

Lanie laughed and ruffled Cody's hair. "You're a deep thinker, you are, brother. Let's go inside and see if we can find something to eat."

"You go on. I've got a few more things I've got to get straight before I go anywhere."

"All right. If you need any help meditating, come and get me."

Leaving Cody to his meditation, she walked across the yard and mounted the steps to the front porch. As she opened the door, she heard Corliss banging on the piano with her stubby fingers. Amazingly enough, she could pick out tunes, and Lanie recognized "My Time Is Your Time," which had been made famous by a radio crooner named Rudy Vallee. Lanie shook her head with amazement. The child had more musical talent than all the rest of the Freemans put together.

She found Aunt Kezia sitting in her rocker in the living room, staring out the window. She was very still and her eyes were half shut.

"Are you asleep, Aunt Kezia?"

The old woman came bolt upright. "Asleep? No, I weren't asleep. What makes you think such a thing?"

Lanie sat down beside her aunt and put her hand on Kezia's thin shoulder. She realized afresh how fragile her aunt was, and thoughts of mortality touched her heart with a cold chill. She had grown to love this old woman who had come to their rescue. Her querulous ways and odd manner of speaking mattered not a whit. Lanie squeezed Aunt Kezia's shoulder and said, "Do you still miss your husband?"

Kezia turned her face toward Lanie. Her eyes were still a startling bright blue despite her wrinkles and shrunken body. "Every day of my life I miss my second husband. I've about forgot the first one, and the last one I'm trying hard to forget."

"Tell me some more about Mr. Butterworth."

"You would have liked him. Everybody did." Kezia's eyes grew dreamy. "He was a fine-looking man. Could have had any woman he wanted, but he picked me."

"Well, he picked the right woman. Was he really as good a shot as you told us?"

"Of course he was. He could hit anything with a pistol or a rifle—even the first time he ever fired a gun! And he was only twelve years old. Said he could outshoot any man in Markley County. Annie Oakley was like that, I heard. Some things are just born in people."

Lanie sat very still, listening while her aunt talked about days gone by. It was apparent to Lanie that Aunt Kezia's days with Calvin Butterworth, in a trail town where he was sheriff, were as real as the life she now led.

Suddenly Aunt Kezia stopped talking and squinted at Lanie. "What's the matter with you, girl?"

"What do you mean? Nothing's wrong with me."

"You're worried about something. I can tell."

"Well, I do worry about Davis and Cody and Maeva."

"They'll be all right. What you worried about Cody for? That boy's got more irons in the fire than anybody I ever saw. He goes at life like a man frightened of bees."

"He's not himself. I don't know what's wrong with him."

"He's fourteen years old. That's what's wrong with him. He's bumping into the hard stuff just like we all do." Kezia took Lanie's hand. She held it, young and strong, between her own withered fingers and stroked it. "He'll have to learn how to cry just like we all do, girl."

The sun had passed the meridian and now was beginning its journey to the west as Cody stopped in front of the church. At first he walked into town aimlessly but soon found himself at the church as if drawn there by a magnet. Except for his father, he had never met a man he admired as much as the Reverend Colin Ryan. He stood in front of the parsonage irresolutely for a moment, and then when he heard a sound walked around back. He saw Colin wielding a shovel over some kind of flower bed, making the dirt fly.

"Hello, Pastor," Cody said. "Need some help?"

Colin turned. He was wearing his usual rather disreputable old clothes, and his face gleamed with perspiration. "I never do work myself that I can get somebody else to do, but I think it'd be a better idea if we went inside and got some refreshments. Think you can keep it down?"

"I can sure try."

The two went inside and sat down at the kitchen table where Colin had put a plate of moon pies and two bottles of Nehi cream soda. They drank straight out of the bottle, and for a time Colin simply smiled and talked about the work of the church. He was an astute man, however, and soon he said as politely as he could, "You know, I can remember when I was fourteen years old. Everything was better then. I can remember onions. I'd just go dig one up, wash it off, and just take a bite out of it like out of an apple. Onions aren't as good anymore. I think only a fourteen-year-old can really appreciate what a real onion tastes like."

Cody grinned. "I eat 'em like that too." He started to say something else and then fell silent.

Colin took a swig from his Nehi soda and said, "Something bothering you? You look a little bit worried. Is it about Davis and Maeva going to St. Louis?"

"Nah, they'll be fine."

"You're not still worried who the Antichrist is, are you?"

"Oh, no. I got all that pinned down."

"Oh? Who is it?"

"I think it's Mae West."

Despite himself Colin had to laugh. "Well, I never heard of her being a candidate for that office."

Cody moved the soda bottle around on the table making a pattern of the dampness, and finally he said, "I—I went to see her in a movie over at Kenton. I was over there with the Emporium, and I saw this picture of her out in front of the movie theater, and I went in and I seen it."

"Sounds like the sort of thing I might have done when I was fourteen."

"No. I don't think you would've. It bothered me, Pastor. She wore—well, she wore revealing clothes."

"That's her trademark, all right. She was in a play, I understand, called *Sex*. That's getting right down to the root, isn't it?"

Many men would have rushed on, trying to pry Cody's problem from him. Colin simply sat there nibbling on a moon pie and waiting.

Finally Cody said, "I can't keep what I saw out of my mind. Some of the things, all about that woman, they keep coming back—especially at night when I'm in bed."

Colin said quietly, "You know, one of the first Scriptures I ever memorized was in the book of Psalms. The hundred and first Psalm in the third verse. It says, 'I will set no wicked thing before mine eyes.' David wrote that Psalm I think, and I often wondered if when he wrote it, he was thinking about Bathsheba. You remember that story?"

"Yes, sir. David got himself into a mess with that woman."

"The Bible says that it was a time when kings went forth to war, but David hadn't gone to the war. He stayed home. And he looked out and he saw this woman bathing."

Colin leaned forward, his eyes intense.

"You know, it's not the first look that's wrong. A man can't help looking or he'll fall down in a hole. Sometimes a tempting woman or something that we know is wrong just pops up. It's the second look, though, that gets us in trouble." He shook his head and added, "If David, after that first look, had shut his eyes and turned around and walked away, I think his life would have been different."

"I never thought about that, Pastor."

"I thought about it a lot. I used to think that it was kind of an instant thing that David saw her and right then he sent for her. The Bible doesn't say, but it could have been something gradual. He could have thought about her on his bed like you say, and that image could have been coming back maybe for weeks. So it got to him at the last."

The two were silent, and finally Colin leaned forward. "You don't think you are the only young man in the world that has trouble thinking evil thoughts stirred up by the wrong kind of picture, do you, Cody? We all have that problem."

Cody looked up, his eyes tormented. "What do I do, Pastor?"

"You do what Joseph did. That's my rule. You remember what he did when Potiphar's wife caught hold of him?"

"I sure do. He ran out of there as quick as he could. So quick he left his clothes in her hands."

"He did exactly the right thing. Of course he didn't give up, but his method was right. What I try to do now, Cody, is when I look at something and it causes me to feel lust or envy or anything that I know is against the will of God—right then I just run. If I have to, I shut my eyes, turn around, and get out of the room. If it's in a book, I shut the cover. Throw it away, in most cases."

"I never thought of it like that."

"Think of that woman as a rattlesnake. You wouldn't keep a rattlesnake and pet it and let it sleep with you, would you? Of course not."

"No, I wouldn't."

"Just remember. Christ is in you, Cody. You're weak and He's strong. That's the way with all of us. When the battle starts and you have a temptation, if you start fighting in your own strength, you're probably going to lose. So what I do is I run and as I run, I pray: God, you fight this battle for me. I'll tell you what. Why don't you and I pray right now?"

"That'd be good, Preacher. I need it."

Colin began to pray for the young man. He prayed the simplest prayer that he knew, for he knew that this boy before him, who would quickly be a man, was at a critical hour. He grew fervent and prayed that God Himself would surround Cody with a bubble so that the evil things in the world could not get in.

Finally, when the prayer was over, Cody looked up, and he had tears in his eyes. "Thank you, Preacher. I'll remember all this."

"We all have to remember it, son. Now, how about another moon pie?"

⊂══✦⊱

Lanie had noted Cody as he headed toward town, and she watched carefully until he came back. He said little enough, but he seemed somehow more at ease than when he had left. She noticed he took Corliss out to look for worms to fish with, and the voices of the two of them were a pleasant sound in her ear.

After supper, Lanie sat down at the table with a glass of tea. Cody came in, and she looked up. "Need something?"

"I'm thirsty."

"Here," Lanie said, "let me pour you some tea." Getting up, she chipped some ice with the ice pick, put it into a large glass, and filled it with tea. She set the glass in front of Cody, who took several loud swallows.

Lanie returned to her seat. "Where'd you go this afternoon?"

"I went to town." Cody hesitated and said, "I had to go to talk to Brother Colin about a problem."

"You want to tell me about it?"

"Not really, but I guess you might as well know." He repeated the story as he had told it to the pastor, and when he had finished he said, "I don't know why I went to that dumb old picture show with Mae West." He looked down at the table and shook his head slightly. "Sometimes, Sister, I don't think I'm as smart as I think I am."

Lanie felt amusement bubbling over, and yet she knew this was a serious thing to this brother of hers. "Well, I expect Brother Colin was able to help you."

"He sure was. Taught me how to fight the devil when he comes. For one thing, I'm not going to no more of those awful movies with Mae West or any of those other half-dressed hussies."

"I think that's a pretty good idea."

Cody downed the remains of his tea, set the glass down, and then turned and put his eyes on Lanie. "Lanie, do girls ever have bad thoughts about men the way men have them about women?"

The question flustered Lanie. Her face colored, and she said, "I don't know what you mean."

"Why, sure you do. I just told you the kind of bad thoughts I had, lustful and all. Do women ever have that kind of lust?"

Lanie tried lamely to avoid the question. Finally Cody said, "You're not answering me. That's not like you, Lanie."

Lanie knew she had to give an honest answer, and she tried to gather her thoughts. Finally she said, "I think women have less weakness in this way than men—but yes. I've had to do exactly what the pastor said, to run away just like Joseph. So you're not alone."

Cody stared at Lanie in disbelief. "I can't believe it! I never thought you'd have thoughts like that."

"I'm sorry, Brother, that you had to find out that I'm such a weak person."

Cody took a deep breath and nodded. "Well, that's all right, sister. I'll pray for you tonight. I'm going to have it out with that red-legged rascal, the old devil!" He got up and awkwardly squeezed Lanie's shoulder, then went off to bed.

Lanie sat alone for a time. Finally Booger came over and sat beside her. He put his big paw on her lap and made noises.

Lanie put her hand on his smooth head. "Bloodhounds have the saddest faces in the world." She reached down and hugged the big dog. "But you'd help me if you could, wouldn't you, Booger?"

CHAPTER 15

The bright shaft of morning sunlight that angled through the window beside Cass seemed to make the dullness inside her heart even more pronounced. As she sat with the needle in her hands, staring down at the baby dress she was stitching, a familiar sensation of grief and hopelessness seemed to fill her spirit. Beau was barking at something outside, and Aunt Kezia was singing in her creaky voice as she worked in the kitchen. Even so, with Davis and Maeva gone, the house seemed too still, adding to her loneliness.

The passing days at the Freeman house sometimes seemed like a dream. Many nights she dreamed of her life before she came here and more than once had wakened, sobbing and trembling with fear. Her future was a blank. She kept it that way deliberately, for when she tried to reason and think and consider how she would live and how she would take care of her baby, a sense of hopelessness almost pulled her down physically.

Suddenly she pushed the sewing aside and got to her feet. She moved across the room carefully as if she were carrying a precious burden. Her time was very near now, and all during her pregnancy she had had strange appetites. They were fierce, voracious hungers that came upon her without warning. Once she thought if she couldn't have a watermelon, she could not live—but that had passed, for there was none to be had.

Now there was a fierce appetite in her for fresh tomatoes. She could almost see them in her mind, red and plump, with their juicy, sharp taste so real her mouth watered. To get her mind off the yearning, she left the house. The sun was high, beaming down with the mild heat of early spring. She walked over to the garden. The soil was broken into small clumps, readied for planting in a few weeks. As she stood there, staring down at the dirt, she felt a lust for a fresh tomato that made her want to burst into tears.

A sound caught her attention, and she looked up to see Nelson Prather coming down the road, driving his team. He had a car, fairly new, but he had told her once, "I like horses better than cars. Cars are so cold, and horses are so nice and warm and friendly."

Cass stood there until Nelson pulled the horses to a halt. He swept his hat off and grinned down at her. "Morning, Miss Cass," he said and leaped to the ground with one athletic bound. "Fine morning, ain't it now?"

"I guess so. How are you this morning, Nelson?"

"Finer than frog hair. I had a cold coming on, but I got to it quick enough and got it all cured up."

"Did you go to the doctor?"

"Doctor! I reckon not!" Nellie smiled. "If you get a cold, don't fool around with a doctor. They can't help you."

"What did you do then?"

"Well, what you got to do is take a woolen sock and it's got to be dirty, worn by somebody else besides you. It's best for a woman to use a man's sock and vice versa, don't you see?"

Cass found herself amused despite the despondency that had gripped her. "What do you do with it?"

"Well, you turn the sock inside out, put the grungy part on the outside, then you wrap the sock around your neck. Be sure that the foot part of the sock covers the worst sore spot on your throat, Miss Cass. You leave it there all night. Smells pretty rank, but I done it, and I woke up this morning. My fever's all gone. Throat felt fine. I recommend it."

"Nellie, do you really believe that a dirty sock can cure a cold?"

Nelson looked at her and then grinned. "Well, my granny told me it worked so I tried it. Trouble is I prayed to get healed, and I tried the dirty sock too. Now I don't know which one it was."

Cass suddenly laughed. "If I were you, I'd rather believe that the prayers did the job."

"I reckon you're right." Nelson smiled. His eyes went involuntarily to the swelling of her stomach, and Cass felt embarrassed. "I hope you're feeling good these days."

"I feel all right, but—"

Nelson looked at her sharply. "But what?" he demanded.

"I get hungry for things that about drive me crazy."

"What kind of things?"

"Oh, different things. Sometimes for a cucumber. Other times for liver."

"You got any special longing for something right now?"

Cass shrugged her shoulders and gestured toward the young tomato plants. "Fresh tomatoes, but of course, there aren't any."

"How much would you bet?"

Cass looked up to see Nellie was laughing, with his eyes at least. "You come with me, and I'll guarantee you you'll be eating fresh tomatoes before you know it."

"Where would you get fresh tomatoes?"

"Why, I got a greenhouse. I keep tomatoes all year round. If there's snow on the ground, I just go out and pick me a nice tomato out of my greenhouse. Takes a lot of work, but I guess I'm like you. I get hungry for things sometimes."

Cass said, "Why, I couldn't do that. Go with you, I mean."

"Sure you can. Come on. Let's go tell Miss Lanie where we're going." He took her arm, and the two walked up to the porch.

As they approached, Lanie came out and smiled. "Hello, Nelson."

"Good morning, Miss Lanie. I'm going to borrow this here young lady for a while. She's got a yearning for tomatoes. I'm going to take her to my greenhouse and feed her tomatoes until she turns red."

Lanie laughed. "I think that would be good. You go along, Cass—and bring me back a big red tomato too."

"I'll do better than that. I'll bring back enough for the whole family."

Cass was entranced by Nelson's farm. As they drove through the fields to get to the house, she exclaimed, "I never saw such a neat farm, Nelson!"

"Well, I take care of it pretty good. Can't stand a messy place. Look. I'm starting a new barn over there. Just work on it when I can. It'll be a jim-dandy when she's finished though."

As they drove up to the house, Cass exclaimed, "What beautiful flowers!"

Nelson pulled the horses up and sat for a moment looking at the daffodils. Indeed, they did make a beautiful sight with their bobbing, cheerful yellow faces. "My ma always loved flowers. After she died, I kept up the flower garden. Seemed like it reminds me of her. You need to take some of them home with you. We'll fix up a nice bouquet."

Nelson quickly ran around the wagon, reached up, and said, "Here. You don't need to be jumping down." He picked her up as if she were as light as a feather. Cass was amazed at his strength. He didn't look that strong, for he was a lean man and tall.

"Come on over and get some of the best water you ever tasted."

She followed him to the well, which was covered. He started to remove the cap, then stopped and turned to her with mischief dancing in his eyes. "You want to see the man you're going to marry?"

Cass looked at him with astonishment. "What?"

"I'll show you the man you're going to marry." Nellie removed the cover, reached into the pocket of his overalls, and came out with some change. Selecting a penny, he gave it to her and said, "Now don't look, but toss this down there. As soon as it hits, you look."

Cass took the penny and smiled. She tossed the penny in and it struck almost at once, for the well was close to the surface. She leaned over and looked.

"You see his face down there?" Nellie asked.

"I don't know what you mean."

Nellie leaned over and Cass said, "There you are. I can see you."

"Well, shucks, you're supposed to see the man you marry when you throw a penny into a well. You'll have to try it again when the water settles."

Cass found herself amused, which was a rare thing these days for her.

"You have any other secrets about marriage and things like that?"

"Oh, lots of them," Nellie said. "For one thing, you know what a bachelor button is?"

"No. What is it?"

"It's a little blue flower, comes out later in the spring. You're supposed to pick it early in the morning when the dew's still on it. Put it in your pocket and don't look at it for twenty-four hours. If that flower's still bright and fresh, still true blue, you'll have a happy married life, but if it's done withered, well, too bad. You'll have a sad marriage."

"Is that true?"

Nellie rubbed his chin thoughtfully. "Well, my uncle tried it, and it didn't work for him. His flower was nice and pretty, but he lived to be eighty-six and never did marry. Sometimes I wonder if I got the hang of all this stuff. Well, come on to the greenhouse."

Cass was surprised that Nellie took her arm and held to it firmly as they walked across the yard. "Some holes in the ground around here. I don't want you falling," he said. He opened the door to the greenhouse and they stepped inside. She looked around with astonishment, for it seemed to overflow with growing things: vegetables of all kinds and colors, herbs and flowers that filled the air with their fragrance.

Her eyes went at once to the tomato plants. "Oh, Nellie, real tomatoes!" she exclaimed.

"Real tomatoes is right. Pick the one you want."

Cass went at once to the tomato plants and reached out and squeezed a huge tomato. "Can I have this one?"

"Have at it. Got plenty."

Cass pulled the tomato off, wiped it with her handkerchief, and then bit into it as if it were an apple. She tore at the rich flesh, the juice running down her chin unheeded. "This is heavenly. The best thing I ever had in my life."

She ate the entire tomato and then said, "I won't have another one now, but I'd like to take some home with me if you can spare them."

"Why, shucks, I can't eat all these tomatoes. Before we go back we'll bring a sack and we'll take enough for the whole family. Come on. I want to show you the house."

The house inside was as neat as the farm outside. Nellie took Cass through it, and then he sat her down and made tea and to her surprise pulled a cake out of the warming oven of the stove. "I made this myself."

Cass tasted the cake. "Why, this is delicious!" She looked at him and said, "I heard about your family, about how you had to take care of your brother and sister and your mother too."

Nellie said cheerfully, "It was quite a chore farming the place and taking care of a family, but it don't hurt a fellow to work." He paused, smiling. "Tell you what. Why don't you just hang around today? I'll cook up something good for us to eat for lunch, and get you home before dinner. That way I can show you the whole place and you can take a nap if you need to."

"Oh, I don't need a nap. I want to see everything."

The day had gone so pleasantly that Cass hated to see it end. After a late afternoon cup of tea, Cass said, "I guess I'd better be getting home, Nelson."

"I guess so. Come along."

She went with him to the barn where he had stabled the horses and waited until he hitched them up. She saw something unusual at the deep end of the barn and said, "What's that?"

"Why, that's a sled."

"Really? I've never been in a sled."

"You haven't? Well, I like sleds. I made that one a long time ago for the kids. Tell you what. Next winter I'll hitch up that sled and take you for a sleigh ride. And the baby too," he added.

Nelson saw something change in Cass's face. "What's the matter?"

"Most men wouldn't want to take a baby—one like mine, I mean, without a father."

"Why, Cass, don't talk like that!" Nelson seemed shocked at the notion. "A baby's a baby. They're sweet and good. It's up to folks to give them a chance to stay that way."

"I wish everybody felt like you do, Nelson."

"Well, I got real attached to my brother and sister."

"It must have been a really hard time for you—losing your father and having to take care of a sick mother besides having to take care of your family."

The late afternoon sun cast its rays on Nelson Prather's face. He was such a cheerful man that she was shocked to see something like sorrow touch his blue eyes. He looked down and seemed to be having trouble speaking. "Me and Pa were close, and when he died it like to have killed me. And then when Ma got sick, I had to take over. I was fifteen years old. I had a younger brother and a sister. Little Johnny and little Florence."

"They died, didn't they?"

Nelson suddenly turned his back, and his voice was muffled as he said in a hoarse whisper, "The flu came. Took all three. My ma and Johnny and little Florence."

Cass stood absolutely still. The tragedy of her life had occupied her heart, but this kind, cheerful man had seen more tragedy than she had. A sudden compassion came over her, and she put her arms around him and whispered, "I'm so sorry, Nelson."

His shoulders shook as he attempted to control himself. Finally he cleared his throat, turned to one side, and pulled out his bandanna to wipe his face. When he turned back to her, trying to smile, he said, "It gets pretty lonesome around here sometimes, Cass." Then he said, "Come on. Let me help you in the wagon. I'll get the tomatoes for the Freemans."

⊂══⋆⊷

Once the supper dishes were cleared away, the rest of the family went into the parlor to listen to *Amos and Andy* while Cass and Lanie sat at the table. Lanie wanted to hear all about Cass's visit, and as she listened, she watched the girl's face.

"It's the neatest farm you ever saw, but you've seen it, of course."

"Everybody talks about Nellie's farm."

"I hate that name Nellie. I'm going to make everybody call him Nelson. You have to start, Lanie."

"You don't think he likes his name?"

"I don't know. But I don't. It sounds like a woman, and he's a strong man."

"I can remember when he lost his mother and his brother and sister. I went to the funeral. I was younger then, but I still remember it. Just about destroyed Nelson. Daddy and Mama always talked about what a good son and a good brother he was."

"I wonder why he never got married."

"I think he didn't even think about such things when he was helping raise his brother and sister and taking care of his mother."

"But afterwards."

"I don't know. Maybe taking care of them and losing them took something out of him."

Cass looked down at the table. "He's such a good man."

"Yes, he is. I'm glad you two are friends."

"He said he'd take me and the baby for a ride in the sleigh next winter." She smiled tremulously. "I told him not many men would want a baby that didn't have a father."

Lanie sensed the longing in the young woman for some security. She reached over and put her hands over Cass's. "It's going to be all right. You'll see."

Cass's lips trembled slightly. "I hope so, Lanie, but I don't see how."

⟶ CHAPTER 16 ⟵

Wednesday morning, Dorsey Pender came whistling down the road, mailbag over his shoulder. "Special delivery," he called.

Lanie came out onto the porch. "Well, hello, Dorsey," she said.

He handed her a bulky package. "Well, here's your new Monkey Ward catalog, but you want to be sure and keep it from them brothers of yours."

Lanie took the package and turned her head to one side. "Why should I keep the Montgomery Ward catalog from Davis and Cody?"

"Because from page forty-eight to fifty-six there's pictures of women wearing their underwears. It ain't good for young boys to see things like that. It gives 'em notions." Pender shook his head sadly. "Notions is bad things for a young fellow to have."

Lanie smiled suddenly. "Are you sure you got the page numbers right, Dorsey?"

"Oh, shore. I'm offering to tear that section out in case you think it'll be too much for your brothers." He waited expectantly, but Lanie simply shook her head.

"No. I think they'll be able to handle it."

"And you got this letter from your pa." Dorsey handed her a small envelope. He stood waiting while Lanie examined the outside and looked disappointed when she tucked it into the pocket of her apron.

"I'll have to read it later. Thank you, Dorsey."

"You shore you don't want to read it now?"

"No. Later will be fine."

"Well, that's as may be," Dorsey said. "I'll be moving along."

Lanie walked slowly back into the house. It was quiet for a change, and the silence seemed to fill the house with a heavy weight. She placed the catalog on the kitchen table, sat down, and carefully opened the envelope. She was surprised to see two pieces of paper inside, one written in handwriting she did not recognize. Glancing down at the bottom of the page, she saw that it was signed Chaplain Buck Jones. It was only a few lines so she scanned it quickly:

March 25, 1932

Miss Lanie, I wanted to slip this little note into the envelope with your dad's letter. As you know, we have to censor all mail that comes in and goes out, and I've been keeping up with you and your family and Forrest, of course, in that way.

I wish I had good news for you, but your dad doesn't seem to be improving any. I know the doctor here is pretty well stumped, but your dad is losing weight and he doesn't have much strength. It worries me a lot, but I know as well as you that God is able to do all things. So, rest assured that I visit him every day and pray for him and with him. I'll continue to do so. I'll look forward to seeing you on your next visit.

Chaplain Buck Jones

Lanie was troubled. Quickly she opened the letter from her father and saw that it also filled a single page. She read through it quickly, but he said nothing at all about his health. He simply told her about some of the inmates and asked her to pray for two or three of them by name. He closed by saying:

My darling daughter, you are the pride and joy of my life. If I didn't know that you were out there taking care of the family, I don't think I could stand it. I thank God for you every day, and I look forward to seeing you on your next visit.

Love, Dad

Fear for her father's health loomed like a black specter in Lanie's spirit. Especially at night when the house was quiet, she could almost see his face thinned by whatever disease was eating at him. She sat there for a moment, bowed her head, and tried to pray, but it was one of those times when it seemed that the heavens were brass and she was talking to herself. She had learned not to accept this but simply told God how she trusted him and asked for complete healing for her father.

A sudden impulse took her, and she acted on it at once. Getting up, she went outside into the backyard where Aunt Kezia was sitting in a cane-bottom chair telling stories to Corliss.

"Aunt Kezia, I need to go to town. Do you need me to pick up anything?"

"Don't reckon so."

"Watch out for Corliss, will you?"

"Sure will, honey. Me and her will be just fine."

"You be good now, Corliss."

"I'm always good."

Lanie laughed. "Yes, you are." She went over and kissed the child on the head and then turned and went into the house. She took off her apron and gave her hair a few brushes.

A few minutes later when she left the house and stepped into the front yard, Beau and Booger came eagerly. They were always anxious to make any journeys offered, but Lanie said sharply, "No! You can't go with me. Now stay here!" As she had expected, Beau went over to the house, threw himself down, facing away from her, abject in every line in his body. He always pouted like this when he was not permitted to have his own way.

Booger sat down and lifted his head and gave a muted but mournful cry. Lanie could not help but smile. The dog's sad face and the even sadder moan were almost comical. She leaned down and hugged him. "Booger, when I get back, I'll take you out into the woods. You can chase rabbits or something. Now, you be sweet."

She left the yard and turned toward town, preoccupied with her father's health problem as she walked. Even so, the fresh air invigorated her. The leaves of the hardwood trees were still tiny flashes of gold. They would turn green soon, and by summer would spread into canopies of shade, giving the street an air of placid tranquility.

She spoke to several of her neighbors as she made her way downtown and wondered what it would be like to live in a city in an apartment house where you didn't know anybody.

I know almost everybody in Fairhope, she thought as she quickened her pace. *That's the way it should be. I hope I'll always live here or in a town like this.*

She passed by the house of the Parks sisters, Effie and Aura, who were called old maids by some or maiden ladies by those who were kinder. They were both in their eighties now and spry as the day was long. They had each, by some strange coincidence, lost an eye, and they were only able to afford one artificial eye to fit in the sockets. This meant that one of them had to wear a black patch over their eye while the other one wore the glass eye. Neither of them liked to appear with the black patch, so often the black patch wearer would stay home while the other would wear the eye to the store or to church. There was something ridiculous about the whole thing.

I wonder why they don't just buy another eye? Lanie smiled brightly and said, "Hello, Miss Effie. Hello, Miss Aura."

Effie said, "Good morning, Lanie. Going to town?"

"Yes. Can I get you anything?"

"No. I reckon not. Be careful. Don't get run over by a truck."

Lanie noticed that they always cautioned her about this. For some reason they had decided that her fate was to be run over by a truck, and no amount of promising on her part gave them any peace about it.

"I'll stay on the sidewalk," she promised. "It'll have to come up there to get me." She smiled and then continued along her way.

When she reached town, she could not help but notice that since the Depression had started, Fairhope had assumed a more somber and even dilapidated air. Several buildings were closed up with "For Rent" or "For Lease" signs in the windows.

She had almost reached the office that Doctor Merritt shared with Doctor Givens when she saw a man standing behind a box. Judging from his faded overalls, large brogans, battered straw hat, and huge hands, he was a farmer. On the box in front of him was a basket full of apples. The sign beneath it read in an uneven scrawl, "Apples five cents."

Buy some apples from that man.

Lanie did not actually hear a voice saying this to her, but the impulse came so strong she could almost vow that she did. This happened to her from time to time, and she had long ago learned to act on such impulses. She well understood that sometimes such impulses were not of the Lord but were simply from her own heart. But she had told Aunt Kezia, "I'd rather be wrong and do something than not do what I feel and disobey God."

"Those are fine-looking apples," Lanie said and smiled up at the man.

"They are right nice."

Hope was in his eyes, and Lanie wondered how many men like this in America were trying to sell apples just to stay alive. "How many do you have there in that basket?"

"I don't know, miss."

"Well, let me count them." Lanie counted out sixteen apples. "They look so good. I'll take them all."

"That's—that's right nice of you, miss." The man quickly pulled a used paper sack out from the interior of the box, put the apples in it, and handed them to her. He put his big hand out, and she saw that it was callused and hard. She counted out the change, and he looked at it as if it were some strange and unusual treasure. "Thank you, miss. Right kind of you."

"Things are a little tight now, but God's in control. They're going to get better."

"I reckon that's right." The man smiled briefly and put the coins in his pocket. "God bless you, miss."

A sadness came over Lanie. Here was a man obviously used to work and who probably longed to work—but there was no work for men like this. The Depression had robbed the country of one of its precious treasures: the right and the opportunity of men and women to work for their bread.

She turned down Stonewall Jackson Boulevard and passed the barber shop, where two young men were leaning against the building. In their twenties, they eyed her as she walked by. One of them let out a long, low whistle and said in an exaggerated, loud whisper, "Now there is a good-looking woman, Fred."

"She shore is, Jack. Looks like she needs some masculine company."

The one named Fred was tall and lean, the one named Jack small and roly-poly. They shoved themselves upright and took position on either side of Lanie. The lean one grabbed her arm. "Hey, sweetheart, what's your hurry? Why don't we go and buy you an RC Cola or something."

"Yeah, we might even throw in a doughnut or a moon pie," the shorter one said.

"Turn me loose, please."

"Oh, there ain't no hurry. Here. Let me carry that sack for you." He reached out, but Lanie pulled the sack back.

"Please turn loose of me." She was not frightened, for it was broad open daylight, and there was really nothing they could do, but it was annoying. "Why don't you two go find a job?"

"You mean work?" Jack snorted. "There ain't no work."

"But we got some money. Let's go stepping."

Lanie struggled to get loose, but Fred held onto her arm.

"You two got nothing to do but make yourselves obnoxious to ladies?"

Lanie looked up quickly to see Pardue Jessup, the sheriff, suddenly appear in front of her. He looked large and at the moment rather ominous.

"Aw, Sheriff, we didn't mean nothing."

"You don't mean nothing, and you don't know nothing. Now you two scat before I arrange with the judge to have you do some road work for the next thirty days."

"You can't arrest us. We ain't done nothing."

"That's right, and that's what's called loitering." Jessup suddenly stepped forward and clapped his hand down on the tall boy's wrist. He cried out in pain, and Pardue said mildly, "You scat before I cloud up and rain all over you."

The two boys turned and scurried away, disappearing into the confines of the pool hall.

"They ain't really mean, Lanie. They just smell kind of bad. Where you headed?"

"I had a few errands to do."

"What do you hear from Davis and Maeva? When they coming back from St. Louis?"

"Any day now. I'll be glad when they get here too."

"Well, I sure hope that fancy doctor up there is able to help Davis with his reading problem. I know it ain't because he ain't smart, because he is." He suddenly snapped his fingers and said, "I meant to tell you. I was out looking for moonshiners over toward where the Satterfields live. I nearly caught some of them, but Logan wasn't with them. He's moved out, you know."

"I know that."

"He's different from the rest of that Satterfield bunch. He takes after his ma. She was a real good woman. I remember her well." He reached into his pocket, pulled out a box of matches, extracted one, and put it in his mouth. Chewing on it thoughtfully, he said, "I was talking to Logan. He don't say much, but I got something figured out."

"What's that, Sheriff?"

"He's stuck on Maeva, but I don't think it'll do him any good."

"Why would you say that?"

"Well, Maeva, she won't stay in Fairhope long."

This thought had been in Lanie's mind for some time, but she was surprised that Pardue had seen it. "I'm afraid you're right," she said. "She likes big things happening, big cities, lots of people and crowds. She wants to be a singer."

"She's got the voice for it and the looks too. But I hope she don't. It's dangerous in big cities."

He turned and she saw devilment in his eyes. He liked to tease her, and she waited to hear what he would say.

"Maeva's got lots of fellas chasing after her, but I reckon you run her a close second. Let me see," he said, counting with his fingers to prove his point. "You got Roger chasing around after you. He's plum gone on you—and then you got that fellow Brent Hayden, that writer fellow."

"He's not chasing after me," Lanie said quickly.

"Oh, I expect he might if you'd wiggle a little bit and give him a little encouragement."

"That's only two and I wouldn't say that's a mob."

The match tilted upward. "Well, there's Doctor Owen Merritt."

Lanie suddenly flushed. "You're talking foolish, Pardue."

"Why, I seen the way you look at him, and I think he's been returning them looks."

"He's courting Amelia Wright."

"So I hear. Good-looking woman. I went out with her myself before she took up with the doc."

"What did you think of her, Pardue?"

"Hard to say. I don't know much about women anyhow. All I know is she's fine-looking and goes to church all the time."

"You're getting to be a worse gossip than Dorsey Pender."

Pardue looked up and said, "Look. There's old Clem Hopkins. Drunk in broad open daylight. I'll have to lock him up until he sobers up." He grinned. "I hope we don't have any trouble between them three fellows. When men get fighting over a woman, I have to step in sometime. Be something if I had to lock all three of them up, wouldn't it?" He laughed and moved down the street. Lanie watched him as he went over and began to talk with the shaggy-looking man. She knew he would keep him from harm until he sobered up.

She hurried down the street until she came to the Doctor Oscar Givens's and wondered why Owen had not added his name to the sign. She entered and found Doctor Givens talking with the nurse, Bertha Pickens. They both looked up and Doctor Givens, a big man in his sixties with coarse salt-and-pepper hair and an old-fashioned mustache, looked at her over his glasses. "Well, what's ailing you today, Lanie?"

"Oh, nothing. I just have something I need to ask Doctor Merritt if he's here."

"He's here." Givens nodded and shrugged his beefy shoulders. "He's in there telling Minnie Sawyer there's nothing wrong with her. She won't believe him, though. I've been telling her that for ten years."

Even as he spoke, the door opened, and a tall woman came out. She was large up and sideways, and her cheeks glowed with health. She was talking as rapidly as she could. ". . . and then I keep having these shooting pains in my back, Doctor Merritt. And besides that I think my heart's palpitating. It beats sometimes like a trip hammer."

"You just take these pills, Miss Sawyer." Owen smiled and guided her to the door. When it was closed, he turned to say to the others, "I wish I had the chance of living as long as she does. She's the healthiest human being I've ever seen. She gets every disease she reads about in magazines and such. Goes to the library and looks them up. Came in one time in tears and told me she had leprosy. It turned out to be shingles. You know, I think she was kind of disappointed. That'd be a right potent disease for her to boast about."

Owen then smiled and said, "Well, Lanie, good to see you."

"Nothing wrong with me, but I need to ask you a few questions when you're not busy."

"I'm not busy now. I was just going to go down to the Dew Drop Inn and see if Sister Myrtle has anything fit to eat. Come along with me."

"Oh, I wouldn't want to do that."

"If you don't, I'll have to talk to some of those other people in there. They'll be wanting free medical advice. Come along." He turned and said, "I'll be back after I get the two of us fed, Doctor."

○═══★─

When the door closed behind Lanie and Doctor Merritt, Bertha said at once, "I heard that Forrest Freeman's not doing too well."

"How'd you hear about that?"

"Well, Maybelle Simms heard it from her sister-in-law Annie Doss. You know she's the one who just lost her third husband."

"Kind of careless, wasn't it, losing three of them?"

"Don't be foolish! Anyway, Mae was in the beauty shop — and I might as well say she sure needs it — and she heard Dorsey Pender tell Mamie D'Orr that he was there when Lanie read one of the letters."

"That man needs to be fired. He's got to know the contents of every letter he delivers."

"He's just interested in folks," Bertha said defensively.

"He's nothing but a gossip."

"Well," Bertha snorted, "it ain't gossip that Doctor Owen is seeing Amelia Wright." She leaned forward and whispered as if the room were full of spies, "He ate supper at her house just last night, and he didn't leave until after ten o'clock."

"What'd they have for supper?"

"Why, I don't know."

"Your spies need to pay a little bit more attention."

Bertha flushed. She had been Doctor Givens's nurse ever since he started his practice in Fairhope and knew she was immune from being fired. "He's too careless with women, that's what!"

Doctor Givens stood for a moment thinking about his young colleague. It had been difficult to fall into a semi-retired position, but he had broken his leg so badly he had to have help. Owen Merritt had come from the big city, Memphis, and when he arrived, Givens did not think he would last a week. But the young man had done well.

He had learned the ways of country and mountain folks, and he was a fine doctor.

Givens ran his hands through his hair and asked in a nervous tone, "You think he's up to no good with that woman?"

"I don't say that," Bertha said quickly. "But you know he just lost one woman. Ever since Louise broke their engagement he's been walking around like a man that's been shot. Same thing happens with men who lose their wives. Both cases somebody grabs them on the rebound."

"You read that in *True Romances*."

"What if I did?"

"Well, just don't be talking it around to other people," Givens said, but he knew that warnings such as this were futile. He turned and went back into the inner office, limping slightly on his gimpy leg. There he settled into his chair and lit a cigar. He watched the smoke rise and thought long thoughts about men and women — especially Owen Merritt and Amelia Wright.

↜ CHAPTER 17 ↝

Owen held open the door of the Dew Drop Inn for Lanie. As soon as she stepped inside, she saw that it was not as crowded as usual. When he moved to join her, he said, "It looks like a local meeting of the ministerial alliance."

Lanie looked over to see Reverend Roy Jefferson, the Episcopal priest, Father Robert Quinn, the Catholic priest, and Colin Ryan sitting at a table. They were laughing at something, and Owen said, "Come along. We'll sit beside them. Maybe we'll hear some good theology."

The three looked up, smiled, and greeted them. Owen pulled Lanie's chair out while she seated herself, and then he sat down and grinned at Reverend Jefferson. "You know, I like it when preachers wear their collars backwards."

Roy Jefferson, a short spare man with blonde hair and blue eyes, looked up with a lively expression. "Why's that, Doctor?"

"Well," Owen remarked, winking at Lanie, "it makes them easier to recognize. I always like to be on my best behavior around the clergy, and when they wear their collars backward I can always spot them. Now you take Baptist preachers. You can't tell one of them from an undertaker. I think you fellows ought to wear something to mark your calling."

Father Quinn, the Catholic priest, was a burly man with a broad face and a pair of sharp brown eyes. His brown hair was curly and needed cutting. "I sort of envy the Baptists," he said. "As soon as I meet somebody, they see this uniform I wear and immediately they're either on their guard or else act so holy that they wouldn't eat an egg laid on Sunday. They're afraid the priest will see them do something. Sometimes I tell them God sees them whether the preacher does or not."

"Well, no one would ever mistake you for a preacher, Brother Colin," Jefferson said. The two were very close friends, and his eyes crinkled as he said, "You look like you bought your outfit from a Salvation Army."

"Well, I think I will get me a collar and turn it around backwards. Then everyone will know I'm a preacher."

"It'd take more than that." Quinn laughed. "You look and act less like a preacher than any man I ever saw."

It did Lanie good to see that the three men had become such good friends. It amazed her that, though they were so different in their theologies, they still had much in common. They seemed unable to fight over their differences because they had developed an enormous liking for one another.

Looking up, she saw Sister Myrtle headed for them, her body thrust forward and her head down like she intended to ram it through an oak door. She pulled up short and pulled a small tablet from her apron pocket. Then she rummaged around in another pocket, came up with a stub of a pencil, but instead of asking for their order, she turned to the Catholic priest. "My brother," she said, "one of your flock is going astray."

"Only one?" Quinn was used to Sister Myrtle informing him about various aspects of his church, and now he glanced at his two colleagues and then back at Myrtle. "Which one is it?"

"It's that oldest Sullivan girl. Her name is Annie. She went to the Green Door, that dive straight out of the pit, with Charlie Danvers. He's already ruined two girls I know of. See to it, Quinn."

Quinn moved his burly shoulders uncomfortably. Sister Myrtle knew everything that went on in the Catholic church as well as she did in every other church. How, he could never figure out. It did bother him that she chose to make public announcements, but he knew that he would never win an argument with her. "I'll look into it, sister. Thank you."

Sister Myrtle then turned to Roy Jefferson. "That sermon you preached on hell last week was wishy-washy. Hell ain't no Palm Beach. You got to make it sizzle."

Roy Jefferson looked up with surprise. "Why, I didn't see you there."

"I wasn't there, but Iris Murdoch she was. She told me about it."

Jefferson looked puzzled. "Why, she's a Pentecostal from your own church. Why did she come to hear me preach?"

"She said she was just curious."

"I expect she wanted a second opinion, Roy," Colin grinned.

Owen found that amusing. "I've been thinking I might shop around a little bit myself. After all, a fellow's got to be tolerant."

"You need to be a Pentecostal," Sister Myrtle said. "That's me. I'm Pentecost at any cost."

Lanie giggled. She had heard Sister Myrtle say this before and it always amused her.

"What will you folks have?"

Lanie said, "I think I'd like a cheeseburger and some milk."

"I'll have the same, Sister Myrtle."

The two sat there and there was little chance of an intimate conversation until they were halfway through with their hamburgers. At that time the three ministers got up, bid them good-bye, and left.

"I think they're going out to play golf. They do that sometimes," Owen said. "I understand it tests their patience not to say bad words when they make bad shots. They know they have to be on their best behavior with each other."

Lanie laughed. For a few moments, they ate in a comfortable silence. Then Lanie said, "I hated to bother you at your office, but I did need to talk to you, Owen."

"Shoot. What is it?"

"It's about Dad. I got a letter from the chaplain. He says Dad's doing worse. I'm worried about him."

"Did he give any of the symptoms?"

Owen listened as she told him the contents of the letter and then he said, "I'll tell you what. Doctor Givens knows the governor's father. I think they went to school together. I'll have him write a letter and get permission to visit your father. And while I'm at it, if he needs to go to Little Rock for further tests, I'll get that done too."

"Would you, Owen?"

"Sure. I don't want you worried about your dad—although, to tell the truth, I'm concerned about him myself."

The two sat there, and Lanie had a warm feeling. It always made her feel better to talk to Owen. Finally she said, "I guess I'd better be on my way home."

"I have a call or two to make."

"Come by for dinner tonight," she said. "We can talk some more."

Owen hesitated and it came to Lanie that he had probably agreed to have dinner at Amelia's house. She watched his face change, and then he smiled. "I'll be there if you make me some fried pies."

"I'll make them. What kind do you want?"

"Apple. I can resist anything but temptation and fried apple pies." He got up and pulled her chair out.

As they left, Sister Myrtle bellowed after them, "You come back, you hear?"

"I wonder if Sister Myrtle can whisper?" Owen said as soon as they were outside.

Lanie had no chance to answer, for Amelia Wright was coming toward them, walking quickly. She stopped in front of the pair and said, "Well, you've been having a meal together?"

"Yes. Lanie and I had a lot of catching up to do. We don't get to see each other much."

"Well, that's nice. Not that you don't get to see each other but that you had the meal." Amelia smiled. "Don't forget about tonight. Come by late. We'll have a late supper." She put her hand on his arm possessively. "I've got some new Bing Crosby records. Come as soon as you can."

Lanie said quickly, "I think I'd better be going. Thank you, Owen, for the hamburger and for the favor." And she turned and headed home.

∘══×∘

As soon as Lanie stepped up onto the porch, the door burst open. She gave a glad cry, for Davis and Maeva came bursting out. "Davis!" she squealed, and he picked her up and swirled her around, squeezing her hard. "Put me down, you brute!" she said. But she put her arms around his neck, pulled his head down, and kissed him on the cheek. When he put her down, she searched his face to see if it would reveal any sort of good news or bad. She had been dreading the worst, but his smile was bright and his eyes danced.

"Come on inside, Sister. I got things to tell you."

Lanie went quickly to Maeva and hugged her. "When did you get back?"

"Just about an hour ago. Where have you been?"

"I was having a hamburger with Owen."

Maeva grinned and winked. "That's right. Keep after him."

"You hush now." Lanie walked inside where all the rest of the family was gathered.

"Did you see Owen?" Aunt Kezia demanded.

"Yes, I saw him. I told him about Dad. He's going to get Doctor Givens to write to the governor's dad. He thinks he can get him to Little Rock for tests."

"Did you ask him about Doctor Christie's galvonic belt and neck bracelet?"

"No, I didn't. It never came up."

"Well, I'll have to go see him myself. I've got to have something to give me a little relief, and I want to know if he can get me a galvonic belt at a discount."

"What's a galvonic belt?" Cody asked.

"It's a new invention," Aunt Kezia said. "You got to know about magnetism and galvanism. When you put one of these things on, it cures whatever ails you."

"I want a belt," Corliss cried.

"Never mind all that!" Lanie exclaimed. "I want to know what the doctor said."

"Come on in and sit down at the table. I've got a lot to tell you," Davis said, seeming barely able to contain his excitement.

Lanie sat down, and he began to speak in glowing terms of the doctor who had examined him. "Doctor Jones found out what was wrong with me," he said. "It's called dyslexia."

"Dyslexia?" Lanie said. "What is that?"

"It's good news is what it is," Davis said. "Maeva was there when he gave me the results of the tests. She can tell it better than I can."

Maeva nodded quickly. "Doctor Jones says it's not a disease, but it's something you're born with and it doesn't mean that the person who has it is stupid or lazy. It simply means there's some kind of hookup in their brain that doesn't work like other people's."

"That's right, and you wouldn't believe the people that have had it. Why, Thomas Edison had it, and so did Alexander Graham Bell. They weren't stupid." Davis paused thoughtfully. "You know," he said, "that's always been the scariest thing for me to think I was so dumb I couldn't learn. But Doctor Jones said he tested me for other things. He says I'm a whiz at a lot of stuff, and he told me I ought to concentrate on that."

"Well, I could've told you that without you going all the way to St. Louis," Cody said impatiently. "You've always made straight A's in math and science and that kind of stuff."

"Is there any kind of treatment for it?" Lanie asked.

"Well, there are some things to do, and I've got all the instructions. But the main thing is, sis, I found out I'm not a freak." Sudden tears glistened in Davis's eyes, and he lowered his head quickly. "You won't ever know how I worried about it."

"Well, you're not a freak," Aunt Kezia said. "You're smart as a whip. I knew it the first time I saw you. So you don't have to worry about that."

"You're going to be a famous baseball player," Cody said. "You don't have to read Shakespeare to throw a curveball. I'd like to see some of those students throw a fastball like you do, some of them smart alecks at school. Why, they're dumb as last year's birds' nests."

Lanie felt a sense of relief. *At least,* she thought, *here's one thing I don't have to worry about.* She got up, went around the table, and embraced Davis. "I'm so proud of you, Davis. I knew you weren't dumb, and now everybody will know it."

❦

Owen, not knowing how to get out of accepting Amelia's invitation, had gone to her home for dinner. He had stuffed himself, and now as he and Amelia sat in her parlor listening to her new Bing Crosby record, he felt almost uncomfortable. "You're a fine cook, Amelia, but I ate too much."

Amelia had worn a thin, ivory-colored dress that clung to her figure. It was rather low-cut, and now when she leaned forward, the curves of her body were plainly evident. "A woman's supposed to cook for a man. The man's supposed to eat."

Suddenly she took his hand and held it and said, "I love Bing Crosby. He can sure sing love songs, can't he?"

"I guess he can sing any kind of song."

The two sat there on the couch for a while, and finally Amelia got up and pulled him to his feet. "Come on. Let's dance."

"Oh, Amelia, I'm no dancer."

"Well, I am, so humor me."

The music was soft, and she came at once into his arms and pressed herself against him. Despite himself, Owen felt old hungers stirring within him. As they moved around the floor, she held him tightly. Their movements were slow, so they were practically just standing in the middle of the floor holding tightly to one another. The thought came to Owen: *I wonder if she knows how she's affecting me. She has to know, doesn't she?*

Amelia looked up. They were barely swaying now, and her face was only inches away from his. She wore a subtle perfume that pulled at Owen, and now she murmured, "You're sweet, Owen." She moved her hand behind his neck and pulled his head down. Her lips were soft and yielding, and Owen wondered if Amelia was purposely trying to arouse desire within him. He had noted it before and had been careful not to put himself into the way of temptation. He had strong opinions about relations between men and women, but Amelia Wright had caused most of them to crumble. Now as he held her, he knew if he stayed there much longer, he would surrender. He knew from how she yielded to him that he could have his way with her.

There was no easy way to do this. Abruptly, Owen pulled back and removed her hands from around his neck. "This is no good, Amelia," he said huskily.

"It is good," Amelia whispered. "I know you want me, Owen, and I want you."

Owen could not deny her words, but when she moved to embrace him again, he shook his head. "It's time for me to leave," he said.

Amelia stared at him, and the beginnings of anger touched her. "What's wrong with you? Don't you have any capacity to love, Owen?"

"This—this isn't love, Amelia. It's—something else. I'll have to leave. And I might as well tell you. I can't come here again at night. It doesn't look good."

Amelia Wright turned pale. She had offered herself to this man and, in her eyes, he had blatantly refused her. Her lips trembled with anger as she watched him head for the door.

He turned and said, "We can be together at church, but this is not good for either of us. Good night, Amelia." He waited for her to speak, but she did not.

When the door closed, Amelia lifted her hands in an angry gesture and began to weep. Moving to the wall, she beat her fists against it. "You're so holy, Owen!" Breathing in short gasps, she ignored the tears of rage that ran down her face. "Well, you've laughed at me. Now we'll see who has the last laugh!"

CHAPTER 18

The first Saturday morning of April arrived with soft warm air and bright blossoming redbuds. Cody looked up from where he was hoeing in the garden, and seeing Doctor Owen Merritt's car, he jammed his blade down in the earth and threaded his way through the freshly turned rows. When he cleared the garden, he called out, "Hey, Doc, wait up, will ya?"

He stopped directly in front of Owen and said, "I need to talk to you."

"Why, sure, Cody, but I've got to see Cass. That's what I came out for."

"Well, you can see her, but first I got a problem you've got to help me with."

Owen smiled. "Is it a theological problem? Something like who is the Antichrist? If it is, I'll tell you right now I have no idea."

"Well, I'll tell you who I think it is. I think it's Herbert Hoover."

"Are you crazy? Herbert Hoover is one of the finest men who ever lived. What makes you think he's the Antichrist?"

"I been messing around with the number of letters in his name. It's got to fit the 666 that's the mark of the beast," Cody said stubbornly. "I don't have it all figured out yet, but he brought all this Depression down upon us. According to the third seal in the book of Revelation, one of the marks of the tribulation is that there are hard times economically."

"Cody, don't you know that there have been hard times economically all down through history?"

Cody shook his head stubbornly. "I'll get it all figured out and then I'll tell you about it. But that's not what I wanted to talk to you about."

"What is wrong?"

"Well, to tell the truth, I been having a problem. I don't want anybody to know about it. Is a doctor like a lawyer that he can't tell anybody what the patient says?"

"I wouldn't ever break a patient's confidence, Cody."

"Good. Well, here's the problem." Cody suddenly looked down at his feet and dug one toe in the dirt. He drew an almost perfect circle, then looked up and whispered, "I been having impure thoughts, Doc. You got to help me with it."

Merritt smiled gently at the boy. "Well, I might as well confess that I have impure thoughts myself at times."

Cody stared at Doctor Owen Merritt as if the physician had just announced that the moon was made out of mush. "You do? You got impure thoughts?"

"That's right. Sorry to disillusion you."

"Well, shoot!" Cody said with exasperation. "I tried to talk to Lanie, and she told me she did too."

"She said that?"

"That's what she said, but don't you tell her I told you."

"I won't," Merritt said, a thoughtful look on his face. Then he shook his head and said quietly, "Look, Cody, that's part of being alive. There's nothing wrong with sex. It's getting it in the wrong place that's the trouble."

"Well, I know that. But when I go to bed at night, I think about, well, bad things. There's one girl in school. She's got too much figure, and she wears tight clothes. She knows it too. They ought to make her wear baggy clothes, that's what!"

"I don't think the school's ever going to pass a rule like that."

"Look, Doc, can't you give me some kind of medicine that'll make me not have these thoughts?"

Owen tried not to smile. "If I had such a medication, don't you think I'd be taking it myself? Don't you think everybody would? That's not the way we're built, Cody. God made us with certain desires, but He also made very strict and limited ways in which those desires could be filled. For example, there's eating. There's nothing wrong with eating. God made us with stomachs and He made food to put in it. But if someone becomes a glutton and overeats, then he's misusing the gift that God's given us."

"I know that," Cody said quickly, "and I can eat less. But I wish them thoughts wouldn't come into my mind. You suppose I could go to a hypnotist and he could hypnotize me so I wouldn't do it?"

"I don't think so, Cody. Look. Did you know that the Bible said Jesus had every temptation that we have? You know that Scripture that says, 'For we have not a high priest which cannot be tempted with the feelings of our infirmity but was at all points tempted like we are.' Jesus was a man, and he had to face every temptation that you or I or any other man would face."

"Well, how did He do it?"

"I think He did it by always taking in the love of God. I think He was constantly doing the will of God, and that's the way He overcame all the temptations that the world gives. And that's what you and I are going to have to do."

The two stood there talking for some time, and finally Cody said doubtfully, "Well, one good thing about it. I probably won't live to be more than seventy or eighty, and by the time I get there I don't guess I'll be having these feelings. Then I'll die and I sure won't."

"Well, that's a rather severe way to look at it. Let's you and I agree to pray for one another that this particular temptation won't get the best of us."

"All right, Doc. I appreciate it."

⌬⚬⌐

Lanie had been watching Owen speak with her brother, and she wondered what kind of outlandish thing Cody was demanding. He missed his father and needed a man to talk to, but there was no way that she could help with that part of his life.

"Thank God Owen's around," she whispered. She waited until Cody finally ran back toward the garden and Owen started for the house, then she stepped out onto the porch and greeted him. "I'm glad you're here. I told Cass you were coming. She's up in her room waiting for you."

"All right. I'll go see her."

After Owen went up the stairs, she busied herself in the kitchen. In what seemed like a very short time he came back down again.

"She's fine, Lanie," he said cheerfully. "As healthy a young woman as I've ever seen."

"That's good news, Owen. I worry about her."

"Why, she'll be all right. Having a baby's hard, especially the first one. But she's healthy."

"But it's her life I'm worried about. I guess her spirit, you might say."

"She's had a hard time," Owen said thoughtfully, "but you've done a good thing taking her in here."

"Well, it was Davis who did it, I guess. He's worried about her too."

"He came by to tell me about his reading problem. It sounds like good news."

"Oh, it is," Lanie said at once, a smile brightening her face. "He was so down on himself. I've always known he was smart, but he didn't think so."

"Well, I'd better be getting back to town."

"Could I catch a ride with you? I need to get some things for Cass."

"Why, of course. Come along."

As they passed the ballfield outside town, Owen said, "Look. There's Davis pitching."

"Yes. They're playing Pine Ridge."

"Let's stop and watch him pitch a little bit."

"Do you have time?" Lanie asked.

"Sure," Owen said. "I don't have office hours today, and nobody's dying that I know of." He stopped the car, and they walked to the wooden stands and took their seats. They watched Davis wind up and fire the ball in. The opposing player took a wild, hard swing and missed the ball by a foot.

"That boy throws like a major-league player."

Lanie turned to see a well-built man with a tanned face and intense blue eyes. He was chewing gum with energy and had a straw hat pushed back on his head. "I seen many a pitcher in the big time that couldn't throw like that."

Lanie glanced at Owen. "I've never seen a major-league ball game, have you, Owen?"

"Oh, sure. When I lived in St. Louis, I went to see the Cardinals all the time."

"Did you now?" the man beside Owen said. "That's who I work for."

"You work for the Cardinals?" Owen asked with surprise.

"Sure do. I'm a scout. Used to play ball, but I got too old for it. We all do." He motioned suddenly toward Davis, who had thrown the sizzling strike. "That boy's going places. He's going to be a professional ballplayer."

Owen grinned. "This is Lanie Freeman. She's that boy's sister."

"Hey, is that a fact! My name's A. C. Tompkins. I'm glad to know you."

"I'm Owen Merritt. You really think Davis has that kind of potential?"

"Why, he could play with some minor-league teams right now. I don't want to get his hopes up, but I don't want to miss out on a good prospect either."

Lanie said nothing, but after the two had left, she said, "I don't know how I feel about Mr. Tompkins and what he said about Davis."

"You don't like baseball?"

"It's fine for a game, but I'm not sure it'd be good to do all your life."

"Well, most young fellows would give a leg to play for the Cardinals—or any major-league team. I used to think I wanted to, but I didn't have the talent for it."

Lanie did not speak, and finally they got back into the car. "Are you going to say anything to Davis about the scout?"

"I don't think so," Lanie replied. "Maybe he'll go away without even mentioning it."

"I doubt he will. It looked like he had real determination. Anyway, where do you need to go?"

"The drugstore, please."

When they got to the drugstore, Owen said, "Tell you what. You go get what you need and I'll take you home."

"You don't have to go to that trouble."

"That's all right. I've got to go make a couple of calls."

"All right," Lanie said. She went inside the store and made her purchases. When she came out she got in the car with Owen. "I'm ready."

"Why don't you go in with me on these calls? Do 'em good to see a pretty girl instead of an ugly old doctor."

"You're not ugly," Lanie said at once. "Don't say that about yourself."

"Well, I never won a beauty contest."

"I never did either."

"The difference is," Owen said, "that you could win but I never could. Come on. No arguing now."

Owen's calls took longer than he thought, but Lanie didn't mind. After greeting each patient, she sat in the car and worked on a poem.

When Owen came out from his last call, he said, "What are you working on? Another poem?"

"Yes," Lanie said reluctantly. "I'm not sure if it's any good. It's about the transfiguration. I've always loved that part of the Gospels. Jesus must have looked pretty ordinary most of the time, but on the mount He was glorious." She began to read the poem.

Once a bolt of lightning caught my open eyes;
Like fiery lace it scratched across the skies
Like a white-hot arm of petrified
Sun-fire that glowed like giant fireflies.

Just so this afternoon my eyes went numb
When Jesus unexpectedly drew down
Into Himself the blazing fiery sun
Glittering like the diamonds on a crown!

His garment glowed like fleecy clouds ignited,
Or like those peaks of frozen snow;
But earth has never seen such fire lighted
Since God Himself touched earth eons ago!

But now He wears again His homespun brown
Instead of vibrant light. Yet still, I ponder
When next He'll call the host of heaven down
And clothe Himself in sun, and awe, and wonder?

"That's a beautiful poem," Owen said quietly. "You know, what I like about your talent is the way you use it for the glory of God."

Lanie dropped her head and could not speak for a moment. "Thank you, Owen," she said finally.

Owen said, "I'll tell you what. I've got to take a prescription by for Billie Simmons. We'll drop it off and then I'll get you home."

"Owen, could you do me one favor?"

"Why, of course. What is it?"

Lanie turned to him. "You're always buying me lunch. You bought my lunch half a dozen times. Let me buy your supper for once."

"Why, I'd deem it an honor. Where shall we go?"

Lanie laughed. "There's only one place open and that's the Dew Drop Inn."

"Well, I like the Dew Drop Inn. You can get a hamburger and a sermon from Sister Myrtle at the same time for one price. Come along."

The meal had been fine. The sermon from Sister Myrtle, as usual, had been sharp and to the point and full of warning, and now Owen said, "Let me drop this medicine off for Billie, and we'll be on our way."

He drove to Bedford Forest Lane. Stopping the car, he said, "I'll be right back. I'll have to look in on Billie, but I shouldn't be long."

"Don't hurry. I'll be all right."

As soon as Owen left, she got out of the car and walked around it, casting her gaze up into the sky. It was a beautiful night, warm, and she could smell the freshly cut grass of the Simmons yard.

Owen was back very soon and saw her looking up. "Counting the stars or waiting for a falling star?"

"One fell just a minute ago."

"Did you make a wish?"

"Oh, I make wishes whether the stars fall or not."

Owen moved closer to her. She whispered, "I look up at the stars and they're all alone. That reminds me of myself."

"Why, you're not all alone, Lanie."

"I feel like I am sometimes." Lanie stood quietly, and as sometimes happened, a great loneliness came to her. She did not want to admit it to anybody, but she felt she could talk to Owen as nobody else. "I get so lonely, Owen. My mother's dead. My daddy's in prison."

"But you've got a family, a wonderful family. You've done a marvelous job of helping them."

"I know it's foolish. But I just—"

Owen leaned forward and exclaimed, "Why, Lanie, don't cry!"

"I–I can't help it, Owen. I know it's foolish and weak, but I get so tired."

Owen leaned forward and put his arms around her and drew her close. Lanie laid her head against his chest. She could feel his heart beating, and while he held her, she felt safe and secure. She lay there against him, and he stroked her hair for a time. Finally she straightened up and tried to laugh. "Just what you need—a weepy woman!"

"It's all right to cry. I do it myself sometimes."

"Do you really, Owen?"

"I have a few times." He took her hand, lifted it, and kissed it. "Come on now. I'll tell you funny stories on the way home, and I'm going to see your dad, and he's going to be all right."

Lanie got into the car, watching as he started the engine and pulled away. She didn't speak, but the moment had been good for her.

⊯

As the car pulled away, Amelia Wright followed it with her gaze, just as she had from the moment it arrived. When she saw Owen put his arms around Lanie Freeman, a bitterness boiled over in her. A flash of quick anger ignited, and when she turned away from the window, she knew that there would be a reckoning.

⊯

Lanie settled back into her pew. The service had been good. The song service had been lively. The choir had sung a special, and Reverend Colin Ryan had preached a marvelous sermon. Three people had come forward for baptism, and it had taken some time for Colin to introduce them and for them to give their testimonies. Finally Colin said, "After the benediction you'll want to welcome these new fellow Christians into the family of God. Now will you stand and—"

"Pastor, could I say a word?" Amelia Wright stood up, her eyes fixed on Colin.

"Why, of course, Mrs. Wright." It was not unusual for people to ask for prayer at a time like this.

An ominous sense of foreboding enveloped Lanie, for she saw that Amelia Wright was as pale as a sheet of paper and her lips were so tight she could barely speak. But her words were clear enough and terrible.

"I committed immorality, and I confess it to the church. The man that I was involved with is Doctor Owen Merritt."

A wave of whispers went across the congregation, and Lanie felt her heart stop. Her eyes went to Owen, as did almost every other set of eyes in the church. She watched as he came to his feet and said quietly, "That's not true, Pastor."

Instantly Colin Ryan said, "Mrs. Wright, there's a right way and a wrong way to handle things like this, and you've chosen the wrong way. Only as a last resort would we bring a church member before the church to confess, and you have brought it before visitors. Right now I ask you to come with me, and you too, Doctor Merritt."

Amelia turned and said in a voice that was as hard and brittle as stone, "He has wronged me."

Anger filled Colin Ryan's face as he stepped down from the platform. "Come along, Mrs. Wright, and you too, if you will, Doctor Merritt."

Lanie watched them go, and it seemed to her that part of the sun had just gone out.

PART FOUR

A Season for Miracles

⟣ CHAPTER 19 ⟢

Bertha Pickens's Bible lay flat on the table in front of her. It was a ruin of a Bible, most of the pages so loose Bertha had to make sure they were still in their rightful places before she began to read. She also had to hold the pages to keep them from scattering in the breeze every time the doctor's office door opened.

Carefully she read the last line on the page, then turned it over. Her eyes ran over the next page, and she gave a grunt of satisfaction as she read the margin notes she had written in a fine but legible hand. In all truth Bertha's Bible was as much her writing as it was the Author's of the Scripture itself, for when a verse spoke to her she believed in underlining it and putting a date and a comment in the margin.

Bertha had lost count of how many times she had read through the entire Scripture. It took her longer than most, for she not only read the text but her own words. Now she paused and read aloud the one note that she had made eleven years earlier. "Jasper Peters is a vile sinner, but I'm not giving up on him, Lord. Save him for Jesus' sake."

The next note brought a smile to Bertha's thin lips. "Jasper Peters saved. Glory to God!" with the date of his new birth.

From time to time Bertha glanced up at the door that led into the office from the outside. She finally was rewarded as she heard the slow, uneven gait of Doctor Givens. It was not long until the old man stepped inside the door. He was wearing his favorite white suit, which should have been donated to a good cause or destroyed some time ago. "That suit is a disgrace, Doctor!" Bertha snapped.

Doctor Oscar Givens stopped and stared at his nurse. "I'll wear whatever clothes I want, thank you!"

"You look like a ragpicker."

"Never mind what I look like. Where's Owen?"

"He went out to see the Satterfield baby. Said he'd be back right soon."

Doctor Givens clawed at his whiskers and shook his head. "Them Satterfields are weak stock. I don't rightly know how they all made it."

He started toward the inner office, but Bertha stopped him. "What are you going to do about Doctor Merritt's problem?"

"What am I going to do? Who do you think I am? I can't do anything about what's happened to Owen."

"Well, that's a fine thing for you to say! You're his senior partner here, aren't you? It's up to you to do something. The whole town's talking about it. Can't hear nothing about anything else everywhere you go."

Indeed, Bertha's words troubled Doctor Givens. Leaning on his cane, he stood in the middle of the floor and tried to collect his thoughts. "You're right," he grunted finally. "But it seems like people should mind their own business."

"It is their business, they think. He's a doctor. He's supposed to be perfect."

"Supposed to be perfect? Well, I'm sorry to inform them that we're not." He was angry and frustrated and grieved by what had happened to Owen Merritt. When Merritt first arrived in Fairhope, Givens had doubted the young man would make it, for he was a city man and knew little about the ways of rural people. He had, however, learned, and now Givens placed utmost confidence in him. Since hearing the rumors about Amelia Wright, he had fumed by day and slept poorly at night. "I don't want to hear any more about this."

"Do you think he done it?"

"No, I don't think he done it," Givens snapped, "and I'm surprised you think so! You should know him better."

"Men are weak."

"So are women. We're all weak. If you shot everybody that was weak, there wouldn't be anybody left to live with."

Bertha opened her mouth to respond with a Scripture which might or might not have had something to do with the situation, but she was cut off when the door opened and Owen stepped into the office.

"Hello, Owen. How's the Satterfield child?" Doctor Givens asked.

"She's all right, Doctor." Owen's face was drawn and there were lines Doctor Givens had not seen before.

"Come on into the office. You can give me your report on her there." He limped through the door, leaning heavily on his cane, and Owen followed him.

As soon as Owen saw the disappointment on Bertha's face, he knew she was dying to hear the conversation. He closed the door behind him and turned to face the older man. "I've decided to leave," he said abruptly.

Doctor Givens stared at Owen blankly for a moment as if he had misunderstood him. "Why, you can't do that!" he exploded.

"I don't have any choice."

"Of course you have a choice. You can stay here and fight this thing out."

"There's no way to fight a thing like this. It'll be my word against hers. Even if I could prove myself innocent, it would stick to me. You know how these things are, Doctor Givens."

Givens had a moment of almost complete despair. He had learned to love this young man, and now the thought of a future without Owen Merritt around to carry on was frightening. "Sit down, Owen. We need to talk about this."

He waited until Owen was seated and then said, "Look. I'm not a Christian man, but you are."

"I wish you were, Doctor."

"Well, I'm not, but I've read the Bible. Let me ask you one question. The apostle Paul. What did he do when things got bad? Did he run away?"

"Of course not."

"And Peter. I understand he was crucified upside down at his own request. He didn't run away, did he, when there was trouble?"

"No. He didn't. But I'm not Peter and I'm not Paul."

Givens leaned forward, and his voice was filled with earnestness. "I read the story of Jesus many times, Owen, and one thing comes out clear. He knew He was going to die a terrible death, and yet He didn't run away. As a matter of fact, He always said that was the hour for which He came. Isn't that true?"

Owen was surprised that the old man knew so much Bible. He'd never mentioned it before. "Well, of course, that's true, but—"

"Then the Bible is full of people that went through trouble and didn't run. Now listen, Owen. If you run from this, you'll never be any good." For the next ten minutes Givens spoke as fervently as he could, saying everything that had been on his heart since the crisis exploded in Owen's life. He was a rough man, gruff in his ways, but his affection for the young man was clear. Finally he said, "You just can't do it, Owen, you just can't!"

Owen Merritt dropped his head. He hadn't slept a wink last night thinking all this out. He did not believe himself to be a physical coward, but the idea of living a life under the shadow of Amelia Wright's accusations intimidated him, and he certainly didn't want to be railroaded into marrying a lying, scheming woman. He valued both his integrity and his reputation, and she had ruthlessly stripped both from him.

Finally he looked up and whispered, "I'm sorry, Doctor. I just can't do it. I want you to make a phone call and find a replacement for me. As soon as you've found someone, I'm leaving."

He got up at once and left the room, leaving Givens there to stare after him. The old man slumped in his chair and whispered, "It's wrong, Owen. You're making the worst mistake of your life!"

The late afternoon sun had begun to throw long shadows from the trees that lined the road back into town. Lanie had brought the emporium out, but it had not been a good experience. She had made some sales, but at every stop, it seemed, every customer had one thing to talk about: the scandal of Doctor Owen Merritt and Amelia Wright. That was the penalty of living in a small community. Everybody knew everybody, and there was little to take people's minds off of the current scandal. A doctor was fair game, of course, and Lanie was sick of hearing about it.

She stopped the emporium, shut the engine off, and got up to greet Loretta Simpkins, a regular customer. The Simpkins were better off than most in Fairhope and Stone County. Her father had been a timber man owning thousands of acres. True, there was not much market now, but Loretta and her husband, Bill, lived in a fine home just on the outskirts of town. They were members of the Baptist church, and Loretta had been Lanie's Sunday school teacher for one year when she was a junior.

"Hello, Loretta. What can I get you today?"

Loretta Simpkins was a small woman not worn down as most rural women were. She had bright blue eyes and was still attractive. "I need some pepper. I'm out altogether, and you might as well give me some garlic too, if you've got any."

Lanie walked through the emporium, Loretta behind her, and pulled items off the shelves.

After Loretta stepped outside and paid for the purchase, she said, "It's just disgraceful. That's what I say. Imagine a doctor doing a thing like that and him a member of our church."

Lanie suddenly flared up. She was not a quick-tempered girl in the least, but she had heard enough about Owen Merritt's problem. She glared at Loretta and said sharply, "You don't know that he's done anything!"

"But that woman says he's guilty. Why would she lie?"

"I don't know why, but I do know that he needs our support now and not a bunch of loose gossip."

Loretta stared at Lanie. "Why, you're defending him. I'm surprised at you."

"Well, I'm surprised at *you*, Loretta. All those classes in Sunday school you were talking about how Christians ought to love one another. You call this love? The first time a fellow Christian gets in trouble you jump on him?" Words tumbled out of Lanie's mouth, and as Loretta's jaw dropped she ended by saying, "Don't ever say anything to me again about this. I'm tired of hearing about it."

"Well, I declare! I didn't know you were such a strong supporter of that man," Mrs. Simpkins said, her face reddening. "If you feel that way, why didn't you stand up and defend him?"

"I will if I ever get a chance. Good-bye, Loretta."

"Wait a minute! You just insulted me."

"Good! I hope you remember it and keep your mouth shut about Owen Merritt!" Jumping into the emporium, she started the engine and roared away under full power. Glancing into the mirror, she saw Loretta Simpkins standing there, hands on her hips, glaring at her. *Well, that was stupid*, she thought. *If I jump on everybody who believes Owen's guilty, I'll never convince them otherwise.*

Shocked at her own anger, she tried to calm down, but she found it was almost impossible.

Soon she came upon Brent standing out by the road waiting for her and wished that he had not. If church members were so down on Owen, unbelievers would be worse. She pulled over, however, and Brent came to the door of the emporium. "Come on in the house a minute. I've got something to show you."

Lanie hesitated but then said, "All right, Brent." Shutting the engine off, she got out. Brent was wearing a white shirt and a pair of gray slacks. He always had the appearance of just having stepped out of a dressing room, something Lanie had not seen in any other man.

Brent opened the door and she stepped inside.

"How about a glass of iced tea?"

"That would be very good," Lanie said, discovering her mouth was dry. She wondered for a moment if anger made spit dry up and then dismissed the foolish thought.

Brent fixed two glasses of tea and sliced a lemon. While he was fixing it, he studied her carefully. "You look bothered, Lanie."

"I guess I am." She drank the tea, and then suddenly the words seemed to rush out of her mouth. "It's this thing about Doctor Merritt. Everybody's talking. I didn't realize we were such a bunch of gossips."

"Didn't you? I would have thought you would have noticed such a thing as that."

Lanie stared at Brent and then shook her head. "You're right. We're terrible. That's what we are."

"You don't think Doctor Merritt is guilty?"

"No, I don't."

"No matter what the woman says?"

"I don't care what she says. I know Owen Merritt. He's not that kind of a man."

Brent took a sip of his tea and then held the glass, turning it slowly and thinking for a moment. Finally he said quietly, "You're loyal to your friends, Lanie. That's unusual in this world." He looked up. "I want to be your friend too. I know if I took some kind of a fall, you'd be right there, wouldn't you?"

"Well, of course. You'd be there for me, Brent. I know that."

"You know, I really believe you would. I don't have your breed of loyalty, but I think I would stand by you. Not that you would ever need me to."

"You never know," Lanie said bleakly.

Brent studied her for a moment. "The doctor will pull out of it, I'm sure. People realize we all make mistakes."

"People have long memories in little towns like this. They'll never forget."

"Sooner or later they will. But listen. I've got good news for you." He moved over to a table and picked up an envelope. "Look at this."

"But it's addressed to you."

"It's for you, though. Look at it."

Lanie opened the envelope and pulled out two slips of paper. She stared at one. It was a check for ten dollars and made out to her.

"Your poem's going to be published in *Poetry Journal*, a national magazine. They don't pay much, but they'll send you ten copies of the magazine and you'll have lots more contracts too. Once you get involved with *Poetry Journal* everybody wants to publish you. Congratulations, Lanie."

Lanie stared at the check and then at the letter, which said that the editor was pleased with her work and would like to see more. For a moment she stood there unable to speak, staring at the check. She whispered, "Brent, I can't believe it."

"I can." He smiled.

"It's all your doing."

"I didn't write the poem. You did."

Lanie finished her tea and could not seem to take her eyes off the check. Finally she said, "I've got to go home and tell my family about this." She put out her hand suddenly. "Thank you, Brent. I owe you so much."

"Always glad to encourage young talent." He held her hand and his grip tightened. "Try not to worry about Doctor Merritt. These things have a way of blowing over."

"Do you think he did it, Brent?"

"No. I only met him twice, but he just doesn't seem like that kind of man."

"But why would she lie?"

"I can't say about that. Now, go home and write more poems."

Lanie went out to the truck. She got inside, stared at the envelope, and stared at the check. If it were not for Owen's plight, she would be bubbling over. But the sadness for him took away the joy of getting a poem published in *Poetry Journal*.

She started the engine and sped home. As soon as she pulled up in front of the house, she saw Colin Ryan's motorcycle. Quickly she shut the engine down and ran inside. She found Aunt Kezia talking with the minister, and she could tell by one look at her face that she was angry.

"What's wrong, Pastor?"

"I been talking to Amelia Wright," Colin said. Colin, who usually had a smile on his face, was now deadly serious. "She won't change her story. She insists that Owen seduced her."

"That hussy!" Aunt Kezia snorted. "She's lying, Preacher."

"If she is, she's doing a good job of it," Colin Ryan said grimly.

"Can't we do anything?" Lanie said.

"I'm going to talk to her again, but I must tell you I'm not very hopeful. She's a vindictive woman."

"She ought to be shot," Aunt Kezia said.

"I guess it's not that bad." Colin grinned briefly, then immediately grew serious. "I'll do all I can. I did talk to Doctor Givens. He told me that Owen is planning to leave as soon as Givens can find a replacement."

"He can't do that!" Lanie cried.

"No. The worst thing a body can do is run from trouble," Aunt Kezia said emphatically.

"I'm going to talk to Owen," Colin said. "You're right. He does need to stay. You two pray, and if you have a chance, encourage Owen not to run away."

With heavy hearts, the two women watched as the pastor started his motorcycle and roared off in a cloud of dust.

⊸⊷∘ CHAPTER 20 ∘⊷⊸

Tuesday afternoon Lanie opened the screen door to find Nellie Prather standing there twisting his straw hat in his hands. There was always a certain bashfulness about this man, but now he shifted his feet and looked even more ill at ease than ever.

"Why, hello, Nelson. Won't you come in the house?"

"I don't want to interrupt nothing, Miss Lanie."

"Why, you wouldn't do that. I'm just washing dishes. Come on in." She stepped aside and when Nellie came through, she closed the door. "I'll bet you could drink a cup of coffee or maybe some iced tea."

"Yes, ma'am, a glass of tea would be nice."

Leading the way to the kitchen, Lanie wondered about Nelson's visit. He had dropped by twice since Cass's visit to his farm, bringing her tomatoes from his garden.

"It's pretty quiet around here," Nelson said as he seated himself at the table. "Where is everybody?"

"Oh, they're in school, and Aunt Kezia, Cass, and Corliss are taking naps." She put the two glasses on the table. "I don't have any lemon, but there's plenty of sugar."

"I don't use lemon, thank you, Miss Lanie."

Lanie watched Nelson drink thirstily. When he put down the empty glass, she said, "I'll get you some more."

"No, ma'am, that's all right. That'll do me fine." Nelson shifted in his chair and said, "How's Miss Cass doing?"

"Well, she's doing real well. The doctor says she's healthy as any young woman he's ever seen. She'll be sorry to miss you. Maybe I ought to go get her up."

"Well, not right now. There's something I have to talk to you about first."

"What's that, Nelson?" Lanie saw that Nelson was twisting the empty glass around, leaving wet circles on the top of the table. "Is something wrong?"

"I guess you're kind of the head of the family around here what with your pa being—" he broke off suddenly and cleared his throat—"being your pa's not with you."

"Well, I guess I sort of am. What did you want to talk about?"

Nelson took a deep breath, and for a moment he looked as if he might get up and run out of the room. "What in the world's wrong with you, Nelson?"

"Well, something's happened that I've got to talk to you about. I've been thinking real hard about Miss Cass and the trouble she's in, and I want to do something to help her."

"To help her? How could you do that?"

"Well, here's what I could do—I could marry her."

Lanie's eyes flew open with astonishment. "Marry Cass? Why, Nelson, I never even thought of such a thing, and I don't think Cass has either."

"Well, *I* have. But I don't ever do anything just because I think of it." He smiled, his broad lips turning upward at the corners. "I think of foolish things sometimes, Miss Lanie. I really do. So I don't act on anything until I get a sign, and I got one."

"You got a sign that tells you you're supposed to marry Cass?"

"That's right."

"What was it?" Lanie asked cautiously. She knew, as did everyone in the county, of Nellie Prather's superstitious nature. If a bird got in the house, to Nelson that was a sign that bad luck was coming. When you moved to a new house, if you moved the cat, bad luck was certain to follow. Most people had some superstitions, but Nellie ran his life according to them.

"Well, here's what happened," Nellie said slowly. "I dreamed about Miss Cass three nights in a row, and you know what *that* means."

"No, I don't know what it means."

"Why, I thought everybody knowed that. If you dream about somebody three nights in a row, it means you're going to marry them. My grandma taught me that when I was no bigger than Miss Corliss."

For a moment Lanie sat there wondering how in the world she could approach this issue. She studied Nellie Prather carefully. She had known him all of her life, and his reputation in the county was excellent. He was a tall, good-looking man in his early thirties, and everyone knew how he had given up his life to raise his younger brother and sister and take care of his mother through her long illness. When finally his mother and siblings died, almost everyone expected Nelson to get married. Many young women and mothers with eligible daughters had tried to bring this to pass, for Nelson had a good farm and was a hard worker, but he had not been interested. He was also a fine, Christian man who could always be depended upon to do the right thing.

Still, Lanie was somewhat shocked at his proposal. "Well, I think you need something more than dreams before you ask a woman to marry you, Nelson."

Surprise washed across Prather's face. "I don't see why. It's as plain as the nose on your face. It's a sign, Miss Lanie. There ain't no doubt in my mind."

Wishing desperately that someone else were present to handle this situation, Lanie knew she had to be extremely careful. Prather was as sensitive as a woman in many things, and she was determined not to hurt his feelings. Still, marriage was too big a thing to be entered into with no more evidence than three dreams.

"Nelson, marriage is a very serious thing. Two people need to love each other, and I'm not sure that you love Cass or that she loves you."

Nellie Prather suddenly grew still. "Well, I don't know much about love. I never did read romances or listen to them on the radio. It seems like those people are just out of one mess and into another one. But I know how to take care of people," he said simply. "I took care of my ma and my brother and sister until I lost them, and now I'd like to take care of Cass and her baby. I don't know if that's love or not, but it's what I want to do."

"You've always been a good man and everybody I know admires you for what you did for your family, but marriage is different. Husband and wife, that's a whole new world. Let me ask you this," she asked. "Does Cass care for you?"

"She likes me. She told me that."

"Well, I like you too, but I can't marry you just because I admire you." Lanie could not help smiling. "There has to be more to a marriage than just a liking."

Silence fell across the room, and Nellie looked down at the glass in his hand. He twisted it around slowly for such a long time that Lanie began to grow nervous. Finally he looked up, and goodness shone in his blue eyes. "Well, tell me what to do, Lanie. I want to take care of Cass and her baby. I want it to be my baby too."

Lanie swallowed hard. "I'll tell you what," she said quietly. "We'll pray about this, and we'll ask God to show us His will. You know Jesus said, 'My sheep hear my voice and they follow me.' That's what you've got to do, Nellie. You've got to know that this is God's will, and then you've got to ask Cass if she wants to marry you. She may not."

"Well, I know she could get a better man than me, but I don't think she could get one that could take better care of her and the baby."

Lanie's heart warmed toward the big man. She put out both her hands and took his hand in hers. "Let's just pray right here." The two bowed their heads, and Lanie prayed a simple prayer asking God to give them wisdom and to guide them in the way that was right. Finally she looked up and said, "Amen."

"Amen," Nellie said. He waited and said, "What do we do now?"

"You go home and pray about it some more. If you still feel strongly for Cass in a few days, you ask her and accept her answer. We've asked God to be in this thing now, so it's in His hands."

Nelson suddenly smiled broadly and chuckled deep in his throat. "I guess trusting God is better than going on three dreams in a row, ain't it, Miss Lanie?"

⊂══⊰⊱

After supper, Lanie went to her room and shut the door. She took her journal out at once and wrote an account of what had taken place. It always helped her to put things down in print, and she finally gave her conclusions:

> *It would be a wonderful thing for Cass to have a husband like Nelson Prather. He's one of the best men I've ever known, and he'd be good to her and the baby. But it won't work unless she loves him. It's hard to tell about Cass. She's a sweet girl really, but she never talks about things like this. She has said a time or two that no man would ever love her baby because he wouldn't be the daddy, but that's not true of Nelson. So I'm going to —*

Suddenly the door opened, and Maeva burst in.

"Don't you ever think about knocking before you barge into somebody's room?" Lanie snapped.

Maeva grinned, plumped herself down on the bed, and looked over at her sister. "Are you writing in that journal again? I think you ought to let me read it. I might be able to help you with some of your problems."

"Why aren't you doing your homework?"

"I heard you moving around in here, and I wanted to know what's wrong with you. You're worried about Owen would be my guess."

"Of course I am. He's in terrible trouble, but that's not what's bothering me right now."

"I bet it is. Let me see that." She reached for the journal and laughed when Lanie snatched it away and gave her an angry look. "Don't bite my head off. I don't want to read your old journal. Wouldn't be nearly as interesting as a *True Romance*."

Lanie always had difficulty dealing with Maeva. Now that she had come to talk about Owen Merritt, Lanie knew she would not leave until her questions were answered. Finally she said, "I'm worried about Owen. I heard he's talking about moving away."

"Well, you've got to go to him and tell him he can't do that," Maeva said simply.

"Why, I can't do that."

"Sure you can. I think he's stuck on you, Sister, and you've been in love with him since you were fourteen. So I want you to scoot over there and tell him."

"Maeva, you have no sense of—of what's respectable."

"I sure don't, but I know what works. You just go over there. Put on some of that perfume you got for Christmas. When you talk to him, just lean on him a little bit. Tell him how much you admire him and that you just couldn't live if he left. Why, you can wrap that doctor around your little finger if you just work at it a little bit!"

Lanie flushed, just as she always did when Maeva spoke to her about Owen Merritt. She thought of every reason possible to prove her sister wrong and, arguing steadily, listed each one.

Maeva paid no attention. She leaned forward, her expression serious, and said, "I don't mean to always be teasing you, but I know you care for Owen. It'd be terrible if he ran away and left this mess. You go on over there now and tell him you're on his side. He probably needs somebody. He's heard enough of the other side."

Suddenly Lanie made up her mind to do exactly what Maeva said—for once. "All right, I will."

"Good!" Maeva got up and went to the door. She turned around and winked. "Don't forget. Put on that perfume."

Lanie at once made preparations to go. She went down the hall and told Aunt Kezia that she was leaving to go to town but did not speak of her mission. She needed no further advice about what to do with Owen Merritt!

━━◦━

When Lanie reached Doctor Givens's house, her nerve almost failed her. *I can't be doing this! He'll think I'm meddling in his business —which I am.* For several moments she stood there struggling and once almost turned and fled back to her own house. Then getting a grip on her emotions, she walked up the sidewalk and knocked on the door. She expected the housekeeper, Mrs. Satterfield, to answer, but instead it was Doctor Givens who stood framed in the door.

"Why, Lanie, what in the world are you doing here? Who's sick?"

"Nobody's sick. I need to talk to Owen."

"Come on inside," Doctor Givens said at once. As soon as she stepped in, he turned to face her. "I hope you've come to talk him out of leaving. I've tried my dangdest, but he won't listen."

"He *can't* leave. It would be wrong."

"In that you'd be right. I'm not a Christian myself, but I wish God would speak to that young man. I'm glad you've come. He thinks a lot of you."

"Where's Mrs. Satterfield?"

"She's gone over to visit her sister at Cloverdale. You come on into the parlor. I'll go get Owen."

Lanie went at once to the parlor but was too nervous to sit down. She went over to the window and stared outside. When she heard footsteps she turned and waited. Owen stepped into the room, and she had absolutely no idea what to say.

"Hello, Lanie," Owen said. His clothes looked rumpled as if he had been lying down in them, and lines of worry crossed his forehead. "What's the matter? Is someone sick?"

"No. Not this time, Owen." Lanie's lips felt dry. She licked them and said, "I–I want to talk to you."

"Why, sure. Here. Let's sit down on this sofa." He motioned toward the sofa, and when Lanie seated herself, he sat down beside her. "Now tell me what's going on."

"I don't know how to say this, Owen, except I think you'd be making a big mistake to leave."

Owen shook his head with disgust. "Everybody in this town knows my business, it seems."

"I know it's terrible. The gossip system works very well here. Better than anything else, I think, sometimes. But you can't go, Owen, you just can't!"

"I have to, Lanie. I can't face the shame of this thing."

"You haven't done anything. There's no shame involved."

Owen studied her carefully. "You're sure about that, are you?"

"Of course I am!"

"Well, that makes at least two people in this town that don't think I'm guilty."

"There are a lot more than that, and you know it. You've made a place for yourself in Fairhope. People love you. They trust you and they need you."

"I just can't face it, Lanie."

"But you're innocent."

"You don't know that."

"Yes, I do. I know you. You've been such a help to me and to my whole family." She took Owen's arm and shook it gently, her voice insistent. "You just can't leave, Owen. God is going to protect you."

Owen sat very still, then he reached over and covered her hand with his own. "I just don't know what to do," he muttered.

Lanie was caught by surprise, for she thought of Owen as *always* knowing what to do. She stared at him, noting the long borders of his face, shelving squarely at the chin. His eyes were troubled, and this disturbed her. Uncertainty had painted its shadows in his eyes and laid its silence on his tongue. She dreaded to see his spirit crushed with a permanent shadow.

"It'll be all right, Owen." She leaned forward and put her other hand on his, noting its strength. "God hasn't forgotten you."

"I feel like I've lost touch with God."

"That's the way all of us feel sometimes."

Surprise washed across Owen's face. "Not you, Lanie."

"Of course! I'd hate for you to know how many times I've felt like giving up."

"You never show it."

"Would you rather I'd make my voice quiver and throw myself on the floor and squall?"

Lanie's words brought a slight smile to Owen's face. "That's exactly what I'd like to do."

"You're too good a man for that."

Owen gnawed at his lower lip, still troubled, but at the same time a light began to brighten his fine eyes. He suddenly laughed. "I'm acting like a spoiled brat." He stood, gently helped Lanie to her feet, then hugged her. "You're good for a man," he said, his voice husky. He stepped back and said firmly, "I'll stay until this thing is resolved."

Though Lanie had visited only a short time, when she started for home, she knew for a certainty she had done the right thing.

When she reached the house and stepped inside, she was shocked to see the whole family waiting: Maeva, Davis, Cody, Cass, and Aunt Kezia. She stopped dead still, and it was Cody who said, "Well, what'd he say?"

For a moment irritation swept over Lanie, and then she began to laugh. "Don't any of you ever mind your own business?"

Aunt Kezia's dark eyes snapped. "This is family, child. It is our business. Now, tell us everything Merritt said."

⤍⇒ CHAPTER 21 ⇐⤎

Two days later Owen appeared unexpectedly on the front porch of the Freeman house, his face suffused with excitement.

"I've got good news, Lanie!"

Lanie clasped her hands. "What is it, Owen?"

"I've got permission to examine your dad and to take him to a hospital if I think he needs it."

Lanie suddenly felt light-headed. "How in the world did you get permission?"

"Well, actually it was Doctor Givens. He's an old friend of the governor. He went to school with the governor's dad. He's been on the phone with him, and everything's been arranged. Monday I'll be going up, and I thought you might like to go along too."

"Oh, I do!"

"Well, there's one problem," Owen said, and his expression turned somewhat sober. "You know how it is in this town about gossip. If we go alone, there'll be talk."

"Don't worry about that," Lanie said quickly. "I'll ask Pastor Ryan along. We'll need his prayers more than his chaperoning!"

⇐⤎

Remembering the trauma of the previous week, Lanie felt restless and nervous all through Sunday's worship service. Owen wasn't there, but Amelia was, sitting stiffly in her usual seat with her face fixed in a frown.

After the invitation had been completed and the church was standing waiting for the benediction, Lanie kept her eyes fixed on the pastor, who looked uncomfortable in his shirt and tie. Lanie's gaze swept the congregation as Colin began to speak, and she saw that Louise Langley was watching him with pride.

"I have an item that I'm going to ask the church to pray for," Pastor Ryan said. "As you know, Forrest Freeman has been having health problems. Tomorrow Doctor Owen Merritt and Forrest's daughter, Sister Lanie, and I will travel to Cummings Prison Farm to see about having more extensive tests made. I want to ask the church to pray that God will work a miracle."

Lanie studied the congregation. She knew that a minority had been unkind in their remarks about Owen, and it grieved her that the church had been divided by Amelia Wright's accusation.

"I would appreciate it," Colin said, "if some of you would come to the church Monday and keep a prayer chain going all day."

"We'll do that, Pastor. Don't worry about it." The speaker was John Stockwell, one of the deacons. "You do the going, Doctor Merritt can do the doctoring, and we'll do the praying."

Lanie's heart warmed toward the tall, ambling man, one who was a true lover of God. She breathed a prayer of thanksgiving for the many faithful in the church who would stand with them.

Kezia looked up at the knock on the door. She had not felt like going to church, and except for Cass, who was resting upstairs, she was alone.

"Who in the cat hair could that be?" She got up, made her way to the door, and through the screen she saw Nelson Prather. "Well, I expected you'd be in church this morning, Nelson. Come on in."

Nelson came in, holding his straw hat in his hand. He was wearing his Sunday clothes, which were not a great deal different from his everyday clothes. He was always a neat man.

Kezia led him into the parlor.

"I'm sorry to bother you, Miss Kezia, but I need to see Miss Cass."

"Well, she's lying down, but I'll get her."

"She's not sick, is she?"

"No, not at all. She was up late last night. I told her to sleep in this morning. You sit down. I'll send her in and leave you two young people to chat."

Nelson Prather stood as Aunt Kezia left. He moved nervously about the room, stopping to look at some of the pictures on top of the piano. He had seen them all before and had always felt envious of the Freeman family closeness.

Hearing a sound on the stairs, he turned as Cass came in. She moved slowly and carefully as if she were carrying something very precious. Her complexion was even smoother than it had been before. "How are you feeling, Miss Cass?"

"Why, I feel fine, Nelson. Why aren't you in church?"

"I wanted to come over and talk to you, if you don't mind."

Cass gave him an odd look. "Not at all."

"Well, here. Sit down on the sofa." He waited until she had seated herself, then awkwardly sat down beside her. Cass waited for him to speak, and finally he cleared his throat. "I've got something to say, but I'm not very good with words."

"I expect you're as good as most," Cass said. "Just say what you've come to say."

Nelson Prather seemed to have trouble putting the words together, but finally he began in a rather halting fashion. "Well, Miss Cass, I envy those people who seem to always know what God's will is for their lives. I've never been able to feel that way. Maybe I'm not close enough to God."

"Well, I think you are. You're in church every Sunday."

"It takes more than that. Now you take Lanie. She really *is* close to God. Lots of times I remember her knowing exactly what God wanted her to do."

"She's a good young woman."

"Yes, she is."

A silence fell on the room, and finally Cass had to ask, "What is it you wanted to find out?"

"Well, I don't know how to say this, and I don't know much about women, Miss Cass. But I've been thinking about you a lot lately."

"You have?"

"A whole lot!"

He turned to her and for one moment she thought he was going to reach out and take her hand, but he didn't. He clasped his big hands together and cleared his throat again. "I want you to be happy, Miss Cass. I want your baby to have a good life. I want him to have a name. I wasted some time waiting for some kind of sign about whether to tell you this or not, but Miss Lanie, she got me straight. I've been praying now all week, and I feel that God wants me to tell you that—well, I care for you." He waited for her face to change and said quickly, "I know I'm not the kind of man a young girl like you would love, but I care for you. As a matter of fact, I–I love you. I wish I were more romantic, but I don't know how to talk to a young woman. I missed out on all that."

Cass was nearly too shocked to speak. She waited for him to go on and when he did not, she finally asked in a whisper, "You want me to marry you? Is that it, Nelson?"

"That's it." Nellie Prather exhaled with relief as though he had been running hard. "I wish I could say it better. I want to be a daddy to your baby and a husband to you. I know how to be a daddy. I've had lots of practice, and I can learn how to be a husband. I know this is not what you dreamed of."

Cass was quiet for a moment, and then finally a warmth came into her eyes. She reached out, took Nelson's big hand, and held it in both of hers. "I've been afraid of men most of my life. They haven't treated me very well. But I've learned to care for you. I'm like you. I don't know how to be a wife, but I'm going to be a good mother. And if we were together and you'd be patient with me, I think I—I could be a good wife to you."

"Then you'll marry me?" Nelson Prather's face brightened, and he began to smile.

"If you want me to, I'll marry you."

Nelson reached into his pocket and pulled out a piece of green cloth. He unfolded it and said, "This was my mother's engagement ring. I want you to have it. I think it goes on this finger."

He put the ring on and she cried, "It just fits, Nelson!" She held it up and the light caught it. "It's a beautiful ring." She turned to him and said, "I'll be the best wife to you that I can, Nelson."

"And I'll be the best husband I can. We'll learn together." He leaned forward and kissed her cheek, and then his face flushed. "Like I say, I'm not very romantic."

Cass leaned forward and put both hands on his face, one on each cheek. "You're romantic enough for me, Nelson Prather!"

CHAPTER 22

The trip to Cummings Prison Farm seemed to take much longer than usual. Yesterday Lanie had been overjoyed by the news of Cass's engagement, and for a time it had taken her mind off of the dark and ominous shadow that hung over her concerning her father. But now as she traveled the long miles, she felt like a hand was slowly closing over her heart. Her thoughts and feelings disturbed her greatly, for she thought they displayed a lack of faith.

Owen drove his big Oldsmobile, with Colin in the front seat and Lanie in the back. Lanie, overcome with worry, barely spoke. She was glad that Colin had come along, for he and Owen had to carry the burden of the conversation.

At the prison gates, Owen pulled the car up, and after showing their passes they passed through and parked. When they got out, Owen said, "They ought to be expecting me. I talked to the warden this morning. It's all arranged for your father to go to the hospital in Pine Bluff if I think it's necessary."

"I can't thank you enough, Owen."

"Well, it's mostly Doctor Givens we have to thank. Come along. We don't want to be late."

⥥

Lanie and Colin stayed in the visitor's room while Owen went with the prison doctor. The clock on the wall ticked loudly, but it seemed to Lanie that time slowed to a crawl. Colin made things as pleasant as he could, praying with her and speaking cheerfully, but when Owen came back into the room and they rose to greet him, his grave expression told them the story.

"I've decided we need to take Forrest to the hospital. They have some equipment there that ought to tell us something."

"How is he, Owen?"

"Well, he's cheerful, but he's lost weight—and I'm not happy with his general condition. I want to do more tests at the hospital in Pine Bluff. Of course he'll be under guard. Why don't you two go ahead? I'll go with the guard and Forrest."

"That's a good idea," Colin said at once. "We'll meet you there."

Owen turned to Lanie and started to say something. He hesitated and then seemed to decide against it.

Once again fear came to her, but she choked it back. "God's going to do something. I just know it."

"That's right. The whole church is fasting and praying," Colin said. "Come along."

Lanie left the prison with Colin. He opened the door for her, closed it, and then walked around and sat down on the driver's side. He put his hand on the key, paused, and turned to face her. "I know it's hard to have faith, but you can't work it up. One of the hardest things I know is to believe God when circumstances look bad."

Lanie nodded and could not bring herself to speak. Colin put his hand on her shoulder. His voice was gentle and his eyes were kind. "You remember the Scripture, 'Without faith it is impossible to please God.' So we're both going to believe God for your dad."

He started the engine and pulled the big Oldsmobile out of the prison yard. The scenery flew by, flat cotton fields spreading out in every direction.

Lanie struggled to find a faith that she knew she had to have.

"Isn't he ever going to come out?" Lanie whispered. Sitting in the waiting room chair, she clasped her hands together to keep them from trembling.

Colin, who was pacing up and down in the waiting room, stopped and looked down at her. "These things take a while, Lanie."

"We've been waiting two hours. Surely they could have found something by now."

Before Colin could answer the door opened, and Owen came through. Lanie rose at once and waited for him to come to her. She studied his face and tried to read what was written there. He was, she saw, keeping his face still by an effort. "What is it, Owen?" she asked, her voice tense with the strain.

"He needs an operation, Lanie."

"An operation? What for?"

Owen took her hands in his. "He has a tumor, but it's operable."

"Will he be all right?"

Owen hesitated. His answer came slowly. "It's a difficult operation, Lanie. A great many patients come out of it and are perfectly well, but ..." He hesitated. "It is difficult."

"Will you do it?"

"Oh, no! It'll take a special surgeon for that. The best one's name is Hancock. His office is in Little Rock. I've already been on the phone with him, and he can do the operation next Monday, April 18. I talked to the warden, and he's agreed to transfer your dad to the Little Rock Hospital."

"I've got to be there for the operation, Owen!"

"Of course you do. I'll be with you."

"So will I," Colin said at once. "We'll all go, and we'll all believe God together."

The two men spoke words of encouragement and hope, but their words seemed to fade. Lanie felt like she was shut into some kind of cell-like room. Outside, a black and hideous fear seemed to hammer at the walls, demanding to be let in. Only by exerting her will was she able to turn the darkness away.

She looked up into Owen's troubled eyes and whispered, "Can I see him?"

"Of course. Come on back. You come too, Colin."

Owen led them from the waiting room to where Forrest waited. With a sinking heart, Lanie saw that he had lost even more weight. He took one look at her face and then said quietly, "Don't you fret about this, Daughter."

"Oh, Daddy, I wish this didn't have to be."

Forrest Freeman held his arms out, and Lanie came into them. She remembered how strong his arms had always been, but now they felt only frail and weak. When she looked into his eyes, though, she saw that he was concerned about her, not himself.

"It's all right, Daddy. God's going to do a great thing. I know He is." She clung to her father, trying not to think about losing him. It had been hard enough to lose her mother, and now the specter of losing her father was a grim and terrible possibility.

"We'll be right there with you, Forrest," Colin said. "And the church is praying."

"I appreciate that, Brother Colin." Forrest took a deep breath and then a smile touched his lips. "It's all right. God's on our side. He'll see me through this."

CHAPTER 23

Because Nellie and Cass wanted to be married before the baby was born, their wedding was quickly set for that very Friday, April 15. That evening, pale beams of sunlight angled down from the window to the right of Colin Ryan, falling on the faces of the two who stood before him. Colin studied the couple carefully as he repeated the ancient words of the wedding ceremony. He was vaguely aware of the witnesses, consisting solely of the Freeman family, but his attention was on the countenance of the young woman who stood before him. His acquaintance with her was but slight, yet when he had been asked to perform the ceremony he had spent several hours talking with her alone. He'd also talked alone with the bridegroom Nelson Prather, and twice during this short week of their engagement he had met with the two of them together.

"Will you, Cassandra, have this man to be your lawful wedded husband?" As he spoke the words, he studied Cass's face. Childbearing agreed with her, for although she had the awkwardness of a woman close to her time, her face was glowing radiant with a joy that he had not seen in her until now. Her eyes, large and lustrous, were filled with happiness, and her skin seemed to glow with a translucent quality.

"I will."

The words were spoken in a low tone and yet were filled with determination and hope.

"And will you, Nelson, have this woman, Cassandra, to be your lawful wedded wife?"

"I sure will!"

Nelson Prather had stood beside Cass wearing a suit bought for the occasion. It was blue, which matched his eyes, and his shirt was so white it gleamed. The tie was red, almost crimson, but the contentment and happiness in the man's face glowed even brighter than his tie.

Colin continued to speak words that the couple before him seemed to drink in, and finally he said, "By the authority vested in me by the State of Arkansas, I pronounce you man and wife. You may kiss the bride."

Colin watched as the tall man in front of him flushed but turned at once and kissed Cass. He had to stoop to do so, and as soon as he stepped back, Colin said, "And I will kiss the bride also." He leaned forward to kiss Cass's cheek and then stepped back.

He felt a sense of satisfaction as the Freemans joyously swarmed in, laughing, kissing, shaking hands, and hugging the bride and groom. *This is a good thing. I wish every woman who's fallen into error could come out of it with as much grace and as much happiness as this woman. He's a good man. She's a good woman. And they'll have a good life together.*

There were plenty of refreshments, and once he had cake in hand, Colin maneuvered himself into a corner with Nelson. He asked, "Will you be taking your bride home today, Nelson?"

"No, I reckon not. I talked it over with Lanie and her folks, and we decided it would be better if she stayed there until after the baby comes." His whole face lit up. "I'm sure looking forward to that baby, Preacher."

"Most men wouldn't look forward to changing diapers and things like that."

"Why, that ain't no never mind. I got used to it with my brother and sister." His gaze went over to Cass, who was laughing at something Maeva said. "Ain't she something, Preacher? Ain't she pretty as a pair of red shoes with green laces?"

"She sure is. You've got yourself a fine woman, and she got a fine man, Nelson Prather."

The morning after the wedding Lanie stepped into the pen to feed the chickens. As usual, all the chickens came scurrying toward her, clucking and gathering around her like a congregation in church. Taking a handful of feed, she scattered it with a sweeping motion. She watched as they began pecking. Not for the first time, she was struck with a strange thought. *I wish I didn't have any more worries than you chickens. The worst thing that can happen to you is that you'll live your life out and have one bad day when you get your neck wrung.*

Ordinarily Lanie would have laughed at her own foolish thoughts, but now she was burdened down with the pressures of her father's operation that was to come in two days. She watched the chickens fight over the seeds and noted that one, a small red hen, undersized and wizened, was being shouldered aside by the larger fowl. The injustice of it struck her, and she marched over to the little hen. "Here, Suzanne!" She dropped a handful of seed and shooed away the rest of the chickens while Suzanne gobbled it up. She did not know why she had made such a pet of the little fowl. Perhaps because she was pushed aside and neglected by the rest of the flock.

While she was stooped over protecting Suzanne, she felt a sharp pain in her right calf. She whirled, only to find a big rooster glaring at her. "Get away from me, Judas!" She had named all the hens and the roosters too, and this one was the meanest she had ever encountered. He made a dash at her, and she lashed out with her foot, kicking him in the breast and knocking him over. He squawked as he rolled in the dust, then came up, his eyes filled with evil. "That's foolish!" she told herself as she left the pen. "Chicken's aren't evil."

She carefully locked the gate behind her, and for a moment memories like a searchlight moved over her mind. She enjoyed most memories, but now with all the problems that had descended on her, it seemed most memories were snarled and tangled on a line nobody could straighten out and that needed to be simply cut away. Lanie sighed heavily as she moved toward the house.

She was greeted by Beau, who reared up on her and looked at her straight in the face. As always, she was fascinated by his eyes, one brown and one blue. "Get away, Beau," she said and shoved him away. Immediately Booger took his place, though instead of rearing up, he blocked her way. When she stopped, he promptly sat down on her feet, which he liked to do for some reason. She managed to smile, then leaned over and stroked his head. "Good dog. Now go sit on somebody else's feet."

Just then the city hall clock chimed three times in the distance and reminded her of other chores. It troubled her that she was not capable of putting her mind on ordinary things. All she could think of was her father's operation. She suspected Owen had not told her the whole truth about the procedure. She had seen him speaking with Colin and wondered if they had agreed not to tell her how dangerous the operation might be.

A sudden notion took her, and she went inside at once, this time moving with determination. Aunt Kezia and Maeva were peeling potatoes. Interrupting them, she said, "I've got an errand to run."

"If you're going by the store, get some garlic," Aunt Kezia said.

"You put too much garlic in things," Maeva said. It was so hot in the house her dress was stained under the armpits with perspiration. She wiped her forehead with the back of her arm. "It makes us smell terrible."

"Garlic is good for you!" Aunt Kezia snapped. "It cleans out your blood."

"My blood is clean enough."

"No, it ain't. Young people got blood that needs to be cleaned out every day. I'm going to give you some of Doctor Stonebreaker's Blood and Liver Bitters. It'll regulate your whole system."

Maeva, who was as healthy as a horse, laughed. "My system don't need regulating. Besides, that stuff wouldn't cure anybody."

"That's all you know. Doctor Stonebreaker saved many a woman from female complaints."

"I don't have any female complaints."

"Well, this will keep you from having any when you get older."

Lanie did not stop to listen to the argument. She knew that Aunt Kezia was susceptible to any advertisement for patent medicine and that Owen was disgusted with all of them.

Lanie washed her face and hands, brushed her hair, and left the house. She had to walk, for Davis and Cody had taken the emporium out on a run and the old Ford had a flat tire.

As she walked, she could not help but think of her father. Her mind went back to the earliest times when he would place her on his shoulders and play games with her.

She had just turned down Elm Street headed for town when suddenly she heard her name called. Turning, she saw Brent Hayden trotting toward her. She waited until he got in front of her and said, "I'm glad I caught you, Lanie."

"What are you doing here, Brent?"

"I had to come to town to get a few things, but I wanted to see you. I just heard your father's going to have an operation."

"That's right. This coming Monday in Little Rock."

Brent was wearing a pair of gray slacks and a light blue shirt open at the neck. He ran his hand through his hair and shook his head. "I'm sorry to hear that. Is it serious?"

"I think it is."

"Is there anything I can do to help? Do you want me to rent a car and take you to Little Rock for the surgery?"

"No. Doctor Merritt and Brother Ryan are going to go. I'm riding with them."

Hayden looked troubled. He was ordinarily a smiling man, but now his lips were drawn tight. "These things are always hard. I went through it with my mother."

"Well, if it weren't for the Lord, I wouldn't know what to do." She saw her words troubled him, and suddenly an impulse took her. "There is one thing you can do for me."

"Anything. Just name it, Lanie."

"Tomorrow morning at the church service, I'm going to ask the congregation to pray for my dad. If you could be there, it would mean a lot to me, Brent."

Astonishment washed across Hayden's face. "Why, Lanie, you know I'm not a Christian."

"You're a friend, though. At a time like this we need all the friends we can get."

Hayden looked as if he wanted to run away, but finally he gave a high laugh. "I'll do it," he said. "I hope the roof doesn't fall in when I walk through the door." He reached out and took her hand and squeezed it. "I wish I were a praying man."

"You will be some day."

He shook his head ruefully. "I hope so. I'll be there though. Probably way in the back. I'll wave so you see me."

Lanie watched as he turned and walked away, and the thought came to her, *He has everything except God—which means he has nothing.* She continued down Elm Street and made her way to Owen's office. She knew he often went there on Saturdays to catch up on patient files and read medical journals. His car was parked outside, a sign he would be doing house calls later.

She went into the small building and knocked at his office door. "Owen? I hope I'm not disturbing you."

Owen looked up from a letter he was reading. "Lanie, I'm so glad you stopped by. I just got a letter I wanted to tell you about."

"What is it?"

"I've heard from my brother Dave. The guys in his police department in Los Angeles tracked down Thelma Mayes, but she took off again before they could question her. Dave thinks she's still in the city, though, and they're going to keep looking."

Lanie's face barely changed at the news. Getting her father back to health had suddenly become more important even than getting him out of jail.

"Are you all right, Lanie?"

"I guess so, but I have a favor to ask."

Owen set aside the letter and studied her for a moment. "Anything. Just name it."

"I know you're embarrassed by what's going on with that woman, but in the morning after the service I'm going to ask the church to pray for Daddy. It would mean a lot to me if you would come, Owen."

Owen dropped his head. Lanie saw the struggle and knew it was difficult. He had not been in church since Amelia had made her charge.

He looked up. "I'll do it," he said quietly, "but it won't be easy."

"Thank you, Owen."

She stood there for a moment as they looked into each other's eyes. They shared a bond that neither of them quite understood. She had been a young girl coming out of adolescence when he had first seen her, and he had watched her blossom into young womanhood. She had watched him too, and now she wanted to say something about their relationship but did not know how to put it.

Abruptly she said, "I'll see you in church in the morning. Thank you, Owen." She left the doctor's office, hoping she had done the right thing.

At supper, Lanie announced to her family, "I got some news. Owen got a letter from his brother Dave."

"The one that's a policeman in Los Angeles?" Davis asked at once.

"Yes." She went on to tell them the bit of hopeful news.

"I'd like to go to Los Angeles and dig that woman up," Maeva said grimly. "I bet I could find her, and I could make her tell what really happened at that shooting."

"Well, you can't go to Los Angeles," Lanie stated, "and that's final. But we've all got to pray that Dave will find her."

The Sunday morning service had gone well, but from her seat in the choir loft, Lanie had been hard put to keep her mind on either worship or Brother Ryan's sermon. Brent Hayden came in during the singing and took a seat in the back. Before sitting down, he looked directly at her, and when he met her eyes, he smiled and nodded. She read his lips as he mouthed the words, *Well, the roof didn't fall in*, and then sat down.

She was also very much aware when Owen entered. As she had expected, many of his friends walked over to speak with him. She almost wished they hadn't, for she could see the attention troubled him.

Finally the service was over. The invitation had been given and several had responded. The congregation now waited for Colin to say, "We'll now stand and have our benediction." Instead he said, "Ordinarily we have a benediction and go home, but this morning one of our fine young women has a word to say. Lanie, the floor's yours."

Lanie did not leave her place in the choir, but as she stood up, every eye was fixed upon her. She had planned what she was going to say, but suddenly she found it hard. She had prayed that God would give her just the right words, and now she said in a voice that carried throughout the whole building, "I think all of you know about our dad. He has a tumor and he needs a miracle in his life. The surgery is going to be Monday at two o'clock. Many times in the past I've asked you to pray for me and for my family, but I'm asking you again to remember my dad and all of us." Suddenly her throat grew thick and she managed to say, "We need him so very much."

A murmur went over the congregation, and Lanie waited and then said what she felt God had put on her heart. "I think all of you know that God loves unity." Her words brought a sudden silence. She waited a moment and then said, "David the Psalmist said something about that. He said, 'How pleasant it is for brethren to dwell together in unity. It is like the precious ointment upon the head, that ran down upon the beard, even Aaron's beard: that went down to the skirts of his garments.' That's in the one hundred and thirty-third Psalm, and

I've read it so many times. The last part of that Psalm says, 'There the Lord commanded the blessing, even life for evermore.'" The silence was almost thick enough to breathe, and she said, "God gave me this Scripture that God's blessing, even life for evermore, would come if our church would pray. But we are a divided church. There are some who have been unkind to a very good man, Doctor Owen Merritt."

Lanie saw that Owen's face was pale. She had prayed hard about what she would say, and now, silently, she prayed even harder, especially for wisdom. "I'd trust Doctor Merritt with my life. If any of you this morning feel that you've been judgmental of Doctor Merritt, please don't pray for my dad. God hates division. If you feel you have something in your heart that isn't right in this matter, please come and make it right with Doctor Merritt and with God."

The profound silence seemed to have a life of its own, but suddenly Mrs. Elvie Pink, the wife of Gerald Pink, moved. She was in the choir seated to Lanie's left. Tears running down her cheeks, she stood, and brushing against the other choir members, she made her way out of the choir. Every eye was on her as she walked toward Owen. When she reached him, she put her hands out and he took them in his. "Doctor Merritt," she whispered. "I've been unjust to you. Please forgive me!"

Owen whispered words of encouragement, but before he could even finish others were coming toward him. Lanie took a sudden breath, for it seemed from all over the congregation people were moving—and all in the direction of Owen Merritt!

Owen stepped out into the aisle and was surrounded by people, at least twenty that Lanie could count.

Owen's face glowed with happiness. "I did the right thing, God," Lanie whispered under her breath. "This is a miracle."

After the last person had made his way to Owen, Colin Ryan said, "This is indeed a blessing and a miracle. Indeed, it is beautiful for brethren to walk together in unity, and I believe now that we have purged our hearts I should declare a solemn fast. And we are going to see God do a miracle in the body of our dear brother. I ask all of you—"

Brother Colin's voice was cut short by a woman's cry. Lanie was confused for a moment, and then she saw Amelia Wright stand and move into the aisle; she had not even known Amelia was in the building, for she had been seated behind one of the biggest men of the church.

Without hesitating, she went straight to where Owen stood.

"I lied about you, Owen," she cried out. She turned to face the congregation, and everyone saw the agony in her face. "God help me! He's been nothing but a good man. I'm the one that sinned. He's innocent." Amelia suddenly turned and fled down the aisle.

Colin cried out, "Brother Merritt, will you please close this service? I've got business …" Colin dashed out the door after Amelia.

Owen said, "Let us pray." His prayer was sweet and fervent and simple, and after it was over, Lanie went to him. He took her hands and said, "God was in this, Lanie. I'm so glad you asked me to come."

Lanie could hardly speak, her throat was so full. She said a few words to him and then hurried to where Brent was waiting.

"Thank you for coming, Brent," she whispered.

"I've never seen anything like this. It's a miracle!"

"My father needs a miracle too," she said quietly. There was an expression in his eyes that caused her to add, "And you also need one, Brent."

He dropped his head and did not speak for a moment, and when he looked up, she saw tears in his eyes. "Don't give up on me, Lanie."

"I won't. God's on your trail like that poem you showed me, 'The Hound of Heaven.'" She gave him a gentle smile. "He won't give up until you're a part of the family of God."

She stepped outside and looked for Amelia Wright, but she saw neither Amelia nor Colin. *She needs the Lord, and I know Colin can help her.*

When she turned back to the church, her family stood waiting. She hurried toward them and cried out, "Now we're going to see God at work!"

CHAPTER 24

At the hospital in Little Rock, Lanie met with her father in his room while a guard stood watch outside.

"You're going to be fine, Daddy. I know you are." Lanie leaned over and kissed her father on the cheek. She reached for his hand, took it in both of hers, and whispered, "The whole church is praying for you."

"Thank you, Muff. I'm glad you're here."

"Everybody wanted to come, but they couldn't all be here."

"I hate to be all this trouble," Forrest said.

"How could you be trouble, Daddy?" Lanie whispered. She smoothed his hair back and then, glancing toward the door, said, "I'll be right out there in the waiting room. Owen and the other doctor will take care of you."

Lanie stepped back, and the guard came to push Forrest's wheelchair through the open doorway. In the hallway, Owen directed them to another room and explained, "We're going to take one more X-ray before the surgery to pinpoint the tumor's location."

Lanie could not speak for a moment, and then she looked up, her eyes swimming with tears. "I'm glad you're here, Owen. I know you won't do the surgery, but it makes me feel better to know you'll be with Dr. Hancock."

Owen took her hand and held it for a moment, then said, "You and Colin go over and do the praying, and I'll be with the surgeon the whole time."

Lanie nodded, then went back to the waiting room and sat down beside Colin, who took her hand in a comforting gesture. There were others seated nearby, and as she looked around, she thought, *Everybody in here is in trouble, or some of their folks are, and I guess they're all praying just like I am. But God can hear more than one person at a time.*

⌖

There were two technicians in the laboratory, a tall man named Louis and Fred, a shorter muscular man who moved in a hurried fashion. Fred leaned over and said, "We're going to leave you right here, Mr. Freeman. We'll develop the X-rays to be sure we got good shots. If it's okay, you'll be ready to go."

"Thanks," Forrest said.

As soon as the two men were out of earshot, the short one said in a low voice, "I don't think this man's got much of a chance. I saw those earlier X-rays."

"I'm afraid you're right, Fred." The two worked steadily, and finally the X-rays were done. Fred handed the film to Lou. "Get these to Doctor Hancock. You know how he hates to wait."

Lou turned and left the laboratory. He found the two doctors waiting in Hancock's office. "Here you are, Doctor Hancock."

Hancock took the X-ray. He was a tall man with a soft voice and sharp gray eyes. He slapped the X-ray up on the lighted glass and took one look at it, then leaned closer and looked again. "This is not right," he said. "Look at it, Owen."

Owen came over and examined the film. "You're right, it isn't."

"Lou, you'll have to take it again. There's something wrong with your machine."

"If you say so, Doctor Hancock."

Lou went back to the lab. "Fred, they want another shot. They say something's wrong with the machine."

"There's nothing wrong with this machine."

Forrest lay flat on his back and listened as the two men argued. Something began to stir within him, and he paid more attention.

Finally Lou said, "Mr. Freeman, we've got to do another X-ray. That one didn't take."

"Go ahead."

They went through the same procedure. Once again they told Forrest he had to wait to be sure the picture was good, and once again Lou took the film into the office where the two doctors waited. "Here you are, Doctor Hancock."

Hancock placed the X-ray up on the lighted glass and for a moment was silent. He studied it carefully, then turned to Owen. "What do you make of that?"

"There's only one thing I can make out of it. Either they're taking an X-ray of the wrong man or—or there's no tumor. Look."

The two men studied the two new images alongside the old one. "The tumor is very clear in this old picture," Hancock said slowly, "but it's not here now."

Owen suddenly straightened, and a light came into his eyes. "How do you explain that, Doctor?"

Hancock stared at the three images, his expression etched with doubt.

"I can't help but think a mistake has been made," he said.

"A mistake?" Owen asked. "What kind of a mistake?"

"Well ... I don't know exactly. Maybe these aren't the right X-rays."

Owen turned and asked the technician, "Where is the envelope these pictures came in?"

"Right here, but there's no mistake," Louis said stiffly. "I made those X-rays myself."

Owen stared at the envelope, then handed it to Hancock. " 'Forrest Freeman,' " he read aloud. "These are his X-rays."

Hancock stared at the envelope for a long time, then shook his head. "Look, Doctor, you and I are men of science. We're both trained to deal with facts. We can't be swayed by what we'd *like*—only by what we can prove."

Owen suddenly laughed, his eyes alight. "And aren't these pictures hard evidence? The machine that made them doesn't have opinions, Dr. Hancock. They record what they see."

Hancock stared at the earlier X-ray as if it were some sort of enemy. "That is a tumor if I ever saw one," he declared. "Tumors of this sort don't just vanish."

"Not as a rule. But this one did."

"Impossible!"

"With God all things are possible," Owen said, his voice not quite steady. "We were both trained to weigh evidence, and that's what I'm doing. The tumor was right there at one point—but now it's gone. The only explanation I can give is that God has healed this man."

Hancock was silent for a long time, his eyes fixed on the X-rays. Finally he threw his hands up in surrender. "You'll have to write up the report. Nobody is going to believe this!"

"I'll be more than happy to do that, but I'll need you to sign it."

Relunctantly Hancock agreed, but said, "You can count on a review, Dr. Merritt. More than one, I'd venture!"

The two doctors talked about the need for more X-rays. After a few minutes Owen said, "I'm going to tell his daughter."

"Aren't you afraid you'll get her hopes up?"

Owen pointed to the X-rays. "The tumor's gone, Doctor Smith. God's done a work. You take all the pictures you want, but I'm believing God."

Owen hurried to the waiting room. As soon as he entered, Lanie came to her feet. He went to her at once, reached down, and took her hands. "Good news, Lanie."

"What is it, Owen?"

"The tumor—it's gone."

Lanie could not speak. Feeling light-headed, she grasped Owen's hands even tighter. "Gone?" Her voice was little more than a whisper. "Tell me, Owen."

"We're going to take more X-rays, but the tumor's just not there, Lanie."

They stood there, looking at each other, completely unaware of anyone else in the waiting room. Lanie's face glowed with happiness.

Owen whispered, "We're seeing what prayer can do."

"Yes," Lanie said. And then she smiled, a wide and glorious smile. Still holding his hands, she said, "I knew God would do it. He's a great and wonderful, miracle-working God."

"Amen and amen." Owen drew her into his arms and hugged her.

← CHAPTER 25 →

L anie rested her head on the back of the car seat and enjoyed the wind blowing in through the open window. It stirred her hair, and she was aware of the sound of the tires humming and the smell of the new broken earth as they passed fresh-plowed fields. The trip from the hospital had gone quickly, and the joy that filled her heart had been more than anything she could ever imagine. In fact, it even drowned out her sorrow that he had to return to prison.

"Don't go to sleep on me now," said Owen, after they dropped off Colin Ryan. "We're almost home."

Lanie opened her eyes and moved her head to look at Owen. The wind was blowing his hair too, and she admired the strength of his jaw. *He doesn't know how good-looking he is*, she thought. "I'm not going to sleep," she said. "I couldn't."

"It's been quite a day, hasn't it?"

Indeed it had been quite a day. The two doctors insisted on more X-rays, and they managed to irritate the technicians, who finally snapped at them, "There's nothing wrong with the machines! Maybe something's wrong with the doctors."

They then took the good news to Forrest, who stared at them for a moment unbelievingly and then said, "Well, I don't think I could ever doubt God again. It's all gone, the tumor?" The doctors assured him that he had no tumor, and he took Lanie in his arms and said, "I do enjoy these miracles."

In the car, Lanie straightened up, ruffled her hair, and said, "Did you always want to be a doctor, Owen?"

"No. I wanted to be an astronomer when I was growing up."

"Why didn't you do it?"

Owen turned, momentarily taking his eyes off the road, and smiled at her. "Because of something someone told me."

"What was that?"

"Well, I always loved to get outdoors and look up at the stars. I've seen nights when the whole heaven seemed to be on fire. Millions and millions of stars all bright and shiny. It excited me, but then this friend of mine told me that what you're seeing is not the stars themselves."

Lanie was puzzled. "What does that mean?"

"He said the stars were so far away that what you're seeing is the light that they sent thousands, or even millions, of years ago. So you're not seeing the stars themselves."

Lanie rubbed her hand across her cheek and thought about that. "That's too much for me," she said.

"It was too much for me too. I didn't want to study something I couldn't even see. Anyway, I'm glad I became a doctor. People are more fun than stars, I think."

Lanie laughed. "I think so too." They were nearing home now, and she said, "I can't wait to see everyone. When I told them the good news about Daddy on the phone, Cody shouted so loud he nearly burst my eardrum, and I could hear Aunt Kezia shouting too."

"I think the whole town's shouting. I made a few calls, and you know how Fairhope is. No secrets from anybody."

"I'd hate to live in a big city where you wouldn't know anybody else. I like knowing the people in this little town."

"It can get a little bit difficult at times," Owen said. "People are so nosy."

"I guess so, but still it feels like a big family sometimes."

Owen guided the Oldsmobile down the street and finally pulled up in front of the Freeman home. Lanie opened the door and got out, and when Owen came around the car, he said, "You're supposed to wait and let me open the door for you."

"I'm so excited I forgot. Come on." She took his hand and pulled him along as she ran down the sidewalk to the porch. They went up the steps and burst through the door. "We're home!" Lanie called out. "Where is everybody?"

They all appeared then, Cody leaping down the stairs, taking them three at a time, with Davis right behind him.

Aunt Kezia and Maeva rushed from the kitchen, and Corliss ran to Lanie, who picked her up and twirled her around. "Did you miss me, honey?"

"Yes!" Corliss squealed.

"Tell us all about it, Lanie," Maeva said. "We couldn't hardly believe it."

"I guess miracles are always a little bit hard to believe at first."

Aunt Kezia, for once, was not saying much, but she had a big grin on her face. "You're not the only one that has surprises. We've got one for you too."

"What is it?" Lanie said.

"Come on. Let's show them, kids."

There was a mass exodus up the stairs, Davis grabbing Lanie's hand and pulling her after him. Glancing over her shoulder, she saw that Owen was coming along, and when they got to Cass's room, Aunt Kezia opened the door and said, "Go on in and see your surprise."

Lanie stepped into Cass's room and then stopped dead still. Cody was beside her squeezing her arm and saying, "Look at what we got."

Cass was sitting in a chair holding a bundle, and she had evidently been nursing the baby because she quickly covered herself up. Then she turned the child around. "Here he is. Nelson Davis Prather."

Lanie gave a glad cry and ran over. She snatched the baby up and cuddled him. "What a beautiful baby, Cass!"

"Do you think so?" Cass smiled.

"But who delivered him?" Lanie said. "Did Doctor Givens come out?"

"Why, land sakes, no! Me and Maeva delivered this big fat baby boy," Aunt Kezia said. "Didn't we, Maeva?"

"We sure did." Maeva was grinning broadly. "No sense wasting money on a doctor."

"Why, sakes no," Kezia snorted. "It was only a baby."

"Nelson was here, and he will be back. He's getting ready to move us to our place," Cass said. There was pride in her expression, and she used the word *our* with almost a sense of wonder.

Lanie cuddled the baby and looked down into the tiny face. "Well, Nelson Davis Prather," she said, "it looks like you're off to a running start."

Afterwards Lanie looked back and remembered that Maeva was behaving very strangely for the week after the surgery. She was excited, of course, about the healing and wrote her father the longest letter she had ever written. She also helped Cass move out to her new home and get settled in, but she was oddly quiet. Lanie did not notice, though, until later, for there was so much going on.

When Lanie got up a week later on a Tuesday morning, the house felt empty. Cass and her baby were gone, the boys and Maeva were in school, and both Kezia and Corliss were asleep. Tiptoeing down the stairs, she went into the kitchen intending to make coffee and fix a big breakfast for herself. But when she reached the kitchen table, she found a single sheet of paper weighted down by a rose vase.

Curious, she walked over and picked it up, seeing at once it was Maeva's handwriting. She started to read, but halfway through she felt light-headed, as if she might faint. She sank into a chair and read the whole thing very slowly, word for word:

April 26, 1932

Dear Lanie,

I am going to Los Angeles with Logan Satterfield. I know this will make you unhappy, but it's something I have to do.

Now don't worry. I'm not sleeping with Logan and he understands that. He's got a job playing in a band out on the west coast, and I almost forced him to take me along with him. He's always said I sing well enough to make money singing, so we're going to find out.

Lanie, please don't grieve over me. I'm not going to California to get into show business, though that wouldn't be bad. What I'm going to do, sister, is find that woman Thelma Mays who witnessed the shooting. She knows Daddy didn't do what the Bigginses said he did. I'm going to find her and make her come back and testify that Daddy's innocent.

I'm going to find Dr. Merritt's brother Dave, the one who's a detective there in Los Angeles, and get him to help me.

Lanie, I knew you wouldn't let me go, so I had to do it this way. You know me, sister. I don't like to hide things but just come right out with it. But I've been thinking about this for a long time, and now I've got to do it.

You've been the one, Lanie, who's had to take care of us all, and now I'm old enough to do something for myself and for my family. You pray for me that I'll find this woman and that I'll find some way to get her to testify. I'll write you as soon as I get there. Don't come after me or send anybody because I won't come home until I get what I'm here for. I'm going to get my daddy out of the Cummings Prison or die trying!

Love, Maeva

P.S. It'll be all right if you want to pray for me. I'll need it, I know.

Lanie put the note down flat on the table and then placed her palms on it. She bowed her head, but she was so confused she could not think straight. Finally she began to pray, and after a long time of struggle, she said, "Oh, Lord, you'll just have to take care of my sister. Watch over Maeva and keep her safe, Lord. Let her find that woman and get her to tell the truth so my daddy can get out of the penitentiary."

She sat still for a long time, then got up to make coffee. When it was boiling, she went over to the window. It was as if, for one moment, she could see all the way from Fairhope, Arkansas, to Los Angeles, California. There was her sister in the big city with everything that can go wrong for a young girl. But Maeva had always been headstrong. Lanie knew she would have to let go and just believe God would keep her safe.

CHAPTER 26

The first few weeks of May were glorious, with bright blue skies, blossoming fruit trees, and just enough rain to keep the grass and gardens lush and green. Lulled by the beauty around her, Lanie almost forgot to worry about Maeva, focusing instead on helping Cass in her new role as little Nelson's mother.

With Cody and Davis still in school, driving the emporium still fell mostly to Lanie. One day she had just packed her last supplies and closed the doors when she heard a familiar voice.

"Can you use an extra hand?"

Lanie was surprised to see Owen. He had not come in his car, so he had approached her without being heard. "Hello, Owen. What are you doing here?"

"I've come to sign on for a voyage. I feel like a sailor about ready to make a trip to some foreign exotic country."

Lanie stared at him and could not help smiling. There was a new bounce in his step, and he looked younger. Since Amelia Wright confessed her wrongdoing, it seemed a mighty weight had been lifted from his shoulders. Even Lanie, until now, had not realized the full impact of the false accusations on Owen during those dark days.

She smiled and said, "Where's your car?"

"It's in the shop and I've got the day off. What better thing could I do than to join you on this vehicle as a hired hand?"

Lanie stared at him. "You mean you want to go with me while I sell this stuff?"

"Right. Why don't you let me drive and give you a break?"

Lanie was pleased but uncertain. "It's not very exciting, Owen."

"Why, my dear, being with you is always exciting." His eyes sparkled as he added, "That was my imitation of Clark Gable. How did you like it?"

Lanie suddenly burst out laughing. "It sounded more like Eddie Cantor."

"You wound me to the heart, dear lady, you surely do. But I insist on going along."

"All right. I'll promise you you'll be bored, but you're welcome to come. You think you can drive this thing?"

"Just watch my smoke."

Lanie watched as Owen got behind the wheel, then she got in and sat down on the seat beside him. He started the truck, then turned to her. "Which way?"

"We're going over toward Summerdale. I've got a lot of good customers there."

"Summerdale it is!"

<hr/>

The trip was no more exciting than usual, but having Owen along made it different. Almost every one of her customers knew Owen, and many made it a point to tell him how happy they were he had been exonerated of the charges made by Amelia Wright.

Once, after one of these encounters, Owen said, "Colin tells me that Amelia's leaving town, but he said she's really had a change of heart."

"Why is she leaving?"

"He said she just wanted to get a fresh start. In a way, I'm glad of it. I don't have any hard feelings, but it would be a little bit awkward. Hey, there's somebody waving us down. Oh, it's that writer fellow."

Owen pulled the emporium over and stopped beside Brent Hayden, who held an envelope in his hand. Lanie got out of the truck to greet him. "Look what I've got. They've accepted another one of your poems at the *Poetry Journal*."

"Really, Brent?" Lanie cried out. She opened the envelope and took out the letter and a check for five dollars. "I'm never going to get rich writing poetry, but it sure is nice to get something."

"Yes," Brent smiled, "not much money in it." Then he turned to Owen. "How are you, Doctor Merritt?"

"I'm fine. I want you to know I appreciate how much encouragement you've given Lanie."

"I wish all of the young writers I know were as sure to make it as Lanie." He turned to Lanie again. "But I wanted to say good-bye."

"Good-bye!" Lanie exclaimed. "Where are you going?"

"I got an offer as an editor in Chicago. I'll be leaving tomorrow."

"Oh, Brent, I'll miss you so much!"

"Well, the mail still runs. I'll be expecting to hear from you. And send me anything new you write that you want me to try to get published."

Lanie put out her hand and he took it. "I'll never forget your coming to church when I asked you to."

Hayden was silent for a minute. "You know, ever since that day I've been thinking about how I need the Lord in my life."

Lanie was ecstatic over his confession. "I'm so happy, Brent. Don't put it off. Promise me you'll listen to what God has to say to you."

"I promise. Now, after you get through with your run tomorrow come by, and I'll have ready all the books and things I don't want to take with me. Leftover groceries too. You can find somebody who wants the food, I'm sure."

Lanie promised, and as the two left, she turned to Owen. "He's been such a help to me."

"He seems like a nice fellow. I thought for a while you were going to get stuck on him."

She glanced at Owen, considering a dozen different reasons why Brent Hayden did not interest her in the least. But she settled on saying simply, "No. It's not likely. He doesn't even know the Lord, but I hope he will."

The emporium had covered a great deal of territory, and the sales had been good. When it was almost twilight, Owen said, "You know, it's going to be dark pretty soon. I'm about worn out." He smiled at her and added, "I bet you are too." He was driving along the road that paralleled the Singing River and suddenly he pulled over into a grove and stopped. "I think we deserve a reward."

"What kind of a reward?"

"Let's have a picnic."

"A picnic? I've got to get home."

Owen seemed very young as he said, "Nope, I demand a picnic. You've got some hot dogs and buns in here and some marshmallows. You've got some matches. We'll start a fire and have a feast."

Lanie protested but not for long. She often got home later than this. Soon they were building a fire beside the river, and when it was crackling hot, Owen whittled two sticks with his pocketknife. He impaled a hot dog on one and then handed it to her. "I'm an expert at cooking over a fire like this," he assured her. "I've had offers from all over for my secret."

Lanie laughed. "I'll bet your secret's just to put that hot dog on a stick and put it in the fire."

"Well, it's all in how you hold the stick. You see it's in the wrist action." He gave her an example and she laughed again. They toasted their hot dogs, put them on buns, and smeared them with mustard. "You see," he said after taking a bite, "a work of art."

They had two hot dogs apiece, and then Owen said, "Now for dessert." They opened a box of marshmallows, and he stuck one in the fire. The marshmallow quickly turned black and burst into flames.

Lanie said, "You better let me do that. You're not supposed to stick them right into the fire."

"I guess not." They had several marshmallows, and then Owen said, "Let's sit on the bank before we go back."

They settled into the soft grass, and the quietness seemed to seep in. "You know this river really does sing. Do you hear it?" Owen said.

"I told Cody once that I could hear the river's voice, hear it singing, and he said it was just the water running over the rocks."

"He's got a lot of theology but not much romance."

They sat there without speaking and around them the sounds of frogs and crickets and night birds joined the song of the river. Finally Owen asked, "Are you very worried about Maeva?"

"No. Not now. I've heard from her twice already, so I guess she's going to be a good letter writer."

"Has she contacted my brother Dave?"

"Yes, and he's going to help her. In the meanwhile she's got a part-time job, and she sings at night with the band."

"She's got enough talent. I think she can make it."

They sat there quietly talking about the family, especially about Cass and Nelson and the new baby and how happy they seemed. "I believe they were actually made for each other," Lanie said.

"Well, he's considerably older than she is."

Lanie turned to him quickly. "That's doesn't matter. He loves her and she loves him."

"In that, I think you're right."

The darkness was almost complete now. The fire was burning brightly and cast flickering shadows over Lanie's face. She was looking out over the river, when suddenly Owen said, "I'm glad you wouldn't let me run away from my problem, Lanie. I should have known better, but I probably would have done the wrong thing if it weren't for you."

Lanie turned to him and laid a hand on his. "I'm so glad you didn't go. It all turned out all right, and Daddy's doing fine. He's gaining weight. I'll be going to see him next week."

The river was murmuring quietly and from far off came the lonesome song of a coyote howling. Lanie was totally caught up in the silence, but suddenly something caught her attention. She whirled to see a large shape moving at a great speed straight toward her. Her first thought was a wolf or a bear, and she screamed and came to her feet. Owen jumped up and caught her in his arms to shield her.

And then without warning the dark shape materialized, and she cried, "Is it a bear?"

"No." He held her tightly and she clung to him. "But it's a large dangerous animal."

Lanie looked around past Owen. She made out the shape of the monstrous animal and laughed. "It's just Booger."

"Well, he's big and dangerous. He might have hydrophobia or something."

"Don't be silly! Now let me go, Owen."

"No. I don't think so. There may be a wolf or something out in the woods. Who knows?"

Lanie felt safe and secure in Owen's strong arms. She had no desire for him to let her go, so she surrendered to the moment.

Owen laid his cheek against the top of her head. "You know, Lanie Belle Freeman, you're the sweetest young woman I have ever known."

Lanie became very still and wanted to hear more talk like this, but suddenly Booger shoved his way in between them. She laughed and pushed Owen away. "You probably tell that to a lot of young women."

"No, I don't, but I've felt that way ever since the first time I saw you. And you were fourteen years old."

"I remember, but I'm eighteen years old now, Doctor Owen Merritt."

Owen put his hands on her shoulders and pulled her closer but made no attempt to embrace her. She lifted her face and looked into his eyes.

He said, "I know very well you're not fourteen."

Lanie waited for him to say more, but he was quiet. Finally she said, "I've got to go home, Owen."

"All right, but answer me one question."

"What?"

"Have you got Roger Langley out of your system, Lanie?"

"Why, I don't know what you're talking about."

"I know he's serious about you, but are you serious about him? I hope not, for he's not the man for you."

A quick anger touched Lanie. "What do you mean he's not the man for me? He's smart, handsome, rich, and has beautiful manners!"

She was very conscious of Owen's hands holding her shoulders and waited until he spoke.

"He's not—he's not tall enough for you."

Lanie giggled. "He's as tall as you are."

"Is not."

"He is too."

"No. I'm taller than he is."

Lanie suddenly began to laugh. "You are a foolish man, Owen Merritt. Come on. Let's go home."

"I'm still hungry."

"I'll cook you something when we get home. Or better still, maybe Aunt Kezia will fix you her specialty."

"Which is what?"

"Fried pig's lips."

"Lanie, never in this world would I eat a pig's lips."

"In that case you'll just have to take what she's got." She turned, and he made a grab for her, but she evaded him. "That's enough of that, Doctor."

After putting out the fire, they climbed into the emporium. He started it up, then reached over and put his hand on her shoulder. "It's been a fine day, Lanie."

"It has been good, hasn't it?"

They sat there in the darkness for a moment, then Owen laughed and started the truck. "Well, I guess pig's lips do sound pretty good at the moment."

The engine suddenly exploded and started, and the emporium moved back onto the highway. Booger followed at a lope, and as speed picked up, he began to bay loudly.

Lanie heard him and said, "Stop the bus."

Owen brought the emporium to a halt, Lanie opened the door, and Booger scrambled in. He got up between them and sat there looking straight ahead.

"He thinks he's a person." Lanie put her arm around him and kissed him on top of the head.

"Stop wasting those kisses on that mangy hound."

"He's not mangy and they're not wasted."

"We'll talk about that later. Right now I'm hungry for pig lips."

The emporium started down the road, and Lanie Belle Freeman and Doctor Owen Merritt, with Booger between them, made their way back to Fairhope, leaving all their troubles behind them.

Be sure to read this excerpt from the next book in the Singing River Series, *The Courtship*

Chapter 1

I don't like the wicked witch, Lanie."

Corliss Freeman was sitting beside her older sister Lanie on the couch. The two of them had been reading for some time, and as always, Lanie was amazed at how quickly the four-year-old was picking up the ability to recognize words.

"Nobody likes the wicked witch, Corliss."

"Then why is she in the book?"

"I suppose books have to have bad people as well as good people." She looked down at the book, *The Wizard of Oz*, and ran her hand over Corliss's blonde hair. "Don't you worry about it. There are no such thing as witches anyway."

"I like the cowardly lion."

"Why do you like him?"

"Because he wanted to be brave but he couldn't. But he will, won't he? Let's skip ahead to the part where the wizard gives everybody what they want." Corliss's blue eyes lit up with pleasure. "The straw man got his brain, and the tin man got a heart, and the lion got courage. I like stories where everyone gets what they want."

An old grandfather clock ticked loudly sending its message across the room that time was passing. The two were oblivious of it, and as Corliss picked out the words she knew—sometimes whole sentences—and read them aloud in her childish voice, Lanie was thinking, *How mama would have loved her! She always was partial to little blonde girls.* A sadness came over her as she recognized that this could never be.

Booger, the bloodhound, and Beau, just a pure hound, had been watching. Beau had been peaceful as long as he could. He got up, came across the floor and rearing up put his front paws in Lanie's lap, his eyes soulful as he sought her gaze.

"No — Beau, you can't get up in my lap! You're too big. Now go over there and be good."

Beau stared at her for a moment, then walked across the room and threw himself down staring at the wall.

"You hurt his feelings again, Lanie."

"He gets his feelings hurt too easy. He's the only dog in the world, I think, that pouts."

"I pout, too, sometimes."

"No, you don't, honey. You're always a good girl. Now, let's go on with the story, but you ought to know it by heart by now. We've read it so many times."

Indeed, the two had gone through the *Wizard of Oz*, ever since Corliss had been able to talk, which was at a very early age. She loved books in general, and the *Wizard of Oz* was her favorite. If Lanie or Davis or Cody tried to skip sections, she called their hand on that immediately. "You're skipping the good part," she would always say.

Booger, the bloodhound, got up, stretched, and the sunlight coming through the window caught the gold medal around his neck. It said simply HERO in capital letters. It had been given to him by the town of Fairhope, Arkansas, when he had used his talents as a bloodhound to find Roger Langley who had been hurt and unable to move in the deep woods. Booger's picture had been in the paper and now was tacked up on the wall with other snapshots of the Freeman family. Booger had been one of the bloodhounds at Cummins Prison where the father of the Freeman family, Forrest, was in prison for a crime he had not commited.

"Booger wants to go out." Corliss put the book down, jumped up, and ran to the screen door. She opened it, let Booger go outside, then came back but didn't sit down beside Lanie. She looked up toward the upstairs and said, "Aunt Kezia doesn't feel good, Lanie."

"I know she doesn't, honey. She's pretty sick."

"She got a new bottle of medicine in the mail, but it didn't help her any."

Lanie frowned and shook her head. "I wish she would stop taking that patent medicine. It doesn't do any good at all." She stirred restlessly then said, " You sit here and read your book, honey. I'll go up and see how Aunt Kezia is doing."

"All right."

Lanie moved quickly out of the living room and mounted the stairs. She was a well-formed young woman of eighteen with a wealth of auburn hair and striking green eyes. Now as she entered the room at the end of the second story she found her Aunt Kezia Pettigrew sitting in a rocking chair and staring out the window. Going over to stand behind her, Lanie was struck again by the miracle of this woman. She was ninety-two now and had lived an adventurous life. It had been God's miracle that when the State was going to separate the Freeman children after the death of the mother and the incarceration of Forrest Freeman that Aunt Kezia had been located and had come to fulfill the State requirement of an adult in the house full of young people. She was a small woman, and age was beginning to tell its tale, but her eyes were still bright and clear. "How are you feeling, Aunt Kezia?"

Ignoring Lanie's question, Kezia looked out over the window and said, "I always liked fall the best of all the seasons. Back when we lived in Louisiana there was no such thing as a fall, not like this one. Look at the colors. The fall brings them out, don't it now?"

"They'll be more colorful in October." Lanie moved over and put her hand on the old woman's forehead. It was immediately struck away, and Aunt Kezia glared at her. "I will not be pawed at thank you very much!"

Lanie had felt the heat from the Kezia's body. "I'm going to get Owen."

"You'll do no such thing. I'll be right fine. I've got me a new medicine." She reached out and picked up a brown bottle and held it high with triumph. "Doctor Oscar Bennett's liver rejuvenator. It's got four secret ingredients."

Lanie took the bottle, unscrewed the top and smelled it. "Why, this is just plain alcohol, Aunt Kezia, with something put in it to make it taste bad."

"It is not! Doctor Bennett was brought up by the Cherokee Indians. An old medicine man gave him this recipe his own self."

"No, this won't do you any good. Don't you remember Estelle Tatum who started taking that patent medicine? It wasn't anything but alcohol. She became a regular addict."

"Well, she stopped aching, didn't she?"

"I guess so, but she was drunk on that patent medicine. I'm going to get Owen."

Kezia cackled, and humor lit her dark eyes. "You likely won't find him."

"What are you talking about?"

"He's probably doctoring the widow Hankins. She's been after him full speed ahead ever since she lost her husband. She sees Owen Merritt as a likely prospect for a new husband."

Lanie bit her lip for she knew that there was some truth to this. In a small town like Fairhope there were no secrets, and she was well aware that every widow and single woman in town were all suddenly enjoying ill health. Doctor Owen Merritt was called constantly to treat women who had nothing wrong with them except loneliness.

"Now, you take that Ella Hankins. She wants a man. She's got her cap set for Merritt. Come to think of it maybe you better go get him. I need to give him some advice on how to take care of these man hungry females that are out to nail his hide to the wall."

Lanie could not help smiling. She reached over and hugged Kezia and nodded. "You just wait right here. I'll be back as soon as I can."

"Take your time, honey. I ain't going nowhere."

Lanie hurried downstairs and went at once to the kitchen where a large black woman was ironing. Delilah Jones was the mother of the Reverend Madison Jones, the pastor of the Methodist Episcopal

Church. She looked up from the cast smoothing iron that she had picked up from the stove, spit on it and watched it sizzle. "This is the way to iron clothes. Them new-fangled electric irons ain't worth spit."

"I'd like to have one all the same, Delilah."

"Them new-fangled inventions ain't gonna do nobody no good. If these solid irons was good enough for my mammy, they're good enough for them women today. They's jist too lazy to work, that's what there problem is."

Lanie had learned long ago that it was useless to argue with Delilah Jones. She had a will as solid as the Rock of Gibraltar, and as far as anyone could figure out, the last time she had changed her mind it had been another century. "I've got to go get Doctor Merritt, Delilah. Aunt Kezia isn't any better. You take care of her and Corliss."

Delilah put the iron down on one of Davis' shirts and quickly smoothed the wrinkles out. She quickly lifted the iron before it could scorch the material and looked up saying aggressively, "I reckon we could pray her through, Miss Lanie. I could get the deacons of our church to come and that preacher of mine. We could anoint her with oil."

"Well, we may could do that, Delilah," Lanie smiled, "but, first of all, we've got to get that awful medicine she orders by mail. I'm hoping she'll listen to Doctor Merritt."

"She ain't gonna listen to nobody," Delilah said vigorously. "She's stubborn as a blue-nosed mule."

And so are you, Lanie wanted to reply but did not. Delilah Jones had been the Freeman's strong anchor ever since the death of their mother. Lanie had been only fourteen at that time and had been forced to take over the raising of her younger brothers and sisters. With the Depression at its worst, they could not afford much, and Delilah Jones had come day after day and year after year to throw herself into the lives of the Freeman children. Lanie loved her dearly and going over, she hugged the big woman's shoulders. "You're a treasure, Delilah. I don't know what we would have done without you."

"I don't know neither. Now you go on and git that doctor. We'll let him try his thing, and then when that don't work, we'll let the good Lord have His way. I knows *that'll* work!"

Lanie left the house and turned toward town. The old Freeman home place was composed of five acres, all that was left of a large plantation that had belonged to Forrest's great grandparents. It was all gone now. Sold off to make city lots, most of it, and as she hurried along, Lanie wondered what it had been like back in the days when this was all open fields with no town at all except a general store.

Turning left on Stonewall Jackson Boulevard, she made her way hurriedly through the town. It was familiar enough to her, for it was the only town she'd ever known. She passed the library where Cassandra Sue Pruitt, the librarian, waved to her, then turning right on Robert E. Lee Street, she passed the Rialto Theater and Planter's Bank directly across the street.

She arrived at the office of Doctor Oscar Givens and entered at once. A short stocky woman with her hair done up in a Pentecostal bun looked up. "Hello, Lanie."

"Hello, Nurse Pickens. I'd like to see Doctor Merritt, please."

"He's not here. He's gone down to get lunch, at least so he said. What he really likes to do is go down and listen to the gossip at the Dew Drop Inn. Who's sick?"

Lanie knew that she could get a full diagnosis from Nurse Pickens but did not want to get into that. The woman had served old Doctor Givens for at least thirty years and knew the ailment of every citizen of the county. "Aunt Kezia's not feeling well, but I'll go find Doctor Merritt."

"You tell him to bring me back Sister Myrtle's special. It's greens and fried pork chops—and bring me a piece of pie. Whatever she made today."

"I'll tell him, Nurse Pickens."

The Dew Drop Inn, being the only café in Fairhope, did a brisk business. It was pinched in between the barber shop run by Deoin Jinks and Gerald Pink's pharmacy. The parking spaces were all taken, as usual, around the Dew Drop Inn, for it was the social center of the town, almost as popular as Bud Thompson's Pool Hall.

Sister Myrtle Poindexter exited from the kitchen carrying two plates burdened down with food. Sister Myrtle was pastor of the Fire Baptized Pentecostal Church. She was a tall, angular woman with sharp brown eyes and her hair done up in a huge bun. She always wore dark clothing, sleeves down to her wrists and no jewelry except for a simple wedding band.

Charley Poindexter, Sister Myrtle's husband, was a short chunky man of few words. This was just as well since Sister Myrtle had enough words for both of them! They had, however, a sound marriage having raised six children all of them turning out well.

The Ministerial Alliance of Fairhope was meeting at the Dew Drop Inn for lunch as they did every Monday at noon. Sister Myrtle did not even bother to take orders. They took the special or there was an argument. None of the preachers ever dared to order anything except the special. The plates were piled high with pork chops, collard greens, squash, corn on the cob, and in the middle of the table was a huge platter of cornbread.

Sister Myrtle slammed the plate down in front of Roy Jefferson, the Episcopal priest, and glared down at him. She had a running feud going with the priest about the collar that he wore. "I've told you before, preacher, Jesus didn't wear no collar like that."

Jefferson looked up. "I don't expect he wore any kind of collar at all."

"Then why do you have to wear one?"

"It's just tradition among our church folks, Sister Myrtle. Now please don't start on me."

But Sister Myrtle plunked down a plate heaping with food in front of Ellis Burke, the Methodist preacher, and turned her guns on Reverend Jefferson. "You've got to make Carl Spivey go to work, preacher."

It was difficult to have a ministerial alliance meeting at the Dew Drop Inn, for Sister Myrtle knew every member of every man's congregation (including all their shortcomings!) and did not hesitate to bring them up in an open forum.

"I don't know how I could do that, sister."

"He lets that poor wife of his do all the work. He's a lazy bum."

"He claims he's got a bad back," Jefferson protested.

"You bring him by our church, and we'll anoint him and get him healed. But it ain't his back. He's just lazy. All them Spivey men are lazy."

Jefferson caved in and nodded in surrender. "I'll have a word with him, Sister."

Ellison Burke, the Methodist pastor, was a small man with sharp, intellectual features. He was grinning at Roy Jefferson when suddenly Sister Myrtle turned to face him. "What are you going to do about that Bowden girl?"

"You mean Alice?"

"How many Bowden girls you got?"

"Well, I guess she's the only one, Sister Myrtle. What's she done now?"

"You need to keep up with your sheep, preacher. She went over to Fort Smith with Aaron Dutton. He's no good, and he's going to get that girl in trouble. I think you got to jerk a knot in her and get her straightened out."

"I don't see I could do that."

"Well, the Apostle Paul would have did it! That girl's trying to be one of them flappers."

"I don't expect she means any harm."

"She wears ear screws. That's flat against the Bible, and you know it!"

"Where is that in the Bible?"

"I ain't got time for no theology lesson. You come by when this meeting's over, and I'll show you. But you've got to stop that girl before she goes plum down the wrong road."

"I'll see what I can do."

Sister Myrtle whirled and disappeared back in the kitchen. She came back almost instantly with two more platters. She put one of them down in front of the Presbyterian pastor, Alex Digby. She opened her mouth but before she could speak Reverend Digby said, "Now don't you start on me, Sister Myrtle. I know some of my flock needs to be chastised, and I'll send them over for some of your sermon."

"Good! I'll give them a sizzling, red-hot dose of Gospel."

"I'm sure they'll profit by it."

Myrtle stared down at the plate of food and then at the rotund figure of Reverend Digby who was not pleasingly plump but was downright overweight. "I've got a word for you from the Lord."

Laughter went around the table, and all the ministers kept their eyes on Sister Myrtle. She always had a word of the Lord for all of them, and Alex Digby flushed. "I don't think I want to hear it."

"Well, you're going to. You need to fast, my brother. You're digging your grave with that fork."

Colin Ryan, the interim pastor of the Baptist Church, was the youngest of the preachers at the meeting. He was twenty-six years old with black hair, dark blue eyes, a widow's peak and a cleft chin. "Do you suppose we could just have the blessing and eat without the theology? These meetings always make me hungry."

Sister Myrtle suddenly laughed. She had a fondness in her heart for the young preacher who was anything but a typical Baptist. He often visited Sister Myrtle's church and was as loud with his "Amens" and "Praise the Lords" as any of her own flock. "You fly right at it, Brother Colin. You Baptists eat better than you do anything else anyhow."

Father Horatio Bates, the Catholic priest, always dreaded these meetings at the Dew Drop Inn. It humiliated him, somehow, that Sister Myrtle Poindexter knew at least as much of the doings of his flock as he himself knew. He bowed his head and said quickly, "Let's have the blessing."

"I'll ask it myself. I ain't sure any of you preachers are in fit spiritual condition to be thanking the Lord anyways," Sister Myrtle said. She prayed in a loud, strident voice as if she wanted the people across the street to hear her. She put in not just a thanks for the preachers and their churches but for every item of food on the table.

Finally, as it went on and on, Colin Ryan broke in and said, "While Sister Myrtle finishes her prayer why don't we go ahead and eat."

A laughter went around the table, and Doctor Merritt, who was sitting at a separate table with the Sheriff Pardue Jessup, whispered, "I like this place, Pardue. You can get your stomach filled and your spiritual needs met."

Sister Myrtle whirled for she had excellent hearing. "I heard that. You missed the last two services at church, Doctor Owen Merritt. You're downright backslid."

"Well, I guess I may be, Sister Myrtle."

Sister Myrtle came over and stared down at the two men, both of them fine-looking and in their early thirties. Owen Merritt was six feet tall, lean with crisp brown hair and warm brown eyes. Pardue Jessup, one year short of thirty, was even taller. He had hair black as a raven's wing, dark eyes, and rough good looks. He was the target of many of the single women. He and Owen Merritt were the prime bachelors of Fairhope. Sister Myrtle looked down at them and said nothing, and finally Jessup grew nervous. "What's wrong now? You want to preach at me about my sins?"

"Well, you need it, Pardue."

"What have I done now?"

"It ain't what you've done. It's what you *ain't* done. It's agin Scripture for a man not to take a wife, and you two need to be thinking on that seriously. As a matter of fact, I've got me a list. I've been thinking about the widows in our church who need husbands."

"We've got two or three of those in our congregation," Alex Digby said, "and I think Sister Myrtle is right. You two need to get yourselves married."

"That's right. You ought to be just as miserable as the rest of us," Aaron Burke said, humor glimmering in his eyes.

The meal continued with Sister Myrtle dispensing food and theology liberally. She looked up when Lanie came in and said, "Well, Sister Lanie, you come to get a bite to eat?"

"No, not this time, Sister Myrtle." She moved over and said, "Owen, Aunt Kezia's not well. Could you come and see her?"

"Why, we'll take this whole bunch of preachers over there," Sister Myrtle said. "We'll pray her well."

"Well, who'll feed the people of Fairhope?" Alex Digby grinned.

"Let them fast. They need it."

"Let's try Doctor Merritt first, Sister, and Doctor Merritt, Miss Bertha says for you to bring her one of the specials and a piece of pie."

Sister Myrtle scurried around and got the pie and brought it in covered with a clean cloth. She gave it to Lanie and said, "I'll be praying for Kezia. That's one fine woman."

Lanie smiled. "Thank you," and left with Owen Merritt.

As soon as the two were out the door, the gossip started. "That young woman's got three men on the string," Sister Myrtle said. "She's a sweet thing, but she don't know much about men."

"Which three is that?" Father Horatio Bates asked curiously.

"You don't keep up with this town much, do you, preacher?" She refused to call him Father for the Bible said, "Call no man on this earth your Father." "She's got Roger Langley downright silly over her."

"That's right. Owen Merritt's struck on her too," Reverend Jefferson said. "That'd be a good marriage even though he's older than she is."

"Well, she ain't doing herself no good running around with that Brent Hayden, that writer fellow."

"I'm sure it's all innocent. She doesn't have anybody to talk to about her writing," Colin Ryan said.

Charley Poindexter came out wiping his hands on his apron. He spoke little, but now he said in a high, tenor voice, "You watch what I tell you. That girl won't marry nobody until she gets her pa out of prison."

A silence fell on the group, and finally Sister Myrtle said, "I reckon you're right about that, husband. She's a fine girl with a strong sense of duty. I wish there was more like her in this town." Sister Myrtle turned and said, "Now, I got a list of Scriptures for your preachers to work into your sermons. Some of them women in your congregation are wearing their skirts all the way up to their knees. I want you to hit that hard, do you hear me?"

⌘

As Lanie and Owen walked back toward his office, Owen was grinning. "You can always get any kind of words you need from Sister Myrtle."

"I like her so much."

"Well, I have one bit of good news. I got a letter from my brother in L.A."

"The policeman there?"

"He's a detective. He says he's got everybody looking for Thelma Mays."

Thelma Mays was a witness that never testified during Lanie's father's trial. Owen looked down at the young woman with admiration. She had pride that he appreciated. He was also aware of the supple lines of her body and remembered the young girl that she had been when he had first met her. She was almost serene in her composure, and her face lightened and grew prettier as he watched her. Her features were quick to express her thoughts and laughter and love of life seemed to lie behind her eyes and lips waiting for some kind of release.

"I'm glad I've been able to help," he said. "I'll send the medicine out."

"Thank you, Owen."

The autumn air was cold in the hills of the Ozarks, and Lanie shivered as she pulled on the flannel nightgown that came all the way down to her feet. She put on a pair of wool-lined shoes and sat down and began to work on a poem. She had been writing poems about the life of Jesus and the people that met Him while He was on earth, and she had been thinking about the rich, young ruler, and now she sat there for ten minutes finishing it up. She put her pen down and then read the poem aloud:

> Seeing you, my son, standing all alone
> In growing dusk, is more than I can bear.
> Your heart is heavy — yet you must prepare
> To live life as a man, without a moan:
> Every day for weeks you've gone to where
> The Nazarene with his glowing eyes
> Entrances you — why, even now you stare
> As if you'd caught a glimpse of paradise.
>
> Paradise? No, Mother, be content;
> This very day I chose to live, not die.
> The Rabbi's price for heaven is too high.
> This solid earth must be my element.
> Sell all he said — but when I passed him by
> A tear of purest rain shone in his eye.

The poem did not please her completely, but her poetry rarely did. She put the notebook aside, then took up the journal and dated it August 3, 1932, and began writing quickly. Cap'n Brown, her cat, had leaped up on the bed and snuggled up close to her. Lanie rubbed Cap'n Brown's head then wrote:

> I was mean to Owen tonight. He tried to talk to me about how people are gossiping about how I go to see Brent Hayden, and I lost my temper. I was sorry as soon as I snapped at him. I know I hurt his feelings, and I feel just awful about it.

It seems strange that here I am eighteen-years-old and a lot of my girlfriends that I grew up with are married — and I'm not. Roger's asked me to marry him, but I can't do it. About Owen, I guess I've been in love with him for years. I thought at first it was just a little girl admiration of a man that had done so much for our family, but I think it's more than that now. I don't know how to say it. And, of course, Brent. He's helped me so much with my writing, helped me to win the national contest, and he's the only one I can really talk to about writing.

She suddenly paused and shook her head fiercely then wrote:

I can't think about a home and a husband and children — not until daddy's out of that awful place!

Three ways to keep up on your favorite Zondervan books and authors

Sign up for our *Fiction E-Newsletter*. Every month you'll receive sample excerpts from our books, sneak peeks at upcoming books, and chances to win free books autographed by the author.

You can also sign up for our *Breakfast Club*. Every morning in your email, you'll receive a five-minute snippet from a fiction or nonfiction book. A new book will be featured each week, and by the end of the week you will have sampled two to three chapters of the book.

Zondervan *Author Tracker* is the best way to be notified whenever your favorite Zondervan authors write new books, go on tour, or want to tell you about what's happening in their lives.

Visit *www.zondervan.com* and sign up today!

ZONDERVAN.com/
AUTHORTRACKER
follow your favorite authors

CPSIA information can be obtained
at www.ICGtesting.com
Printed in the USA
LVHW111025070321
680804LV00020B/1030